It was pure rapture. Rand's kiss grew gentle for an instant while his arms crushed her to him; then his lips slanted hungrily over hers as his tongue sought to explore and taste her open mouth, so willing, so provocative.

Chelsea's knees were weakening; her hips wanted to begin the primitive rotation that came so naturally, instinctively.

He swept her up into his arms and cradled her satin-covered body to him while he carried her into a darkened room. There he gently placed her on a bed slashed with light from the hall.

"Where...are we?" she asked with a quiver, hypnotically clinging to his leather-covered shoulders, strong and rippling, as he eased the length of his body down beside her.

"My bedroom, my bed," he breathed huskily, passion shortening his words as his warm hands found the pearl-smooth contours of her breasts, her waist, hips, thighs....

ABOUT THE AUTHOR

Rianna Craig is a film producer and
screenwriter who once spent three years living
abroad on an old schooner sailing to various
ports of call. She now makes her home on
land in Texas with her husband and five
children. This is her first novel.

Love
Match

RIANNA CRAIG

Harlequin Books

TORONTO • NEW YORK • LONDON
AMSTERDAM • PARIS • SYDNEY • HAMBURG
STOCKHOLM • ATHENS • TOKYO • MILAN

Published May 1984

First printing March 1984

ISBN 0-373-16056-9

Chapter One

A coastal fog crept willy-nilly through the Biloxi boat-yard. When it found the rickety wharf, it settled, enfolding the wooden boat and those aboard in an isolating wall of misty gray.

Chelsea sat shivering on the deck of the captain's cabin. She felt like an enchanted mermaid pulled from the sea. The handsome hunter circled closer to study his captive prey. Like one hypnotized, she glanced up and dared to return the stare of the brooding, flaxen-haired god commanding her submission.

She was fascinated by the appeal of his rough-hewn, wind-tanned features: a not-so-perfect nose, slightly scarred full lips. And the arrogant glint in his amber-brown eyes held her tingling as he approached with the determined strength of steel.

Silent messages tantalized her sensuous nature. She felt an undeniable magnetism, a raw attraction binding them mutually in an illicit intrigue. Chelsea willingly obeyed his unspoken order and prepared to bare her perfect young body.

Swiftly he knelt beside her, encircling her shoulders with his powerful arms. His warm breath caressed her ear, her neck.

Wanton, she obsequiously lay back on the deck. Her wide emerald eyes, framed by luxuriant, smoky lashes, messaged tremulously: I need to explore what I feel for you.

He pulled back to appraise again her fully matured, female contours. He seemed perplexed at the willingness of this woman he desired.

The charged atmosphere altered slightly with the sound of her name spoken in a sultry whisper. "Chelsea." His voice timbre was incredibly appealing. Slowly he continued, "Where have you been...so many years...you've changed...."

The intensity of his emotions compelled her to meet his gaze more closely. She propped up on one elbow and leaned near to his face. Before she answered, she tossed her long, tawny ringlets to one side, then purred with lover's adulation, "Rand, I've always wanted you, but you didn't know I was...alive."

In husky, honeyed tones, warmly colored with his unique Mississippi–Cajun accent, he drawled, "Let's see just how much you've changed." His heartbreaking smile reassured her like the sun breaking through clouds to warm the earth. The deepening dimples in his cheeks distracted her from his fingers, which expertly worked the buttons on her blouse. Then a flash of teal blue rustled, and she gasped. He had pulled her blouse open and captured her arms in a vice of twisting silk.

"Rand." Her expressive, moist lips quivered as his fingers began to trace the fullness of her now fully exposed breasts. His hot, calloused hands, rough against her satin skin, intensified her desire. With each stroke of his scratchy fingers he increased the pressure. A heady, tingling pleasure flooded her pulsating triangle like a current of electricity.

She loved being naked in front of him. She had dreamed of this long before leaving Biloxi at fourteen. "Now, Rand, now!" she begged as eroticism flamed in the depths of his golden-brown eyes, a vortex to his soul.

The only response was a low moan as his curly mass of salt-water blond hair tickled her throat while he kissed a wet, tantalizing trail around her quivering breasts. His wildly flicking tongue sent tremors that hardened her nipples and caused tiny explosions below like the hills and valleys of a distant siren.

Ecstatic, she breathed, "Free my arms. Then I can hold you, as I've always dreamed." Her heartbeat and pulsating nerves equaled Rand's.

He raised his head, and through half-open eyelids his eyes, dilated with passion, confirmed her arousal. Satisfied, he released her blouse.

Suddenly he seemed tense. "What's the matter?" she asked.

Rand whispered his concern. "What if, what if... someone... interrupts?"

Chelsea quickly curled her slender arms about his neck and felt another surge of pleasure warm her as she assured, "Not tonight. There's no world at all tonight. Only us." His male scent was a rhapsody of promise as he lifted her, half naked, onto the starboard bunk. The confining blouse fell away from her arms with ease, and for a moment he paused, then magically stripped her of all remaining clothing, her perfect proportions a feast to his senses.

Urgently she again linked her hands at his neck and brought him down to her lips, parted to receive his. She groaned when his kiss seared her mouth. Chelsea clung, her legs intertwined with his, as his full body weight settled atop her. In the fervor of their unrestrained passion, her breasts were crushed against the hardness of his chest; there was no air to breath....

A sweet, warbling siren signaled—danger. Stop! Stop, she thought.

It was a moment before Chelsea realized that the distracting sound she heard was the wail of a police siren. The flashing red and blue lights completed the destruction of her powerful daydream. Reality screamed behind her.

"What—what's happening?" she whispered aloud to no one.

Then a glance at the speedometer and she started to slow her sports car and pull off the interstate. The rush of adrenaline had given her a lead foot. I can't believe I...it was so real. Oh, what a...fantasy. I could feel his kiss...his...I'm still shaking. She eased the car to a stop. I know how I've changed, but...I wonder what *he's* really like now. I haven't thought of him in years. A strange smile sat idly on her face.

It was unappreciated by the gruff old Louisiana State trooper who was totally removed from her sensual aura. He stooped over and leaned on the low sports car door as she lowered the window. "Young lady," he began slowly. "Kindly remove your presence from this here minicar and show me your license, please," he twanged lethargically.

"Yes, sir, uh. Well, certainly," she stammered, embarrassed and unable to make sense of what was happening. She got her purse and stepped out into a blast of January cold. She unconsciously smoothed her wrinkled white wool slacks and zipped her beige down vest against the damp, wintry gusts that whipped about her as the four-lane traffic zoomed by.

At the back of her car she joined the officer who rested his booted foot on the bumper of her 1946 MG. On his knee he balanced a clipboard of tickets where he busily wrote her license plate information.

"Where in Texas you from, Miss, uh...?" he droned.

"Houston, sir. I'm Miss Norquist, Chelsea Norquist," she smiled nervously. "I'm sorry if, I mean, have I done something wrong?" she asked his mirrored aviator's sunglasses. All she could see of her own distorted reflection was the long, frizzy hair that beat around her face. Then his gray moustache moved. "Pardon me. What did you say?" she shouted above the intermittent highway noise.

"Your license for driving, please," he repeated impatiently. "And take it out of your wallet."

The license stubbornly resisted Chelsea's fumbling attempt to free it. Her mind was still addled from her imaginary encounter with Rand. She absently chattered, "I, uh, seem to have lost track of where I am."

He stopped writing, crossed his arms over his barrel chest, and shot her a look of suspicion as he supplied, "Oh, 'bout thirty miles this side of Baton Rouge. You got some kind of e-mergency, Miss Newquist?" He rocked back on his heels, cocked his head like an owl, and thrust his double chin forward of his square-set jaw.

"Norquist," she nervously corrected, worried by his judgmental stance. "I guess no emergency, but, you see, my grandfather died...last fall—" she stopped; the license came loose. "Oh, here!"

He accepted her license. "Sorry to hear that, ma'am." Sighing, he resumed writing on her ticket.

She felt a compulsive need to cover her fragmented composure with conversation. "I'm on my way to Biloxi, Mississippi, now to sell the family boatyard, what's left of it." Her expressive emerald eyes began to sadden as she rambled, "I loved it there as
when my folks died...Grandpa sent me to live with my aunt in Houston. I haven't been back since their funeral, twelve years ago." Her voice drifted lower, "I don't think I could have faced Grandpa's funeral, even if I had known about it in time." She added, more to herself than to her listener, "I know I should have been there."

The authoritative officer seemed kinder now as he shook his head in understanding. He had stopped writing to listen.

She smiled enigmatically. "I could never go back, though. I like those big city lights now, and 'life in the fast lane,'" she added whimsically.

Her humor was lost on him. He was writing again.

"This your correct address? Hmmm. Better check your license renewal date too."

"Yes sir. I'm twenty six," she explained.

He cleared his throat and handed her the ticket, "Miss Norquist, you have seriously broken the law. I clocked you at seventy eight miles per hour!" Her eyes widened as she slowly absorbed his words. "Have you ever had a speeding ticket before?"

"No-o sir, never. I had no idea I was going that fast. My mind was on...what I'm going to find...in Biloxi—"

He interrupted with a tired sigh. "Okay, okay. Come on." As they walked toward the car door he added, "You pay this fine on time, now, and drive this car under the speed limit. All right? Now, get out of this cold," he ordered, opening her door like an old southern gentleman. "Don't forget now!"

She cautiously steered her low-slung antique back on I-10, shifted gears, and headed East again. She was genuinely shocked. The ticket in her lap proved how fleet-footed the little green turtle was.

Six years ago her 1946 TC-MG had been "a mechanic's delight." A dubious birthday gift from her mother's widowed sister, Marianne McClure, who took her role as Chelsea's guardian to heart. The car came with a course in auto mechanics. "One more opportunity to gain independence on the way to self-actualization, control of your life, and thus, happiness," her aunt had reiterated. Marianne's philosophy had been a shaping influence for six years by then. Chelsea was reluctant at first, but soon discovered her natural ability with engines and actually enjoyed rebuilding then maintaining her little British sports car. "This old MG never ran this well. Seldom ran at all, in fact!" Marianne admitted. She was proud of Chelsea's new expertise and dogged determination.

With part of her mind automatically assigned to driving, the highway blurred; her thoughts took a magnetic drift toward true north—Rand Korbet. He had claimed her attention once she left Houston traffic behind and, except for the speeding ticket, he was still holding center stage. She paused in her reflections to marvel at how fascinating someone forgotten for years could now seem.

She eased her foot onto the brake as she joined the traffic coming off the Mississippi River Bridge into Baton Rouge. When she left the city in her rearview mirror, she was easily absorbed again by Rand-colored thoughts. Had he married? If not, might they have a future?

It was easy to remember when she had first discovered him. She was twelve, full of romantic daydreams and hopes for a real prince charming in her future, but timing and hormones were late; she still looked like a frizzy-headed little boy. Rand was about twenty and so in command the day he had docked his dad's steel pushboat at the Norquist yard to talk business with her father and granddad. She had watched his every move while she swept leaves and wood shavings from the porch, in hopes he would notice. He hadn't. Who noticed twelve-year-olds but other twelve-year-olds? She admired everything about him: the sun-bleached blond hair, the darndest gold-brown eyes, the irregular features that were strangely appealing.... And he was built just right, about five feet ten. Her crush had been genuine. He was flawless in her eyes.

Her folks had liked him. They had said he was a "natural water man" with his grandpa's flair and ambitions. Then, when she was fourteen, they had expressed disdain that the Korbets were converting totally to steel-boat construction. "The only good vessel was a wood vessel," they had held, true to their Norwegian traditions of six generations.

A few months later her folks were dead, victims of a boating accident. So much for traditions.

Aunt Marianne and her philosophy had supported

Chelsea through the pain of their loss. Right or wrong, she had blocked all thoughts of her past. She had leaned on Marianne and learned to live in the present with an eye to the future.

Over the years her grandfather had visited her in Houston so she could avoid the trauma of a return to Biloxi.

Her aunt's high-spirited values shaped Chelsea's young life considerably. She joined her aunt at philanthropical efforts she supported as well as the opera and symphony season after season. Though money was no problem, her late husband had invested wisely, and the widowed Marianne encouraged independence in Chelsea.

She worked her way through the University of Houston, then after several short-term jobs, started as Assistant Art Director-Photographer at the Houston advertising agency of Sherwood/Graham. When she moved into her own efficiency apartment near her office in the Galleria, her bond with Marianne remained close. Her career goals were clear-cut—she would have her own agency some day. Her personal life was happy. She dated, but not compulsively, as some of her girl friends did. Marriage was an option for sometime in the future.

Now her fascinating thoughts of Rand were shading the future.

Chelsea shivered as a crack of lightning jigged across the darkening gray sky. She hadn't realized she was driving into a storm. Abruptly a crash of thunder seemed to join her in the front seat. Then the banks of low, scudding clouds dropped a blinding wall of water that reduced visibility to zero. Now her attention was riveted on driving—and the pesky leak starting to drip into her lap from the car's cloth top. "Damn, I've had that seal on order for months!" she cursed.

A steady downpour drowned I-10. Although intermittent daydreams had crept in with Rand fantasies, the extra attention required for driving in the storm dampened any further stimulating scenarios. Besides, she told herself, I will be seeing him, in his own appealing flesh, tomorrow. How ironic, she thought again, to be selling him the yard, "her" yard, after all these years.

She relished the idea and was now grateful her grandfather's lawyer, old Dwight Connors, had insisted she come to the closing of the sale. She had hoped to handle it all through the mail and never confront her past. But now, she told herself, I wouldn't miss meeting with Rand for anything. With building excitment she fanned the flames for what might still be, even though she was weary from the long day's drive.

The rain-filled sky was getting dark fast as she turned the car left off East Bay, the hard-top road that skirted Back Bay, Biloxi. Instinctively she slowed to glance at the old wooden arrow that indicated the Norquist Boatyard was indeed still there.

A glimpse of the name on the old sign sparked a pride in her family that had been flickering all day. Suddenly she stopped the car to admire the sight. I don't know if it's the gloomy weather or my purple nostalgia, Chelsea mused, but this is a picture I may never see again. She retrieved her faithful Nikon from the camera bag in the back and quickly rolled the window down. After checking the meter for light, she focused and, through a soft filter of rain, shot the weathered sign, receding in the mist.

A cool, wet gust sprayed her Nordic cheeks, a welcome refresher after the long drive. By the time she clicked off several more exposures, crystaline droplets had dampened her naturally kinky, fawn brown hair into tiny tendrils that framed her almost pretty face.

She slowly eased the low-slung car forward into the once oyster-shelled, now slimy, mud ruts that led to the shipyard office. The barnlike structure was down a slight incline near the water's edge.

Through the on/off view furnished by the diligent windshield wipers, she saw a dim yellow light in the small first-floor office window, but the old family house at the edge of the yard was dark. Once the car engine was off, the sound of the relentless rain increased as it pounded on the old cloth top. Even with the leak, somewhat plugged with tissues, it seemed cozy inside compared to the deluge that awaited her.

Chelsea debated whether to go on to the motel in Ocean Springs where lawyer Connors had made her reservations or take a quick look around the yard in hopes of meeting the foreman, Lafe Sorensen. Connors said the Sorensen family lived in her old home there, but it looked abandoned now.

It was almost dark. She pulled her car lights on to illuminate the path and, she hoped, attract the attention of anyone inside the office. She waited. She honked the horn. Impatient, she rationalized, I've come a long way after a lot of years—and I'd like to get a look around, *now*! She honked again.

Snapping the full length of her down vest, she pulled the collar up, placed her leather handbag snug against her middle, and wished for an umbrella as she opened the car door. Her white wool slacks bore the brunt, absorbing the gusting water. She leaned into the windy rain, slammed the door, and rushed for the inviting office light that held a slim promise of life.

The oozing muck sucked at her comfortable deck shoes, slowing her approach. She was thoroughly soaked when she finally reached the office porch and shivered under the overhang as she tried the doorknob. Locked. She gave a series of futile, frustrating loud knocks on the door. Nothing.

"Damn!" she cursed aloud. "I should have had a key sent me before I even left Houston."

Cold, wet, and completely discouraged, she stepped off the porch and headed for her car, barely visible twenty feet away. Grousing in her mind, she admitted,

I'm really crazy! First I'm so disinterested I didn't even want to come here to sign the sale papers. Now I'm so eager, I'm going to drown, or at the least get a case of pneumonia.

Filled with self-reproach, she stomped forward, determined to reach her car more quickly. But, with the next step, the suction of the soggy soil held her right shoe firmly planted, and she lost her balance. Her shapely five feet six inches plunged head first, and she slid, facedown, a few feet closer to her destination. From ground level she perceived a pelting brown fog. The earth tasted salty. She gasped for clean air. Spitting grit, she wiped her eyes with a muddy silk sleeve and blamed a deck shoe that, instead of gripping the slick surface was sucked under.

While making a shaky attempt to stand upright, she failed to see the red and green running lights of the Korbet tug, *Sampson*, or hear the twin engines as they reversed, backing the fifty-foot vessel into the slip by the building ways, roiling the waters angrily at the bulkhead. If she had seen, she would have been aware of the ease with which the commanding figure in the yellow foul-weather gear hanked a line around a bollard on the dock near the vessel's bow and casually jumped ashore.

He strode easily. The tred on his high rubber boots afforded a firm grip on the slippery ascent. In a few moments he was at the toolshed near the office.

Chelsea was almost on her feet when Rand Korbet rounded the corner of the building. His flashlight caught the jerky brown movement of her attempt at an upright posture. The light startled her. She jerked toward it, slipped again, and this time fell flat on her back. Stunned, the breath knocked out of her, she was outraged at her lack of control in this situation. Then, as everything on her backside started shouting with pain, she was more aware of her misery. The accident had occurred with incredible speed, yet it seemed like

endless slow motion. She had to admit she needed assistance—for the first time in a long time—and started
to cry weakly, "Help! Help!"

The blinding light flashed in her eyes. Rubber boots
sloshed near; then two very strong arms lifted her
easily and swiftly to a standing position. Large, warm
hands maintained a protective, firm hold on her arms.

"You all right? You hurt?" His authoritative voice
had a distinctive Mississippi—Cajun accent. "Can you
walk? Is this your car?" He played the flashlight from
the car to her body.

Still shocked by it all, Chelsea didn't respond.

"What are you doing here? If you're looking for Sorensens, they went to Mobile for the weekend." Before
she could organize her thoughts and respond, he swept
her up in his sinewy arms and carried her toward the
car.

Feeling grateful to this vaguely familiar stranger, she
managed, "I'm...fine, fine," and leaned against the
security of his broad chest. "I *was* hoping to meet Mr.
Sorensen, but—"

"Well, that's a relief. I thought maybe you were
making mud pies." He huffed and puffed to humor-
ously exaggerate his effort. "The mud you're wearing
is heavy enough!"

Blinking to clear the rain and muck from her eyes,
Chelsea gazed into the face under the rain gear's yellow
hood. His words sounded remote as she absorbed impressions of his features, tanned and rugged in the dim
glare from his flashlight aimed at her car. She blinked
harder to get a clearer vision as she glimpsed a slight
scar on his upper lip. Then she knew! This was Rand
Korbet. Without even catching his eyes, the knowledge
of him fully electrified her senses, dulled as they were
from the flood of chaos. Disaster!

She struggled to get out of his arms as she stammered, "The rescue, thanks for the rescue—thanks
very much! Oh, my shoe, I, back there, it's stuck—"

She broke off, suddenly mortified with just how awful she looked. She wanted to get out of his sight immediately. This was not at all the way she'd planned to meet him.

He carefully put her on her feet and kept one strong arm around her waist while he opened the car door. Then he picked her up again, as if she were a delicate feather, and set her in the driver's seat. "You're mighty welcome, Miss, uh ... ?" She didn't offer her name, preferring anonymity at the moment. She felt as inundated by her emotions as by the cold shower sluicing off his rain gear. "Anything else I can do for you?" he offered. "Give a message to the Sorensens, or ... Just a minute, your shoe." He disappeared, but his male scent, mixed with aftershave and diesel fumes, lingered on.

Chelsea fished in her muddy vest pocket and retrieved her car keys; then he returned. He held two muddy objects dripping before her, slightly resembling her deck shoe and purse. "Oh, thanks!" she murmured, trying to anchor the key in the ignition.

"Course, if you'd rather stay and play in the mud, I won't interfere anymore. I'm just here to check on the yard so old Lafe could have a weekend away." She didn't dare look at him, but his voice held a teasing grin, she was sure.

She wondered at his sense of humor. Why would he tease her, a perfect stranger? The little four cylinder motor kicked over, responding to the light feathering of her foot on the accelerator. It was all ruined. She desperately wanted to leave the emotional maelstrom of his presence. She revved the engine slightly; content with the sound, she let it idle as she stammered, "Thanks again. Uh, that's fine, Mr. ... ?"

"Korbet, Rand Korbet, Miss ... uh, Norquist, is it?" he pronounced with a straight face then choked on laughter as he stepped back and pushed the door shut. "You'll probably catch Mr. Sorensen tomorrow. Don't

forget your hip boots. Rain's forecast again,'' he yelled
through the rolled-up car window. With that he walked
away, a yellowish blur in the distance, before she could
think of anything else to say or do.

Ohhh, how did he know who I was? she asked herself,
embarrassed and angry. How infuriating, since he apparently knew who I was, that he laughed at me. Ohhh.
Then she rationalized that if he wanted to do business
with her, he would have shown some respect, decorum. But he had laughed! Chelsea fumed as she drove
east on the Highway 90 causeway to Ocean Springs and
the Motel Haven. Her pride was bruised and battered
along with her body.

Her failure to meet Lafe Sorensen and scout the yard
was nothing by comparison to the turbulent emotions
she felt from her brief, untimely encounter with Rand
Korbet. An entire day of delightful fantasies, she
thought wistfully, and then this; he finds me, my body,
hair, clothes, my face—all in the muck!

How could he have known it was me? she asked herself again and again. She reached for some Kleenex in
her purse, amazed and grateful to him that she still had
it, though it now resembled a rectangle of fudge.

''Don't ask!'' she dared the startled desk clerk, staring at her from behind his clean counter, cozy and
warm. Her reservations expedited the matter of a
room key and settling into the sanctity of the humble
motel room. The clerk asked no questions at all. He
seemed frozen wordless as he handed her the key and
gestured to the left for room 108. She offered no explanations.

Oblivious to the torrential shower by then, she un-
loaded her bags from the car, hobbling; only her left
foot wore a shoe. A moan of relief escaped her lips as
she closed the door behind her and leaned against it
with a feeling of accomplishment. Her bones and
muscles were beginning to ache. She felt weary as she

sat her camera bag on the dresser and stared at the image reflected in the mirror. It was more than a little funny. No wonder Rand had laughed.

Probably good for my skin, she optimistically rationalized as she undressed in the bathroom, careful to place the whole muddy mess of clothing in a plastic laundry bag. She hoped the white slacks and expensive vest of down were salvageable, but she knew the teal blue suit blouse of silk was totally ruined. Then there was that mud-filled deck shoe. I'll work on it tomorrow, she decided, standing under the hot shower. The jets of heated water removed the outer layers of earth clinging to her face, neck, hands, and right foot. Then she drew a luxuriant tub of steaming hot water for a long, soaking bubble bath.

Only then did she relax; the undulating movement of the fragrant, foamy water eased the tensions of the long day and excruciating evening. Try as she might to mentally schedule tomorrow's activities into an efficient operation, every bubble in her bath tingled sensually on her responsive skin, sending her into a mesmerizing replay of Rand's rough hands in her racy fantasies earlier in the day. She soon ignored the aches and bruises from her fall as she turned the warm water on full blast, laid back in the tub, and let the churning jet of water further stimulate her to a self-satisfying crescendo.

Well spent in the bathtub, she let the remembered aura of Rand slowly recede. Relaxed and tired, it took great effort for her to get out and dry.

With the pleasant fragrance of Lilly of the Valley misted on her throat, thighs, wrists, and under her breasts, she wrapped her well-proportioned torso in a bright orange bathtowel, a gift from aunt Marianne. Her face welcomed the soothing cleanser she smoothed on it. Then she stretched across the bed, wiped away the creamy residue, and vowed that tomorrow she would meet Rand looking the best she knew how. She would dare to try every makeup trick she knew to help her "almost pretty" face make Rand forget just how awful she had looked tonight.

That's my plan, just like Aunt Marianne says, "'Cause if you don't have a plan, someone's gonna have a plan for you!" Which reminded her. She called her aunt and her lawyer to let them know of her safe arrival.

Marianne was out; Chelsea left a message on Marianne's machine announcing her safe arrival and the motel phone number should she wish to get in touch.

When Dwight Connors heard her voice, his kindly countenance came through. "Chelsea child, is that you?" His warm chuckle was infectious. "With this weather I was really getting worried about you. Just get in? You okay?"

She assured and reassured him that all was well, preferring for the moment to skip her encounter at the boatyard. "I'm fine, but exhausted. In fact, I'm already in bed. And thanks for arranging this motel. It's pretty close to your office, if I remember. Uh, straight down Washington, turn right?"

"Yes indeed. You've a memory like your granddad. My, how the windows of time open and close. Mighty glad you made it safely."

"I'm glad you insisted I come." She stopped herself before she said why. "See you at your place in the morning, about nine."

"Good night, now," he crooned, his mellow Mississippi tones reminding her of voices from her childhood.

With a sigh of exhaustion mixed with anticipation, she turned out the light, snuggled between the sheets, and enjoyed the sensation the cool linens made against her sensitive naked skin. She puzzled over Connors's remarks for a few moments, but soon her empty stomach reminded her she had eaten nothing but apples and cheese she'd devoured in the car for breakfast. The sound of the blustery rain helped her determine that sleep was a far more important need.

She easily drifted into sweet, memory-laden sleep, her fulfilling night dreams uninterrupted.

Chapter Two

Chelsea slowly opened one eye and then the other. She felt disoriented, but in an awakening, feline stretch, her still sore muscles reminded her of the preceding day's events. Suddenly wide awake, she remembered that today she would see Rand Korbet—on equal terms—to sell him the boatyard.

Her watch on the bedside table read 7:15. Then she noticed the rain had stopped. Rand was wrong about more rain, at least. Welcome sunlight poured through the slight opening in the tan draperies. That set the tone for the day. She went into action.

Starving, she phoned room service. The alert voice assured her, "'Bout fifteen minutes you'll have a pot of coffee, orange juice, two scrambled eggs with biscuits tossed on the side, and yes, plenty of strawberry jam."

Anticipation coursed through her veins as she splashed bracing cold water on her face and brushed her teeth. Well motivated by the challenge of totally fascinating Rand Korbet at the meeting today, she dressed and made up according to her plan. She wanted to see that look in his eye and return to Houston with the knowledge that she was well remembered by this man of her fantasies. Doing business with him was quite incidental at the moment.

She moved fast in the January chill, which hardened her nipples as she slipped on her ecru and lace camisole and matching bikini briefs. In her rush the dainty seed-pearl buttons on her camisole jumped a loop, and she had to start over again. Slow down, she told herself, while goose bumps urged her to hurry.

She donned a lemon-yellow angora sweater and welcomed the immediate warmth. She checked the bra-less, natural contours of her firm breasts in the mirror as she zipped on the silk-lined, cashmere wool-blend slacks that echoed the same yellow. A swirl of orange and yellow silk tied casually on one side of the boatneck sweater added the extra dash she sought.

She hit a snag as she threaded on her knee-high nylons in preparation for her dainty ankle-strap, four-inch heels—hip boots! Ugh! If I want to impress that man, I can't possibly wade through mud and still look my best at our meeting in this outfit. Get it right, Chelsea, she thought impatiently.

The arrival of her breakfast momentarily took the edge off her distress. She drank the juice and devoured the eggs and biscuits, forgetting to taste them in her haste. Her mind was on revisions in her great plan of what to wear.

This she pondered with a companionable cup of coffee while she applied her makeup. Though her skin was good, she had been taught to moisturize before she smoothed on a light covering of olive-beige makeup base. With a clean, spongy triangle she lightly buffed the creamy color into her hairline, over and beneath her eyelids, the corners of her nose, and under her chin, careful to use an upward stroke. A lighter shade under her eyes and lower jaw line set up her facial contours to receive a highlighting dusty-rose blush on her high cheekbones. Now she had a perfect oval canvas on which to create a "fascinating" face.

Her eyes bore color like a peacock before she started to blend the shadows on her brow, mauve to dark brown in a triangle below, and a tiny touch of sky-blue at the inner and outer corners of her eyes. A delicate sponge tip subtly enhanced the colors. A soft black liner to both top and bottom eyelids was quickly smoothed away, leaving an upturned smoky appearance. Her thick, dark lashes needed only a light coating of mascara. She brushed her brows into their natural, neat, angular arch. Finally she outlined her cupid's bow and the rest of her lips carefully with a thin line of dark plum, then filled the center with an apricot gloss.

To doublecheck her cosmetic art, Chelsea took a hand mirror to the window and in the natural light used a quick brush here and a deft touch there. Her sea-green eyes looked intriguing, her face attractive. For an "almost pretty" girl, she told herself, you look positively striking.

Her confidence buoyed, she hurriedly pulled the wire-pronged brush through her tangled mane of long, kinky ringlets, still damp around her face from her enthusiastic cold-water face wash. The static electricity from the cold air added even more body to her wild hair, perfecting the tawny, leonine elegance. She was happy with her image.

Suddenly, like a gift from heaven, she had the solution to her clothing problem. She almost laughed aloud as she rushed to her car, retrieved from the back the stained but clean coveralls worn when she worked on her car, and hurried back into her motel room. When she put them on over her sweater and slacks and zipped them to the top, all that remained of her "great" look was a bit of silk scarf gaily peeking from the collar.

She checked her watch as she wiggled a foot into a cowboy boot. She was late. According to her plan, she stuffed her dainty, yellow leather spike heels into her camera bag; just before the meeting with Rand she would unzip her cocoontype camouflage and emerge one hell of a butterfly.

With one last sip of the now cold coffee, she made a dash for her car and the 9:00 A.M. lawyer's appointment. She stopped midstride, ran back into the motel, grabbed a damp towel, and wiped the dried mud from her car's front seat. Then she headed down Highway 90 for Washington Avenue, the main street in Ocean Springs.

In an area where the only change is usually wrought by hurricanes, Chelsea saw few differences. Ocean Springs looked just about as she remembered it twelve years ago. As she turned on Washington Avenue and headed south over the railroad tracks, she noted the old L & N depot had received a face lift. It was now a gift shop called The Whistle Stop. The two-lane main street, lined with moss-drooping live oaks, sported a freshly painted divider stripe, untouched by Monday morning traffic.

She had to admit the area felt like home, though she still preferred the Houston bustle to the meandering pace of this Mississippi Gulf Coast.

She parked her MG in front of the barber shop just off Washington.

Though Dwight Connors had always handled her family's legal affairs, he had been more a part of their lives as an extra "uncle" and her grandfather's dearest friend.

She walked up the dusty flight of stairs to his office and wondered how much he'd changed in twelve years. From the unkempt look of things, clients hadn't beaten a recent trail to the heavy mahogany door, beautifully carved at the turn of the century. The worn brass knob turned loosely in its fittings, ready to be retired from duty. Chelsea pushed, and the door opened slightly; the fragrance of freshly brewed coffee beckoned. She closed the door and marveled. The wall to wall, floor to ceiling bookcases spilled memories from too many yesterdays. The office spoke to her like an excavated mine but the dust made her sneeze.

A chair squeaked to her right. Its stately occupant startled her. He looked like a clean-shaven Santa as he swiveled his dilapidated Morris chair away from the live oaks framed in the bay window. He looked over the gold rims of his half-framed glasses, precariously perched at the tip of his nose, to focus on the disturbance.

"Uncle Dee," she greeted, her voice warm and soft.

"Chelsea child." He bounced around a desk that time left stacked so high with debris she could hardly see his white hair bobbing toward her. "Oh, it's so good to see you." The old elf grinned, removed his glasses, and tilted his head an ounce to the left in a boyish show of bashfulness. Then, like a restrained southern gentleman, he graciously took her hand, squeezed it gently, and patted her folded fingers.

Affection tinged with nostalgia swelled in her heart as she smiled and gave him a bear hug and peck on his shiny dome. "It's...really great...to be here," she said slowly with sincerity.

He stepped back as she released her arms. "Why, honey, you're a beauty." He took a long look. "Course, you always were a darlin', but my, oh, my, what those years have done. Wish your granddaddy could see you now," he added, slightly melancholy. "It was a fine funeral...." His voice faltered. "But without family..." His head drooped.

In a quiet voice she apologized. "I'm so sorry. It was like I told you. I didn't know until it was too late. Aunt M. came...for both of us." Suddenly her grandfather's demise seemed as freshly painful as the day she'd heard the news upon her arrival back in Houston from a fashion shoot in the remote Big Bend National Park.

"Here, now. This is no time of day for gloom. I'm happy to see you dressed sensibly for a long tour of the yard," he commented with a chuckle that brightened both their spirits. "How about a cup of my famous coffee?—I even added a few fresh grounds for the occasion—then we'll get right to the business of these contracts of sale." Without waiting for confirmation he poured a cup for her.

"I'm glad you approve of my coveralls. I learned about mud when I stopped by the yard last night...."

He didn't seem to be listening. He was concentrating on the cup of hot, black liquid that threatened to spill as the delicate bone china cup rattled in a matching saucer that was cracked. "This was my Anna's favorite cup," he announced. "She died long before you were born." He placed the coffee shakily on the desk before a chair, which he motioned Chelsea toward.

"You must be very lonely, Uncle Dee," she sympathized, and slipped into the maple ladder-back chair.

Connors slumped into his seat, "To tell you the truth, child, when your grandpa Henry went, that was it. He was like my own brother, you know. I decided that probating his estate would be my last act as a lawyer. I'm as good as retired now. I farmed out my old clients to some younger men around." He changed abruptly. "Would you listen to me! I didn't insist you come halfway across the Gulf to talk about *me*. Now, let's look at these papers and then get to the yard. For heaven's sake, you must see your granddad's pride and joy, his half-finished Biloxi Schooner." He reached to pull open his desk drawer.

"Never mind," she nodded. "Whatever you have on those papers is fine with me. After all, if I can't trust you, who can I trust?"

He beamed. "Well, thank you, darlin', but—"

"I'm really eager to see the yard, and meet Mr. Sorensen."

Connors leaned forward in a most positive manner, braced his hands on the desk top, his voice stern. "Now, Chelsea, be aware of what you are signing. However, in this case, after all the depts are paid, you will have a rather handsome sum. Rand Korbet has agreed, with Herschel's full approval, to give you more than the fair market value. Course he doesn't regard the half-finished vessel as worth a plug nickel." Disapproval ran heavily in his voice.

She was amazed. "Are you sure? I mean, not that you wouldn't be.... I, uh, just didn't expect anything much."

"Oh, it should be somewhere between enough to start your own small agency in Houston, or"—he raised an eyebrow in expectation as he finished—"enough to finish building your grandpa's schooner."

"Ohhh, no, you don't. I'm not a boat-building Norquist. But my own agency, wow! That's something. I figured maybe in twenty years. It's possible now!" Her eyes widened with delight and looked more jade than emerald. In her enthusiasm she took a sip of the potent brew, and her expression changed to a pucker of distaste. It was much too strong. She put the coffee down. Restless, she announced, "I've had too much coffee already today. Let's go now. You can fill in the details while we drive." She stood as if to leave. "I'm eager, in case you can't tell. The sooner we sign these papers the better. When do we meet with Rand Korbet?"

"Slow down, child," he counseled. "You been in that big city too long. Things get done just as well if we take 'em as we find 'em. At least, here on the coast. However"—he picked up the receiver and started dialing—"I've had the papers ready for months, and young Korbet's been itchin' too. Let's see what time he can make it."

Chelsea nervously started to pace, her mind jumping from fairy plums to chocolate cherries in anticipation of a couple of dreams about to come true.

"That you, Herschel?" Connors yelled into the receiver. She listened attentively, though she kept walking back and forth. "Back still bothering you, uh? Sorry to hear that. Say, is Rand around there, close to the phone?"

Connors held his hand over the mouthpiece and explained, "It will be a minute. Rand's being paged. He's out on the dry dock. You remember Rand's granddad, Herschel? Has a bad back and—'' He broke off. ''Fine, fine, Rand. I'm calling to let you know Miss Norquist is here and set to meet with you as soon as possible. What?... Well, she looks just fine to me!'' He gave her a quizzical glance. ''And she seems as eager to sell as you are to buy.... Three o'clock?'' He looked to her for confirmation. She nodded in agreement while wishing it were sooner. ''Sounds fine, Rand. Is your mom going to be our notary? Fine. See ya'll at the Norquist office then around three.... What? Just a minute.'' He handed the receiver to Chelsea. ''Rand wishes to speak to you.''

As she took the instrument in her hand a ripple started somewhere below and tingled all the way up to her blushing face. ''Hello, good morning, I—''

''Good mornin' to *you*, Ms Norquist. How are your bruises after last night's battle with the mud?'' he drawled languorously. He had the same effect on her over the phone as he did in person, and in her daydreams. Her palms were warm and moist and her heart skipped and thundered in her ears as her breath grew more irregular and her mind refused to work her tongue.

She stumbled for words. ''Well, I, uh, well, how thoughtful of you. Uh, fine, I'm just fine...uh, and, well...'' Where was her natural, sharp repartee when she needed it most? ''See you at three.'' How dumb, dumb, she told herself. She had bidden him good-bye with a voice frothy from the verbal contact.

''I'm ready.'' Dazed, she floated toward the door.

If Connors noticed he didn't show it. ''Just a minute. I'll get my things. That yard will be one loblolly after all this rain. You got any rubber boots?'' he asked as he pulled his gear from under his desk.

Boots held little importance to her at that moment. ''No, just my rawhide boots, see?'' She pulled her pant legs up to show him. ''Will these do?''

"Can't say they will. If you don't mind, we'll check your grandpa's things in the loft for a pair. You got to go through that stuff anyway."

As they left, Chelsea noted Connors didn't even lock his office door. She wondered if that was because he didn't care or because he held a great deal of trust in the integrity of the local people.

For a seventy-six-year-old, he had little trouble easing down into the seat of her classic sports car. He appraised it immediately, commending her on her inherent good taste.

The ten-minute drive to Biloxi's Back Bay allowed small talk that, Chelsea slowly realized, carried some heavy overtones. Connors started with a not-so-subtle observation that, "To sell the yard to Korbet Shipbuilding Company would not only close the Norquist boatyard to wood boat construction and repair, it would effectively bring the end to an era, the end to a certain set of values, and the end to an almost extinct art form. "No more," he pontificated as he gave a history lesson, "No, no, sir, no more shallow draft schooners, ever, to work the rivers and bays as well as the Mississippi Sound and the Gulf." He recounted the qualities of the sea-going wooden workhorses that had fished and shrimped and hauled cargo; they had brought life and industry to the Gulf Coast states long before railroads, trucks, and planes.

As she turned the car into the familiar muddy ruts that led to the boatyard office, he finished his dissertation with, "If I had my way, you, Chelsea Norquist, would carry on quality wood boat-building in the Norquist tradition."

His remark touched a nerve grown more sensitive since she arrived in Biloxi; a pride in her family that she had purposely forgotten twelve years ago. Then her more practical Houston self told her these were the ramblings of an old man, out of touch with reality.

She parked the car exactly where she had last night, but an old yellow pickup truck with a slight list to port sat nearby. As she was debating the merits of new springs for the GMC, an Ichabod Crane incarnate waved from the office doorway. His six-foot seven-inch frame was topped with a huge Adam's apple that bobbled below a tiny onion head. A round smile wreathed his bony face, and his infectious warmth pulled a smile from Chelsea, already waving in response.

As he spryly exited the car, Connors bellowed, "Lafe, how was Mobile this fine, wet, winter's weekend? Oh, oh...that's goldarn slippery," he yelled, and grabbed the door handle. "You stay put, child, or you'll sink to your knees."

About that time a younger version of the older Sorensen appeared. He effortlessly carried several long planks with which he created a dry path from the office porch to Chelsea's car. All the while he answered his dad's questions in a language she soon learned was Danish. All six feet seven inches of him dutifully offered his hand to assist her.

Once they were all inside the office, Connors made the introductions. "Lafe, Eric, this is Henry's granddaughter, Chelsea." Duplicate grins and bobbing heads accompanied their greetings.

"How nice to meet you at last." The older man curved his wide, infectious smile earlobe to earlobe.

"Nice to meet ya," the younger, better looking, stammered bashfully.

"I'm Lafe Sorensen, Miss Norquist. My son, Eric," he offered in a thick Danish accent, as he extended a strong handshake. Eric's handshake lingered a moment.

Chelsea liked them immediately. What a delightful surprise. She felt both maternal and filial affection for them.

She bubbled, "I'm the one who's happy to meet you—at last. Thanks again for taking care of Grandpa and everything here at the end. I want to meet your wife and thank her, too." She nodded toward the old house.

"Uh, Mom won't be home from the hospital until after three. Boy, does she ever want to meet you!" Eric interjected. Now more engaging, a smile half as wide as his dad's blessed her.

"Hospital?"

"She's a cook, not a patient," Eric happily explained.

"And she's a *great* cook, wasted on that hospital," Connors volunteered. "That woman helps me keep my weight up." He patted his full girth and chuckled.

"So-oo, you want to look around now, Miss Norquist?" Lafe invited, indicating the whole area.

"Why, yes. I surely do. I remember some things, but..." She stopped rather than get into discussing the past. "Please call me Chelsea, if you will," she trilled, then curtsied unexpectedly, pulling out her pant pockets for want of a skirt. Her clownish joy enhanced her femininity and charmed her audience.

"You'll need rubber boots." Lafe forewarned matter-of-factly. Eric nodded agreement.

"I thought Henry's things in the loft might yield a pair for the time being," Connors advised.

Eric eagerly offered to check and left through a side door that slammed with a blast of cold air. The warmth of the office stove and the sunny day had helped Chelsea forget the chilly January winds.

"Ya, Eric will handle it," Lafe assured them as he shuffled across the cement floor and opened a beat-up old wooden filing cabinet. "While we wait, might as well look at some of these. For instance, this inventory of tools, molds, heavy equipment." He stopped as Chelsea cocked her head quizzically. She didn't think she needed to know any of this. He thought she needed further explanations. "Heavy equipment—you know, like the diesel engine we use on the ways. The railways, you remember, that's how we pull a vessel out of the water to work on the bottom," he prodded.

Her memory somewhat primed, she nodded her head yes, still only half-interested in this technical information.

Lafe continued his dutiful accounting in a dull monotone. Her attention soon wandered to penciled notes and phone numbers scrawled on the once tan utility walls of the huge room, banked with wood-sash windows on three sides. There her eyes lingered on a familiar collection of framed photos whose silver frames had aged into a gold-tinged, dusty rose. In one picture she recognized her dad and granddad among a crew of workmen she didn't remember. They stood in front of a clipper-bowed schooner ready for launch. Another picture revealed a vessel half-finished; the workmen proudly held various work tools that designated their individual skills.

Among the haphazardly hung pictures, several calendars from years past still remained. Jobs were marked on several days. She squinted to read the words from where she stood rather than risk rudely interrupting Lafe's lecture. She could read, "FAYARD out—caulk garboard." Another said, "MAPLE LEAF III—out, one plank aft." The office itself was familiar, but strange without her dad or granddad or mom around.

Connors wisely noted Chelsea's interest in the calendars as Lafe droned on and on. Then Eric returned. He carried four rubber boots and a huge, faded army surplus jacket in tatters.

Connors broke in. "Thanks Eric," he said as he took both pairs of boots to examine. "Surely we can get two out of four," he declared, scratching his white head of hair.

Eric then held the jacket open for Chelsea to slip her arms into. He beamed as if he were presenting her with a trophy. "This has been worn by just about everyone, including your dad and granddad." The years of character that had been worn into the coat made it a work of art.

"You really think I'll need this?" she giggled as she put it on and was promptly lost from sight. The frayed collar tickled her ears, the sleeves hung to her knees, the cuffs were stiff with an accumulation of soil and paints. She sniffed pungent aromas, dimly recalled as copper-bottom paint, creosote, linseed oil, tar, barnacles, and a variety of marine paints splashed from topsides work: red, white, black, blue and green. The quilted lining was still soft and warm, but only one button was left to fasten the jacket. One pocket was half torn away; the other, taut and bulging with a variety of oddities that included bronze screws and thick wood coins Eric called wood plugs.

Connors handed her two mismatched boots. "These ought to do it."

When the three men agreed finally that she was properly shod and protected against the cold, they squired her about the yard.

Connors was full of "remember whens" and "what might have beens." Lafe remained technical with his informative comments. She learned that in the past six months he and Eric had continued repair on some of the old regular wood boats, but had no time or money to take on new construction.

Her near contemporary at twenty-four, Eric strode easily beside Chelsea as a natural confidant. "Right after you moved to Houston, my dad sort of took over the job your dad had done. I've apprenticed here since I was ten, alongside Dad and your grandpa." He bent his towering frame down to speak confidentially. "After we moved into the old house, we became another family to Henry."

As the foursome inspected the parameters of the yard, the worn bulkhead, the barnacled, worm-eaten pilings and dilapidated wharf, Eric automatically took Chelsea's delicate hand to help her jump puddles and the wide, muddy chasms eaten away in yesterday's storm.

Eric continued in unabashed admiration for Chelsea and her Norwegian forebears. "Norquist traditions fit mighty well with our Danish ones." Cold winds howled, then tousled his black hair. He hunched into his CPO jacket a little further and kept talking.

"Mom, Dad, and I go home to Troense, in southern Denmark, every three years or so. I love it." He drew a verbal picture, comparing the Norquist yard to his grandfather's, where three- and four-masted wooden cargo ships were built for the Baltic trades. "I know it sounds corny, but those trips renew my dedication to wooden boat-building. Just to be at the yard where my dad grew up!" He raised black, bushy eyebrows heavenward in appreciation, widened his smile, and demonstrated contentment with a nod of his head.

She learned Eric had been born after his mom and dad moved to Nova Scotia. Work and warmth eventually brought them south.

"What will your family and you do, uh, now that I'm selling the yard?" she queried, just beginning to realize an entire family was about to be displaced.

Lafe and Connors, who had been walking ahead of them, dropped back on that remark. Eric deferred to his dad. "Young Korbet, uh, he's a fair man. We've jobs promised by him as finishers for the interiors of his steel vessels."

"He uses wood and formica," Eric added. "We'll probably have to move, but at least it's a job in Biloxi. We won't have to go North."

Just the mention of Rand Korbet's name assaulted her mind with his presence and the ambivalent emotions he had caused last night.

Eric caught her eyes. Sensitive to the flickering emotions at play in her deeply green orbs, he offered, on an upbeat note, "Hey, the best is yet to come, and it's out of the wind!" He inclined his body toward the shed, his hands jammed in his pant pockets for warmth. She followed, grateful to this newly acquired big younger brother and friend. Connors and Lafe fell in line as Eric continued, "Inside is your grandpa's supreme joy."

As they all entered the drafty, high-ceilinged old building, Lafe explained, "There she is. Though she's only half-finished, you can see she's some kind of special design."

"He gave her the last three years of his life," Connors said, more to himself than the others.

Chelsea gazed at the great wooden skeleton. "How big is this boat—uh, vessel—going to be?" she asked in their vernacular.

"Thirty-six-feet length over all," Eric chimed.

The older men were already walking around, touching the various planks, discussing the amazing craftsmanship. Eric remained beside Chelsea, whose gaze was drawn around the shed's interior. To her mind, time had not altered a thing. Odd shelving lined some of the walls with assorted, strange-looking tools, some rusty from lack of use, others finely oiled and sharpened. The bandsaw, which had been a relic when she was small, remained, as always, at the front of the building. Near it were the spur-of-the-moment wood stairs built in a day by her grandfather to make do until later. Later never came. The access to the mold loft remained as it was when started. Never even painted. The handrail well oiled by human hands full of sweat and dirt and tired engine oil. Some of the shed's wood siding was missing down near the water's edge, but other than that, it seemed as she remembered.

She gave her attention back to the framed-up keel and told them her first impression. "This reminds me of a huge turkey skeleton, resting on its backbone and picked clean at a Thanksgiving dinner." She smiled at her comparison, pleased with the thought.

That was a mistake. The statement challenged the three men to see to her enlightenment. They were serious as monks in their effort to help her share their appreciation of this beauty before her.

She was walked round and round the schooner-to-be, the collection of mud on her over-size boots now collecting sawdust and wood shavings from the earth floor. She could hardly move her feet by the time they finished pointing out the quality of the wood and the shipwright's ability in the stern, stem, frames, and their placement onto the keel. She did love the smell of the various woods involved already. The hardest white oak was starting a new life as the keel, stem, sternpost, and frames; long-leaf yellow pine as dead-wood.

Standing at the clipper-designed bow, the three professors reprogrammed Chelsea's values. "It's a design peculiarly suited for the Gulf Coast," Lafe enthused. "This first one is a gaff-rigged schooner."

"It was to be a prototype on speculation," Connors interrupted.

Lafe continued, "With this forward cockpit design"—he indicated an area just forward of the center—"Henry envisioned a watch kept easily on the luff and trim of sail for the main and jibs. Most all line to be handled from the comfort of the cockpit."

Eric jumped in, unable to control his zeal. "Now, doesn't that make sense?"

Chelsea nodded, trying to acknowledge and absorb what she was being told and saw, but she was unable to focus on what she was feeling.

"With this long keel she'll have a beautiful run." Lafe gestured the full length, a few inches up from the keel. "Good, uh?"

Eric interrupted before she could answer, "She'll be especially fast reaching and off the wind!"

Chelsea was dazzled by the smiles from three happy but expectant faces, awaiting her response. Her emerald eyes opened wide in a plea that matched her plaintive voice. "Is there a, a picture, or maybe a drawing of how she'll look completed? I guess . . . I could better understand, maybe?'' she grimaced with one finger tapping nervously on a pretty white tooth.

Connors jumped at the idea, eager to sell her on finishing out this one last sailboat, to take up where Henry had left off. ''Good, good idea. It's in the office. Yes, let's go to the office.''

As they all took turns and raked the mud off their boots on a scraper near the office door, Connors continued in an enticing, fairy godmother manner. ''Chelsea, child. Can you remember when you were just a wee thing, your folks would take you out to sail? As you sat by the rail and the boat worked her way into the Gulf, remember how the salt spray off the bow felt as it washed your senses clean of the land?'' he asked, his voice lilting.

''Sort of,'' she said vaguely, having blocked memories of her childhood for twelve years.

The quartet circled the desk, which had been wiped clean of grit and dust with one long sweep of Eric's sleeve. Lafe unrolled a large, colored rendering of an artist's concept of how the vessel would look, schooner rigged and under full sail.

''Just look at this high freeboard, the flaring bows,'' Connors whooped, losing himself in the fantasy. ''A great beam, eleven foot three inches to be exact, with this cockpit extending completely across the boat.''

Lafe took over. Chelsea turned to face him, impatient to speak. ''All this with a shallow three-and-a-half foot draft, centerboard up, and seven foot, board down. As we say back home, 'one wood-swimming lady this be.'''

''Wait, wait, enough,'' she begged. ''I'm properly impressed, even as she stands, slightly naked.'' She gathered her diminished Houston perspective, took a deep breath, and asked, ''One question: Why isn't the vessel finished?''

All three men tried to answer at once.

"We ran out of money, simply money," Lafe admitted.

"Ran out of wood," Eric alibied.

"Simple truth is, your grandpa ran out of time. If he were still here, he'd be slogging forward as the money came in and the wood available." Connors's answer had the finality of a eulogy.

For a moment she felt her grandfather's ghost. Then she turned to the task at hand. "It's pretty obvious, this place hasn't turned a profit in sometime."

The men seemed a little uncomfortable with that fact.

Chelsea started to say something; instead, she let a sunny smile light her face. "You know, for a while now I've felt I needed a lawyer to protect me from my lawyer and yard foreman and his son." That received the desired response. She had their attention and sympathy. "I got your message, boys, and it seems silly to have to defend myself in this matter, but here goes: I'm a Norquist who trained for and became an art director and a photographer, for a fine Houston advertising agency. I like my work. I'm good at it. I like my life." She was just warming up. "As I told you, Uncle Dee, I want my own agency eventually. You do see in what a different direction I've gone? Building boats in Back Bay, Biloxi, is out of the question—as if I could!" She finished and took a few steps in a circle. As an afterthought she added, "How different it would all have been if Dad had lived and carried forth.... But my training is in a totally unrelated field. Don't you agree?" As if their mute voices still argued, she added, "It's impossible for me to take up where Henry Norquist left off—if he couldn't make it pay, how could I?" She was exasperated at the idea and had worked herself into a high-pitched key. She walked to the window to stare into the yard. A moment later her good-natured self turned, looked at Eric, then at Lafe, and stopped on Connors. The three wise men remained wholly silent. She laughed and placed her hands on her hips. "Give me a break, ya'll. In fact, I'll buy lunch if you'll promise to make it a propaganda-free shrimp salad over at Fisherman's Wharf. How about it?"

On that they could all agree.

Chapter Three

Business was booming at the small restaurant on Highway 90. The parking lot was nearly full. With Eric crammed like an accordian in the seat next to her, Chelsea followed Lafe's pickup to the far corner of the parking lot.

A satisfied grin tugged at one side of her mouth as she recalled the impact she'd had back at the office when she'd pulled off her rubber boots, stood up, turned away from the three men, and slowly, oh so slowly, unzipped her coveralls. They had all quit breathing. Then she let the masculine attire drop to the floor, stepped out, and turned to face them—the perfect yellow butterfly of her design. A benign Lafe nodded; a wide-eyed Uncle Dee said only, "My, my, my, oh, my." Slack-jawed, Eric's eyes saucered, saying everything. At that point he insisted he could fit in her match-box car for the ride to lunch.

Eric sprung from his side of the car and flung her door open before she even had the engine off. While he watched, she changed from her cowboy boots to her dainty ankle-strap high heels. Lafe and Connors went on ahead to get a table. Eric glowed with his role as her escort.

Gulls screeched overhead, then dived for their dinner of refuse from the small shrimp boats docked next to the restaurant built on stilts over the water. Bitter, cold winds whipped off the Mississippi Sound and bit through Chelsea's flimsy angora sweater. She was so cold she shuddered in spite of herself as she walked toward the restaurant. Her plan did not call for wearing the army-surplus jacket once she left the yard, but then she hadn't felt those cold winds as she made her plan. Eric, sensitive to her every breath, quickly removed his plaid wool CPO jacket and slipped it around her shoulders.

"Th-h-h-anks," she chattered through clenched teeth. "My down vest would feel great about now. I'll give this back the minute we're inside."

"No problem." He was aglow. "Keep it as long as you wish."

"Do you know a dry cleaner for down vests?" she asked as they reached the door.

The question went unanswered as they stepped inside. In the steamy warmth she removed his jacket and held it out for him to reclaim. So enamored he couldn't take his eyes off her face, he failed to grasp the jacket, and it fell to the floor.

"Uh-oh." He stooped to get it.

"Oops." She bent over to pick it up at the same moment, bumping heads with Eric.

"Oh, uh, oh." They giggled and stood up, rubbing their matching bruises.

"I've got it," she said, abruptly retrieving it before his lanky bones could start to bend again. She carefully placed the coat in his hands, clasping them together around it before she let go.

Lafe and Connors missed most of this action as they followed the hostess to a red-checked, cloth-covered table near one of the windows fogged by the battle between hot and cold. Beyond those windows, barges, pushboats, tugs, and shrimpers plied the main channel to the Sound.

One Fisherman's Wharf customer, Rand Korbet, had not missed a thing. He was seated with a clear view of the front door. He watched the shapely yellow valentine, fascinated as she walked to her table. He easily forgot the gorgeous woman at his side, considered by the men at Korbet Ship to be the best-looking female on the entire Gulf Coast. Leslie Borba's breathtaking beauty bespoke her Teutonic heritage. Naturally slim, her tall, haughty carriage reminded one of a duchess at least. Haunting eyes, more gray than brown, left their mark wherever they roamed. Her skin was Dresden peach molded over a bone structure designed in heaven. The only feature to achieve more sighs was her hair, which flowed about her shoulders like burnished copper, rich, thick, and silky.

It was no secret that she wanted to marry Rand Korbet. Leslie had staked him out and let it be known that she was his girl. He was her territory, and it was just a matter of time. She loved his money and his aggressive drive to gain more land and power. She wanted to love his steel-hard body more, but he was stingy with it, always showing more interest in his work than in bedding her.

To Rand, Leslie was a beautiful boost to his ego—he liked to be envied—but he'd had his fill of trickery in women with his marriage and subsequent divorce a long time ago. She was tolerable, but her constant conniving kept him away more often than not. He had no interest in marriage or even in a long term relationship.

When they finished dining, Leslie excused herself for the powder room. Rand casually sauntered over to Chelsea's table.

"Hello, Dwight, Lafe, Eric." He greeted them, nodding to each. Then his eyes feasted on Chelsea. She had just taken a mouthful of delicious chunk shrimp in a Remoulade sauce, and her ability to speak was impaired. She met his bold gaze and hurried to chew her food, feeling much like a cow with fodder. Rand just watched, beholding her sunny effervescence.

Connors dabbed his napkin to his mouth and spoke up heartily. "Why, Rand, my boy. We're just about ready to meet with you, and here you are." He nodded to Chelsea, chewing madly. "You spoke with Miss Norquist this morning. Rand, this is Chelsea, Henry's granddaughter."

She took a long drink of water as Rand said, "Hello officially. You look better every time I see you, Chelsea. Nothing like last night. Certainly not like that frizzy-headed little boy who years back lived at the yard." He dared to laugh at her again, just as he had last night.

She choked on the last of the water. The more she coughed, the more she choked. She was still digging for a breath when Rand came around behind her and jolted her with a couple of rough pats on her back. She nearly landed in her plate, but still she coughed, marveling that her lungs could produce a wheeze when starved of oxygen. The man in command then jerked her arms above her head and in the process pulled her out of her chair. The other three men were frozen on the edge of their chairs at this emergency. She managed one tiny gasp as tears welled from her lack of air and inner exertion.

At that untimely moment Leslie arrived at the table and beheld Rand holding Chelsea a prisoner, her arms firmly above her head.

"Why, Rand, darlin', she's too frightened to run away. She's cryin'. You can let go now," Leslie said soothingly in her most affected and outlandish southern belle accent. Her territory was threatened. She eyed Chelsea; instinctively she knew how to deal with her. The fox and the hare.

Rand tersely introduced Leslie to all while continuing to hold Chelsea, but changed his life-saving technique to a bear hug around her tiny waist, letting his arms feel the soft mounds above her ribs. With her hands freed, Chelsea brusquely elbowed the good Samaritan's arms, who was rapidly doing more damage than good. She extricated herself, grabbed a napkin, and dabbed at the black tears of ruined eye makeup painting her cheeks and her chin. She ignored Leslie's presence, bid a raspy, "Excuse me," and fled to the privacy of the ladies' room.

Once behind the closed door, she finished coughing and spasmodically cleared her throat. She frowned with disgust at her mirrored reflection, red-faced and owl-eyed from the rearranged mascara. My plan! she wailed inwardly. My great plan. I really impressed Rand Korbet. That's the second time I was not in control, and he rescued me. I won't have this. I've never had this. I'll be in control again! she angrily told herself, thoroughly humiliated.

She took several deep breaths, cleaned her messy face as best she could for the moment, readjusted her lovely slacks and sweater, and stepped outside the ladies' room door to face a terribly concerned Eric. He asked if she was all right and kept on asking as he steered her back to the table.

"Rand's friend had an urgent appointment, but he was anxious about you and reluctant to leave. He said he'd see us at three, as planned, unless he heard otherwise," Connors dutifully reported.

She was relieved he was gone, but agitated. What is this with me? she thought. She skipped the rest of her lunch and ordered a cup of coffee while the others finished dining. Among other disturbing thoughts, she wondered who was this Leslie "beautiful" and what she had to do with Rand.

Connors interrupted her musings and directed her back to business. He forgot his promise as he spoke again of the little thirty-six-foot yacht, "No doubt about it, your grandpa's design would have proven so popular that mass production would inevitably have been required. That would have revitalized a lot of this community. Eric here is the only youngster for years that has cared enough to pass up the promise of 'big bucks,' as they say in other professions, to stick by his roots and apprentice himself to this craft of building wooden boats.''

Chelsea studied her coffee.

Lafe sang his verse of the song. ''Ya, you know Henry's perfected design will be lost. Rand has no interest, none, in building anything in wood, only steel. True, they make money. He has even bigger plans now. Rand wants to make this entire side of Back Bay, Korbet Ship. He's well on his way, too. He's a big employer around here—for fitters, welders, crane operators, materials preparations men—'' Lafe stopped as the waitress delivered the check.

True to her liberated word, Chelsea handled the check, much to the consternation of her lunch guests. She was grateful the waitress had interrupted when she did. As proud as she was of her Norquist boat-building traditions and the inherent quality it signified, she knew her life was in Houston. She was simply going to sell the yard to Rand, bid these fine folks adieu, and be on her way home. Of course, if Rand wanted to take her to dinner before she left, that would be okay, too. A business clincher.

However, from the looks of Leslie Beautiful, Rand was taken. Of course, that life-saving bear hug did seem a little unnecessary, she argued, then decided her great plan was in a cocked hat. Why kid herself, and dream further? But those fine daydreams were harmless, and they sure had made that long trip from Houston a cinch.

When they arrived back at the yard, she asked the three men to leave her alone for a while in the loft; she wished to go through her grandfather's things in solitude. She felt at home when she entered the cold, silent mold loft.

A small mountain of wooden crates and bulging cardboard boxes beckoned. There was an incredible, dreamlike quality to everything as she sorted through objects belonging to her parents that had been stored by her grandfather. Sweet memories, buried too long, crystal-ized with the family photo albums, crisp and deteriorat-ing from age. There was one thing undamaged by time and elements: a dark green strongbox. She unearthed it from the bottom of one of the crates but could not find a key or a clue to opening the lock. She set it aside and forgot it as she spied, upside down, her mother's wed-ding portrait, preserved under glass in an ornate wood-en frame. She felt prickles tease her spine, her neck, her forearms. The sweet young face that, Madonna-like, inclined her delicate head toward the formal bou-quet of roses and lace intertwined with flowing ribbons, was crushingly familiar. Chelsea had never realized she'd matured into her mother's double—not until that moment.

She wasn't half through when Eric stuck his head in and announced Rand's arrival. "Thanks, I'll be down in a minute," she said, and nodded.

She took a few minutes to touch up her makeup, though a cloud of melancholy made her question why she should bother. Her wilted spirit wondered just what really mattered anymore. How much of her was miss-ing that she didn't even know about? Her healthy sense of wholeness was being nibbled to death by moths.

As she descended the stairs from the loft those same moths nibbled at her firm resolve to sell the family yard and thus, squander her fresh treasure—roots.

Though her mind was flooded with familial images, preservation of the species momentarily surfaced as she entered the warm office; she was immediately at-tracted to Rand's magnetic presence. Chelsea was re-lentlessly drawn to just a quick glance but instead made a low, slow survey from his black kid shoes up the soft, flannel wool slacks that molded his thighs and lean hips; then her eyes flitted awkwardly to the topaz-brown sweater that absolutely matched his eyes, which were waiting, already fastened on her. She could not

look away. He held her gaze until one strand of untamed, sun-blonde hair that had fallen across his forehead seemed to beg her to smooth it away.

"Here, sit next to Mrs. Korbet," Eric's voice interrupted. She reluctantly turned away from Rand to look
at the spot Eric indicated on the wooden bench under
the window. The older woman seated there smiled
warmly as Rand introduced them. "Chelsea Norquist,
my mother, Mrs. Karl Korbet." He kept his eyes on
her.

"She's our notary today," Connors supplied.

The woman's sincere, dark brown eyes and her
lovely open smile welcomed Chelsea to sit down. In a
melodic voice tinged with a familiar Cajun accent, Mrs.
Korbet quietly started a slow, reminiscing flow of idle
Back Bay conversation.

Mrs. Korbet was a startling combination of dignity
and warmth. Somewhere in her early sixties, Chelsea
judged, with vestiges of her youthful beauty strongly in
evidence. A dramatic ribbon of gray streaked the right
side of her chestnut hair, naturally curving to the neat
bun at the nape of her neck. Her matronly figure was
dressed with simple good taste: a black, business-like
soft gabardine jacket dress with a white tailored collar
that separated the black from her face, which was full
of good healthy color. Perhaps Rand's deep, windburn
tan was partially his own mother's genetic endowment,
Chelsea mused, glancing at him as he stood beside his
mother and leaned against the wall.

Lafe and Eric stood next to the filing cabinet, appear-
ing to prop it up like duplicate bookends. Chelsea was
still awed by their extreme height.

Connors was seated at the old desk. The rendering of
her grandfather's pride and joy was carefully rolled up
and lying to one side of the stack of legal papers. These
she guessed to be contracts of sale.

Assuming the mantel of lawyer, Connors began.
"Since we all know why we're here, I guess we can

begin." He looked tenderly at Chelsea. She wondered how long this would take as she unconsciously dried her moist palms on her yellow slacks.

Eric spoke up brightly. "Remember, Chelsea, when Mama gets home, you're gonna come in and meet her—*at your old house.*"

Did he emphasize it, or was she just sensitive now? She would like to finish confronting her past, the ghosts, the memories. "Thank you; yes, of course. I, I, uh, want to meet your mom and see the house. She took care of Grandpa right"—her voice cracked—"just like my mother would have...." Heads snapped in her direction.

Connors queried in alarm, "Before we begin, Chelsea, is there something you wish to say? Something that might alter what we are about to do here today?"

She couldn't utter a word. She shook her head no in confusion while her mind skittered about, a lost lamb looking for direction.

"Very well then," Connors began. "Six months ago Henry Norquist suffered a heart attack. Slipped away from us, rest his soul. His true will and testament lies before us today...." His voice droned on in legalese while she shut it out as best she could to fight the mounting pain. She heard his final remarks with her name. "... leave to my only surviving progeny, my granddaughter, Chelsea Clynne Norquist, who resides in Houston, Texas."

Connors took a breath, nodded to Rand, and continued. "Rand here has been wanting this boatyard for several years now, as we all know. As we discussed earlier, Chelsea, he knows what he wants and is prepared to offer more than a fair price. A generous, I feel—" He stopped as he took his eyes from Rand to see her head sag.

Her throat constricted with a knife that stuck. She swallowed desperately. She couldn't raise her eyes. The worn gray-and-black patterned tiles on the floor began to swirl. Hot tears quietly slipped out and cooled on her cheeks as they fell on her lap.

"I...I...I'm sorry, I—" The cathartic flood of tears held back twelve years poured forth. She covered her mouth with her hands to muffle the awful sounds as they increased in volume. She wanted to run from the office. It was so hot and stuffy. Then Mrs. Korbet took Chelsea into her arms, "There, there, now, don't cry so. It's all right," she soothed.

No longer embarrassed, Chelsea, in uncontrollable, spasmodic sobs, wept for her mother, and for her father, and finally, for her grandfather.

Mrs. Korbet patted the heaving shoulders until the shuddering sorrow was quelled.

Someone placed a handkerchief in her hands. She pulled away from Mrs. Korbet's wet shoulder to use it and saw Rand crouched before her. "Th-thank you. I'm so sorry to have—disrupted..." She hiccuped in the aftermath of her dreadful weeping.

Her wet lashes were strikingly dark against the pallor of her skin. She dabbed at her nose and her wet cheeks while Rand stared, seeing her for the first time, for he gazed into her soul. She let him look. She couldn't hide what he'd already witnessed: her vulnerability. And in return she was allowed a glimpse into his true nature, as benevolent as his mother's, yet deeply moving to her with his masculine sensuality. Though no words were uttered, the looks they exchanged spoke volumes. There is no world out there. Only us, her inner voice recalled.

Then Rand broke the spell. "You okay now?"

"Sure." She sniffled. "Sorry, I don't know why, I—"

"No problem," he assured quietly. "We'll try again tomorrow, when you feel better." He glanced around for everyone's agreement.

Mrs. Korbet was still holding Chelsea's hands, studying her tear-streaked face. "You need some rest now, dear."

Ill-timed as it was, Connors couldn't resist advising, "And give a little more thought to selling—your inheritance."

Lafe abruptly ordered, "You come with me, now. Stay with us tonight. Thyra will be here any minute." He smiled sunnily.

"I, uh, don't think so. I'm all set, at the motel."

"No, enough talk," Lafe continued. "Eric, go start the water for tea. We all gonna have some of Thyra's cookies with tea."

"I, for one, think Chelsea should have solitude. I'm also needed back at the Korbet office, anyway. Right, son?" Mrs. Korbet looked at Rand for confirmation.

He contemplated Chelsea for a moment, paused, and agreed. "Mom's right. I'll phone you later to see how you're doing."

Chapter Four

The penetrating seriousness of the nonjoking Rand Korbet was even more appealing, Chelsea decided, curled up in the worn-out, Naugahyde recliner. He was so pleasant to contemplate, and she was so weary. She felt like a stone, lodged in the chair.

From the kitchen the sounds of the Sorensen men preparing tea were distant, tinkling on the edge of her awareness like remote temple bells.

For some reason she felt quite small. Never in her adult life had she perceived herself as small. At 118 pounds, five feet six inches, she was average to tall. Perhaps, she mused, I left a little piece of myself in the loft with my family's stuff.

Her swollen eyelids felt heavy as she scanned the pine-paneled walls, darkened with age, in the living room—the front room as they had called it when she was a kid. When she was a kid.... A few more memories surfaced: learning to roller-skate on this same hardwood floor as her father held her hand; her aproned mother frying a delicacy caught by her granddad—softshell crab—then serving it to a timid six-year-old who winced at the idea of eating the shell.

The three-bedroom house had been considered quite grand when it was built in the twenties. By now it had withstood a few hurricanes. Other than the brown siding that now covered the original white-wood exterior, it seemed about the same. Why brown siding, she wondered? Everyone here knows you paint boats white to deflect the sun's heat—the same principle should apply to houses.

Thyra's arrival interrupted Chelsea's reverie. Lafe and Eric carried the sacks of groceries from her car, which was parked near the back door. After a brief conversation in hushed tones, Thyra came to meet Chelsea, a boneless mass in the old chair.

Chelsea tried to sit up and lower the foot rest to greet her hostess. The short, plump, middle-aged lady, jolly in spite of her attempted restraint, extended her work-worn, chubby hands as mirth lighted her eyes. "How do you do, Chelsea Norquist." Her head bobbed with the Danish rhythm of her spoken English. The motion accentuated her short gray-blond hair that didn't just grow—it sprouted. "I'm Thyra Sorensen." A grin broke free and absolutely frolicked across her face.

Chelsea was enchanted and sounded timid as she said, "Hi, Mrs. Sorensen. Nice to meet you at last. You took such great care of my granddad. That was very dear of you."

Thyra blushed with modesty. "Henry? Oh, no. He took care of us, just like we were family, for years," she demurred as she tied a faded print apron around her large bosom and little round shoulders as well as her ample tummy and hips. She still wore a white nylon uniform with a hospital emblem on the breast pocket.

"No matter what you say, I thank you for being here and for caring," Chelsea declared as she gave up on the foot rest and awkwardly extricated herself from the stubborn recliner. "May I help you with anything?"

Thyra pursed her lips and peered owlishly over her glasses, then her gamin smile returned. "I was told you had quite an afternoon and needed rest, but if you feel like joining me at the kitchen table, that would be lovely."

"Ah, I'm fine now, really. I've rested, and now I'm ready to work," she stressed. As she followed close behind this maternal gnome, Chelsea kicked her diminished self-image and rose to her full height when they reached the cheery kitchen. "I want to know all about you and Lafe, of course, Eric, then Denmark and boat-building in Troense and your years with Grandpa and—"

Thyra interrupted with her look of incredulity. "Well...sure, sure," she said, nodding her head. "But we're just plain folks mostly, I guess." She automatically started stowing the cans and fresh foods. "Now, you'll stay here, of course. Eric has made up the bed in your grandpa's room. After dinner we'll go check you out of that motel."

Chelsea didn't wish to appear ungracious, but the invitation, well...

"Here, sit here." Thyra pulled Chelsea into an old pine catkin high-back chair at the round oak table, then placed a grocery sack of fresh green beans in front of her and tore it open. "We'll just snap beans while we get acquainted, though I do feel I know you, from all Henry said." Thyra sat down beside her, put a mixing bowl in her lap, and handed Chelsea another. The two women plucked away at the mound of beans, snapping and talking so fast they hardly noticed when Lafe and Eric sat down at the table with them and served the almost forgotten hot tea and Thyra's delectable, buttery spritz cookies.

The afternoon pleasantly fused with evening as the four talked and joked and felt like a family through Henry Norquist. Thyra had already started dinner preparations when Chelsea made up her mind and announced to all three, "I know you'll understand why I'm staying tonight at the motel. I'm afraid if I stay here, with all these memories, my ambivalence will only get worse. I do appreciate your asking." She smiled, her eyebrows raised to encourage their acceptance.

Of the three serious-looking faces, Eric was the most

disappointed. "Please, stay. I've got you all set in your grandpa's room, and we can talk all evening and—"

"Now son, she knows what's best for herself," Lafe interrupted. He was about to say more when the phone rang, and he answered it.

"Uh, hel-lo. Yes, Rand. She's fine, just fine now. I think she can. Just a minute." Lafe called Chelsea as he held out the receiver, "It's Rand."

Her heart skipped, then doubled its beat as she took the receiver. She had definitely returned to "normal" she told herself. When she spoke her voice betrayed her attempt to sound casual. "Hi. Thanks for calling. I need to apologize for delaying the closing as I did." She was rushing. "Tomorrow, early tomorrow, if we can—"

Rand cut in, "If you feel like it, let's meet now, over dinner. We probably need to talk…about all this business…don't you think?" his heavenly, husky voice coaxed.

Well, of course, she had to agree. Sometime earlier today, wasn't that what she had wanted? "That's a lovely idea. I would like to hear your plans for the yard, although I've heard *about* them, from others," she said in a lilting voice.

"Do you remember where the office is at Korbet Ship? Same old house out front. The only thing that hasn't changed over here." His pride was showing, or was he just a little smug? "I'll be waiting out front. Just back out of the Norquist driveway and head east on the blacktop. Half mile later you can't miss me." He laughed. "Five minutes, okay?"

She was giddy. "Oh, well, sure!" She replaced the receiver with hands that were definitely shaking. She felt bubbly joy until she turned to tell the Sorensens. One look and a fistful of guilt dented her delight.

"Rand suggested we meet, to talk, uh, to discuss all this business before tomorrow's meeting." She hurried on, "I'll just stop by his office on my way back to the motel now.'' She colored the truth just a little and skipped the part about dinner, to spare their feelings. ''I'll see ya'll in the morning,'' she threw over her shoulder as she gathered her car keys and purse from the living room.

Thyra was hot on nourishment and wailed, ''But you haven't eaten dinner yet, and I'll have it on the table in another hour or so. Just come on back after your meeting!'' Oh, how logical, Chelsea thought. Now what do I say?

''I know you're a marvelous cook, Thyra, and I'm a fool to pass up a chance to dine like royalty. But there's no way I'll know how long this meeting will take, and I won't have you spoil your dinner waiting for me. I'll just get something back at the motel later.'' God, one little fib to spare feelings and now this. Will you never learn, Chelsea? she glumly asked herself.

The whole family followed her to the car, expressing regrets but assuring her they understood. Thyra insisted she plan dinner with them tomorrow night, for sure. Eric plaintively extended the invitation again for tonight, should she change her mind.

Two tiny thoughts flashed through her mind as she streaked for Korbet Ship: I wish I were as fresh and well put together now as when I left the motel this morning, and, after that intensely compassionate moment when Rand viewed my naked soul, what effect if any, will it have on this ''business'' meeting tonight?

The moment Chelsea pulled into the paved drive, Rand came out the front door of the office and headed for her car. As he opened her door his lusty smile answered her question. She was definitely affected—all over. ''Business'' was going to be laced with pleasure if nothing else.

''Just leave your car; we'll get it later,'' he ordered. Both glorious dimples stated his intentions. ''We'll take my Blazer!''

Her instincts told her better. ''No, thanks. I'll just

follow you to the restaurant; then I can go directly back to the motel from there." That's a girl, she told herself. Keep your options open.

Rand smiled wickedly. "Suit yourself." He winked, and added, "But follow closely, now. This big city could swallow a young thing like you, alone, at night. We're heading for the Old French House restaurant by Highway Ninety." He shut her car door and in three brisk strides was behind the wheel of his four-wheel drive, no-nonsense Blazer. That impressed her. He was a stable business man in a workingman's vehicle. Perhaps he *was* only interested in her health and her yard with no hanky-panky intended. *I've probably read into his words and actions what I had hoped, wanted, dreamed. And I'm just damned attracted to him.*

Therefore, it was prefectly natural for her to try to look her best. She attempted to touch up her makeup, dab on some lip gloss, and brush at her hair while she drove behind him, one eye on the road and the other on her reflection in the rearview mirror.

Though her attention was divided, she did notice they were driving through narrow, two-lane streets where old homes served as small businesses. In one block the neon-sign company had struck gold: every glassed-in front porch flashed colorful tubing that competitively shouted each specialty, from fashion to hardware. Few if any conglomerates did business here.

The MG cuddled up to the Blazer in the parking lot of the ancient Magnolia hotel. They faced a motor bank just off Highway 90 that resembled a white antebellum home. It was a charming area of Biloxi, perfect for an evening that promised to be, at the least, enchanting.

She planned to enjoy this meeting with Rand Korbet. From the moment he opened her car door and she accepted his extended hand in assistance, real or imagined, the singing tension between them began. She thrust her long, shapely legs to the ground, and he took a slow, deliberate survey all the way to her well-turned ankle and enticing sandal-strap high heels.

"Thank you," she said, looking up into hot, amber-brown eyes that grabbed her breath.

"And thank *you.* Sights are lovely tonight." His warm, husky tones scorched with insinuation, as did his big, hot hand at the small of her back while he guided her across the parking lot.

As they neared the courtyard entry to Mary Mahoney's restaurant, Chelsea shivered from the cold night air, and ran ahead of him into the brightly lighted Creole courtyard, laughing, "Here I am, freezing without a coat again."

He rushed to keep up. "Wear my jacket," he ordered, breathless as he reached her. She gazed up at him, and above his head a black velvet sky crackled crisp and clear and held a handful of twinkling diamonds temptingly near.

"No, no thanks," she chattered. "I never allow gallant knights to rescue me more than three times a day. I've only been here twenty-four hours, and you've saved me from sinking in mud, choking to death, and drowning in tears." She wanted to say something about his offered compassion, but a look crossed his gorgeous eyes at the wonder of it all. She said no more.

He took her hand in silence and led her to the hallway entrance. It seemed dark and clandestine, and she half expected to be asked the password. With Rand beside her, it felt warm, appealing, with a hint of mystery that excited her silly sense of intrigue.

"What is this place?" she asked in wonder as they followed a hostess past a wall adorned by one huge oil painting, stepped up a level, and continued through a narrow doorway that led to a very small room at the back. The wall plaster appeared to have crumbled off in several places. The floor felt as if a thin layer of concrete had been poured over unlevel earth. It was cracked and patched. In contrast, they were seated at a small table covered with formal white linen and set with crystal, silver, and fine china. Flickering candle tapers in elegant silver holders cast an intimate glow.

"This used to be slave quarters. It's believed to have been built about 1737," Rand supplied, his interest in Chelsea's face, not history. Under his intense stare she blushed and looked away.

Few patrons shared this almost private dining room, she noted as an attractive waitress greeted Rand. "Hi, honey!" The bottle-blonde kept her back to Chelsea. "Whatever you want, I can handle it tonight." She wiggled her hips to emphasize her intent.

Chelsea fumed. Rand let it slide. With only one dimple slightly cracked, he said, "We'll start with this wine, Wanda Lou." He handed her the wine list and dismissed her with his full attention back on Chelsea.

Could he see the prickles of irritation, she wondered as she fought the jealousy provoked by that witchy waitress? But his caressing brown embers calmed her sparkling emeralds, and soon Chelsea felt all warm and happy. He was exactly as she had fantasized, especially the way he was looking at her.

Her mouth threatened to give away her inner excitement with an idiotic ear to ear grin. She struggled to control her lips in an easy, sincere smile, to keep her voice tone casual, as she said, "Nice place." That's all she could manage.

His response was a smile that broadened slowly, wickedly deepening his dimples. He took his time, leaned forward to rest one elbow on the table, then bathed her with his sexy, husky voice, all honeyed at the moment. "I wish all my 'business' acquaintances were this pleasant—and lovely to look at."

Chelsea pictured just how beautiful Leslie was and suspiciously had to wonder at his sincerity.

Then, abruptly it seemed to her, he launched into business, though still in those heavenly, honeyed tones. "I want to thank you for selling me the Norquist yard, excuse me, *your* yard. I've wanted to expand Korbet Ship in that direction for years. Because I know it's a wise move for me, and because the Norquists have always run a fair yard, I'm willing to pay more than the market value. Senseless to some, but, just good business to my way of thinking. I know the inventory well, the outstanding debts, the back salary to the Sorensens, who, by the way, have a job with me waiting for them."

Concentrating on Rand, the blond waitress interrupted. County-wide bosoms fell into his face as she leaned forward to place two long-stemmed crystal glasses before him. Her performance was hard to ignore as she bounced everything from her bleached curls to her ample hips in an exaggerated production of opening the wine. Suggestively she passed the fragrant cork under Rand's nose for approval, a little longer than was necessary. "For heaven's sake, Wanda Lou." He glowered. "I'll pour and we'll order later," he said, sharply dismissing her. Undaunted, she siddled away, Chelsea noted, and marveled at how well the waitress handled rejection.

The reflected candlelight danced in the vintage white wine, and once again their attention was well centered. Rand proposed the first toast: "To the many generations of boat-building Norquists that I have been privileged to know!" Their crystal kissed, and he added, "I want to thank them... for making the last one a female." He savored Chelsea's pinkening face as well as the fine wine aroma, then sipped heartily.

His words echoed with double meaning. She looked into the lively liquid, aware of a slight annoyance, then dismissed it and took a long, saluting sip that stimulated her to her toes.

Rand continued. "I want to know more about this female." His smile, his eyes, his voice.... Was there no end to this warmth that poured over her body like hot, fragrant oil? "Tell me what you're all about, Chelsea Norquist," he gently demanded.

All her fantasies paled by comparison to the potential of the moment, the evening, the...night.... "I, uh..." She inhaled, cleared her throat, and tried to sound casual, calm. "First, I wish to propose a second toast." She lifted her glass. "To Korbet Ship and the generation that sits before me. I've a hunch this one's a real man!" She nearly died. *Why did I say that?* "I mean, I meant to say, I was glad this one was a man!"

Rand roared, tossed back his head, and said, "I'll drink to that." Then he held his glass to hers while their eyes exchanged confused messages for an eternity. They finally remembered to sip the heady elixir.

The candlelight flickered as the electrical current between them took energy from each other. Her cheeks felt flushed. He was so warm, he promptly pulled off the crew-neck sweater that matched his amber-brown eyes to sit more comfortably in the white dress shirt he wore under it. She watched with pleasure as he rolled up the sleeves and confessed. "You'll never guess how surprised I was to find you at the yard last night—and in the mud. You don't look too bad in mud-brown," he teased, "but this yellow fluff is much better. When I saw you today at Fisherman's Wharf, I—"

She foolishly interrupted this lavish praise to ask, "Did you really think I was a boy—as a kid, I mean?" she coaxed, not wanting to believe that as fact.

"'Fraid so." He chuckled.

"Well, I knew you were around, anyway. And I never doubted that you were—a man." She batted her long eyelashes for emphasis.

He took that stroke as if it were well deserved, grinning all the wider. "Which brings up my almost-forgotten question. When did you turn into this girl, uh, this woman, who sits before me?"

Much more interested in what Rand had been doing in the last twelve years, she gave him an abbreviated version of her years from fourteen to twenty-six. As she concluded with her career goals they finished the bottle of wine, and both lingered in a golden fog. Delicate fingers of candlelight played about her wild, tawny mane, her satin cheeks, perky nose, and in her soft emerald eyes.

Talk about timing. Wanda Lou materialized out of pure thought. Her own. "Ya'll ready to order dinner now?" she twanged, once again giving her back to Chelsea.

Rand seemed slow to react, and when he did, his eyes remained locked with Chelsea's while his voice echoed on another plane, "Uh, the snapper, Wanda Lou, Mary's German fries, Roquefort on our salad, and a repeat on that wine." His eyes had asked Chelsea's agreement with each item ordered.

"Fine, sounds fine, great," she concurred.

"You heard the lady; that's it, Wanda Lou," he ordered, not glancing at her once. Chelsea felt as if she were suddenly in a contest to keep Rand's attention. Without blinking an eye, Chelsea lifted her water glass, sensuously held it to her downy pink cheek, then slowly rolled it to her moist, full lips, which were pouting in thirst. Rand was hypnotized. Triumphantly Chelsea shot a sidewise look at the now impatient waitress, still poised with pad and pencil.

Then, with a mere glance, Rand dismissed her. "That's it—please bring the wine now." Wanda Lou shrugged and moved away.

Heaven was Rand's undivided attention, and that little taste of power whetted Chelsea's appetite. Food had never been this delicious.

While they dined, she managed to draw from him a few of his plans for the yard and for Korbet Ship, which she perceived as synonymous with Rand Korbet's life.

"For a while I'll utilize the railways and move our small vessel repair and production over there, but as soon as possible, I'll put a marine travel lift that'll quickly handle pulling 'em out and putting 'em back in. I need to add another big dry dock at our place, so your place will take up the bread and butter work." He was rolling with his vision when he said, "I'll get around to the new machine shop when I tear down the old house."

It took a moment before the impact of the words hit her. She was inexplicably shocked at the thought and nailed him with a sharp look.

Not to be deterred, he dropped a small apology, his mind still in the future. "Sorry, but it will have to go eventually. I intend to expand Korbet Shipbuilding Company, Incorporated into a shipbuilding empire greater than even my grandfather once planned." With derision he added, "It's a dream my father certainly couldn't handle. He was so out of place at the shipyard. He should have been over with your granddad, reliving the past, building in wood. He had no appreciation for steel or market demands. He held Korbet Ship back," he said with stunning bitterness. "His death came none too soon. When I took over, Korbet Ship came to life again." He looked away, slightly embarrassed. "I didn't mean to get into all this."

Rand was still caught up in memories when coffee and cognac were placed before them by a now totally inconspicuous waitress.

Chelsea ventured in a soft voice, "Why did your dad, uh, how did your dad, die?"

"Just lost interest in living!" he snapped, then, more composed, added, "Let's get off this subject and back to your plans."

Reluctantly she acquiesced, aware she was in tender territory. His mother had been wonderful a few hours earlier, piquing Chelsea's curiosity, but she would wait. The fragrant coffee was delicious but sobering, or maybe it was the turn in the conversation. The golden glow had diminished somewhat when she began, "Well, as I said earlier, owning and running my own agency has been my ultimate goal. I can start those wheels in motion about twenty years ahead of schedule with the money from the yard. I believe I can get a line of credit with it from a banker friend who..." Rand's gaze seared as he raised questioning eyebrows. She felt compelled to reiterate, "Yes, *friend*. Business acquaintance, dinner occasionally, and that's all." Once again she was slightly annoyed with dear Rand. Chauvinist Rand.

He dug his hole a little deeper. "So, you'll be working at a nice, clean desk, or entertaining clients at dinner or— Sounds like women's work," he declared, his tone a little too smug for her to overlook.

Women's work! She bit the inside of her mouth while silently counting to twelve. It didn't help a bit. "I, uh, can easily see why a big outdoorsman like you would consider advertising as 'women's work.' Much is done indoors, although we have occasional location forays and battle the front lines of the weather. We are guilty of wearing clean clothes to an office that is somewhat orderly." Then she clinched her growling tirade more sarcastically than intended. "But the real difference lies in personnel—no mindless muscle allowed."

He blanched at the caustic remark but immediately apologized. "I'm sorry, Chelsea." He did look sincere. "It's just that shipyard work is one of the toughest, roughest...Even some men, like my dad, for instance, couldn't handle it, so I—"

"Naturally thought a mere woman should sit on a powder puff," she finished humorlessly. Disappointment provoked her angry glare as she looked him directly in those innocent amber-brown orbs. "I'll bet you've assumed for six months now, that I, being a mere woman, would naturally have to sell the Norquist yard." Her voice was steady but threatening.

"For God's sake, of course." His voice was incredulous. "I mean, even your grandfather couldn't keep the yard going."

"And he was a *man!*" She glowered and ground her pretty little teeth.

"How did we get into this? Not only was he a man, but his business was going broke. No one wants the maintenance of a damn wood boat, so construction of them was a thing of the past. Hell, he knew that. Then, what few wooden shrimpers or snapper boats that come for bottom work and repair are almost gone. His old customers from over Mobile, Pascagoula, Moss Point, they were still loyal, but a man can't make a living on that, let alone pay employees and build a business." He was shaking his head, adamant at the thought. "And those few old boats can't live forever, either."

Chelsea's polished fingernails nervously beat out a riff on her coffee cup. She looked away, then thoughtfully asked, "What do you propose to do with the half-finished thirty-six-footer of Grandpa's?" Naturally there was no smile on her face.

He shrugged. "I had thought of letting Lafe and Eric work on it and purchase it out of their salaries, but it would cost them too much of Korbet Ship's money and time. Besides, the vessel is taking up a railways that will be valuable space for my steel hull work." He hesitated, then flatly declared, "It's probably best to cut it up for firewood."

"What! You'll *what*?" She gasped, mounting emotion in her voice. "Are you saying, you'll destroy, just like that?" She angrily snapped her fingers. "A thing of beauty my grandfather so valued that he devoted the last three years of his life to it?" She was almost screaming. Seething, she was surprised at how strongly she felt about this.

"Chelsea, this is business," he corrected sharply, as if that should settle the whole matter.

Several patrons gawked at the feuding pair, whose voices were decibels louder than the intimate atmosphere allowed. He called for the check. As they walked through the bar and out the door it seemed as if someone had turned up the volume on the last strains of *The Way We Were*.

She was so upset, she didn't notice the cold. Silence, heavy between them, was broken only when they reached her car. Her voice was shaking with the weight of her angry decision. "Rand, I will *not* give you the opportunity to destroy that boat. I'm going to see it completed, and in record time, since I have another business to run in Houston. Then and only then will I sell you the Norquist yard." She opened her car door and slid in. "Thanks for dinner. Doing 'business' with you is a rare treat!" she snarled with intended sarcasm, and slammed the door. The MG whined as the engine coughed to life; she roared away to the sanctity of her Ocean Springs motel room one more time. The last glimpse she had of Rand was reflected in her rearview mirror. He postured like a charging dragon, flames leaping from his mouth.

Chapter Five

"Another two weeks! No way, there's no way, Chelsea," Art Graham flared, a little grumpy at being awakened in the middle of the night. "I can't find anything now!" he pointed out. "We still have our regular production schedule, which you promised to catch up on as soon as you were back, new clients waiting— No, another two weeks—uh-uh. We really need you here."

"Of course, Art," Chelsea responded, not really listening to what he was saying. Her mind was already at work on the plans to finish building the boat.

Her earlier conversation with Lafe had started the wheels in motion. He calmly took the news of her postponing the yard sale until the boat was launched. He willingly agreed to take charge of finishing construction and assured her they would have volunteers from the community to help bring the boat to completion in the two to three weeks allowed by her job. Lafe thought he could also get some materials contributed in the name of a just cause, the launch of the last of the Back Bay, Biloxi, schooners. She would then get the cash needed in loans from Aunt Marianne and her banker friend; her credit cards would have to handle the rest.

"I hope you agree," Art declared.

"Oh, I fully agree, Art, absolutely," she contributed, putting her seal of approval on his last statement, whatever it might have been, before drifting off again to recall her phone call to Connors.

Delightfully surprised, then immediately trium-
phant, Connors had said she was doing the "right
thing" and that he was available to assist in any way he
could. He offered to cosign a note at the bank with her;
he would paint; he would bring in old friends—retired
shipwrights and caulkers—to instruct in the finer points
of finishing the wooden hull if not work themselves.

"Did you hear me, Chelsea?" Art boomed in his
most majestic bass tones.

"Uh-huh. Yes, Art. You're absolutely right," she
conceded, totally unaware of what he had said. "Now,
I'll see you in two weeks, maybe three. I know you can
do it, Art. And I'll be devoted slave labor when I get
back," she finished, disregarding his attempted objec-
tions. Her voice was so positive and final, he gave up.

Defeated, he bawled, "Oh, all right, Chelsea. See
you in a couple of weeks."

Her mind was reeling from the sudden change of
events and mental scheduling for the job ahead. The
impossible job ahead, she reminded herself, not daring
to ask herself why she was attempting it. This much she
did know: Mr. Rand Korbet was going to bear witness
to one woman's dogged determination if nothing else.

Tuesday morning Chelsea checked out of the motel
and into her grandfather's room at the Sorensen's. It
made sense for her to be near the yard, she decided;
besides, they sincerely seemed to want her there.

By midafternoon Lafe had almost everything organized; a schedule had been drawn up by which the work
would be completed, names had been assigned to various jobs, some materials ordered and some already
arriving. The atmosphere at the yard had gone from
apathetic to positive and productive, making it an environment Chelsea thrived in, similar to her job in Houston.

A truckload of oak, pine, and cypress planking was
due to arrive from Lakeshore, Mississippi, freshly sawn

at a small hand mill in Kiln, Mississippi—all on faith in the Norquist reputation and Lafe Sorensen's personal popularity that they would be paid when the yard was sold.

Principles are worth what they cost you, Chelsea told herself as the debts mounted rapidly. She and Lafe were headed for the ship chandler to purchase the many fastenings and incidentals for the boat. Eric was to help unload the truck when it arrived and answer the phone that never stopped ringing now that the word had gone out, like oil through a pipeline, on what was being attempted.

Pitalo's—"the best ship chandler this side of Mobile," as Lafe said—was located in an old glass-front grocery store in the heart of boat-building Biloxi and across the street from the original Pitalo family home. Both buildings were modest, white-frame, one-story dwellings with high-pitched roofs.

Once inside, as the glass doors rattled shut behind them, Chelsea was fascinated by the marine hardware supply. The wide-planked floor, worn bare and smooth, gave a hollow echo to her footsteps. Lafe went about finding exactly what he knew they needed in copper, silicon bronze, and Monel screws and bolts. Chelsea walked among the shelves stacked with unfamiliar hardware and marine equipment, catching a whiff here and there of unrecognizable aromas that teased her adventurous senses. A crazy feeling of potential power welled within her as she imagined the many inventions she could create from this inventory of foreign objects. She would, however, soon come to know and love the forgotten smells of tarred hemp, caulking oakum, manila line, oiled metals, antifouling paints, marine varnishes, creosote-filled wood preservatives, and old-fashioned linseed oil.

She felt at home in this atmosphere of anything is possible, especially as she charged it all to her credit cards.

Over the last ring of the cash register she heard the now-familiar voice that filled her with electric excitement. His Mississippi–Cajun accent rolled out on husky tones that crackled as he spoke to his companion.

Her heart skipped, then doubled its beat, as she unconsciously turned toward him. Rand's wild, strawlike hair was captured under a black watch cap. His plaid wool shirt was open at the neck, the sleeves rolled to the elbows, revealing his thermal underwear cuffs. Her eyes stopped at his worn Levi's, which fit like a second skin, all points of wear faded extra white: the knees, thighs, pockets, and the bulge below his zippered fly. She had drifted in her mind to romantic moments of their ill-fated dinner when his introduction jarred her back to the present.

"Herschel, meet Chelsea, Henry's granddaughter." She smiled at the elderly, barrel-chested man as Rand continued with a touch of derision. "And the latest in a long line of Norquist boat builders. Chelsea, this is my grandfather, Herschel Korbet." He nodded casually. "Morning, Lafe."

Chelsea heard Lafe respond, "Morning, Rand, Herschel." Then she acknowledged, "Nice to meet you at last, Mr. Korbet. I've heard a great deal about you." She smiled, a perky tilt to her head and green eyes sparkling.

The square-headed, bald giant of a man dominated the room as his gravel voice rumbled a greeting. "Miss Norquist, the pleasure is all mine." For a man in his eighties, the twinkle in his eyes was certainly the forerunner to his grandson's. "It's very good to meet you. I seem to remember a tyke at the Norquists a few years back." He attempted an intimate whisper as he continued, "Don't you believe a word you hear about me unless you ask me first," he joked as he took her hand, squeezed it between his meaty palms, and roughly patted the tops of her fingers. "Oh, please call me Herschel. Now then, what is all this talk I hear about you and 'boat-building'?'' he demanded, looking down his bulbous nose like an inspector general, not a smile or a dimple anywhere.

Still unnerved by Rand's presence, and now confused by the elder Korbet's personality, she responded rather shakily. "Oh, I presumed... that is, didn't Rand tell you? I'm going to finish, that is, *we*—Lafe, Eric, and many of their friends—are going to complete Grandpa's thirty-six-foot design." Nervously she stuck her hands in the back pockets of her grungiest blue jeans, shifted her weight, and glanced at Lafe for reassurance. He nodded slowly.

Herschel pursed his lips, lowered his bushy eyebrows, and pretended to pout. "But I thought you were selling the yard to us? Does this mean you're leaving Houston, returning to Biloxi, and—"

She interrupted, her face a study in seriousness, "Oh, no, nothing like that. I'm still basically a city girl. I like my work in advertising." She looked at Rand directly in the eyes and without batting one tiny eyelash, declared, "I'll be selling the yard to Korbet Ship in two or three weeks, when we launch, uh, *Triumph*." The name just bubbled up, but she stated it defiantly, like a proclamation, her chin up and shapley chest out.

Lafe looked surprised at the name given the vessel, then interjected, "Yes, *Triumph*; home port: Back Bay, Biloxi."

Chelsea allowed a lavish smile to cross her face as she turned to the elder Korbet. "You, sir will certainly be invited to the launch, as will all of Korbet Ship," she delivered, casting a special look at Rand, half challenging, half inviting.

He took the challenge. "A few weeks, hell. You'll never finish that boat, *Ms* Norquist," he said, emphasizing the address sarcastically. "Why are you attempting the impossible, anyway? Just because I said something about women's work? You gonna prove something to me or to yourself?" She could feel the heat prickle her scalp as she inhaled sharply with anger. His gorgeous honey-brown eyes were cold and mocking, but his wonderful voice held only contempt. "Just admit you let your mouth overload"—slowly his eyes undressed her—"your Levi's, out of insecurity or anger or whatever. Save yourself the grief, money, and my time. Let's get this over with today and be done with it. I've got a two-week tow coming up tomorrow, and I need to sign those papers now, before I leave." He glowered then twisted the knife. "No doubt you are a fine art director-photographer, as you say, but those are not the qualifications that build ships...or even small wooden sailboats."

Chelsea was livid. His words had scratched raw nerves. Why was she doing this, anyway? Who was *he* to prove anything to? After all, she had her life in order, back in Houston. Her body was shaking, quivering, as she struggled for composure. The clear tones of her voice did not betray her. "Rand Korbet, you're not listening to me—and I've no more time to waste. *Triumph* awaits us, Lafe," she managed through clenched teeth, backing toward the door. "We've a boat to build. See you at the launch, Herschel." Without looking back she opened the heavy glass doors, and Lafe scurried out behind her. Herschel smiled to himself and chuckled. Rand spit out a lengthy chain of oaths to no one in particular.

Ten days and nights and eleven workmen later, the carvel oak planking had topped the battens from the garboard strake at the keel to the sheer strake near the deck beams. The white pine deck had been laid, and now the real elite of the old wood shipyard workmen, the caulkers, took over. These two men were in their late eighties, but the various craftsmen had ranged from as old as ninety-three to a couple of young apprentices in their late teens.

When Leon and Abe, the last of the local caulkers,

started to work on the garboards, Lafe and Eric caulked on the deck. For a time Chelsea, with camera and note-book, documented the old-timers and their soon to be extinct skills as the completion progressed. A sense of history and urgency dominated her consciousness.

She had lived in her oldest blue jeans, a sweat shirt over a cotton turtleneck, and her mechanics coveralls over all that. The slop-chest army surplus jacket had come in handy along with her comfortable cowboy boots. She had tried her hand at just about every part of the operation, learning quickly some of the unwritten secrets involved in building a wooden hull well.

Connors had been tirelessly rounding up and chauf-feuring the old men from the surrounding area to pro-vide the expertise in all phases. Lafe was great, but considered the elder shipwrights indispensable to the quality of the operation.

Eric reveled in his role of instructor to a willing and capable student. After Chelsea watched and worked with the ancient specialists in various phases, Eric went over it all again, patiently explaining and demonstrat-ing.

"Now, let the mallet do the work. You'll hear that solid ring when you've hit the iron on the right density of oakum, not too full and not too loose." He had his arms around her, enclosing her shoulders in his tall, lean frame as one hand held the caulking iron and oa-kum, the other gripped her hand along with the caulk-ing mallet. "Now, did you hear that difference?" he asked as he hit two different sections to show a per-fectly caulked seam and one that was just a little too loosely packed. A few more swings with the foot-and-a-half long wooden mallet and the sound was that of per-fection.

Chelsea gave it a try by herself. The mallet was amaz-ingly heavy, and she feared hitting her fingers, which awkwardly held the oakum and the #1 making iron. Timidly she swung at the quarter-size head of the iron.

Ka-thunk. She winced as her aim narrowly missed her fingers, the mallet bouncing off the side of the iron and hitting the lovely oak hull. "I guess I'll need a little more instruction?" she said meekly. "I usually find I'm fast to learn and much better coordinated than this." She scratched her babushka-covered head with frustration as her green eyes darkened for the moment. The predominantly tar smell from the oakum filled her nostrils as she beseeched her surrogate brother, friend, teacher.

Eric eagerly repositioned himself to patiently explain and demonstrate again the art of caulking a wooden boat. Adoringly he wrapped the oakum through her fingers.

Two hours later she had mastered enough of the art to be assigned the butt seams. Under his watchful eye, of course.

That night she needed aspirin to dim the pain in her aching muscles as she fell, wonderfully exhausted, into her grandfather's bed. It was only at bedtime each night that thoughts of Rand Korbet filtered through her busy mind to plague her dreams, in which she no longer found fulfillment. She had heard that his two-week trip had taken him to Tampa, Florida.

The job was going to take every bit of three weeks, she learned. After two phone calls to Aunt Marianne and a second call to Art Graham, the third week was arranged.

At fourteen days and counting, it was still magic time in the old shed. The finishing work was being done; the cockpit floored, centerboard fitted, rails and coamings ready for sanding, as well as the deck and hull planking. Some of the faces of the volunteer help were quite familiar by now, but Connors was still recruiting new people with different skills needed for completion of the now "community" *Triumph.* Everyone liked the name and especially liked Chelsea.

Her attitude had taken her out of the narrow confines for women in the area. There was a growing respect for her willingness to take on the job and work "like a man" to complete it. At the same time no one forgot there was a very sensual woman under her Tugboat Annie appearance and scrungy shipyard work clothes. There was something about the way she moved and talked and generally conducted herself that made her appealing to almost every man, old or young. She realized she had never experienced this intangible power before. Her presence inspired women and mesmerized men.

Eric was the worst hit. To him Chelsea represented all and more than he had ever hoped to find in a mate. They not only shared the value of the emerging *Triumph*, but she was fun and energetic and all woman, sexy in her dirty coveralls, smelling of shipyard and unladylike perspiration, her unique face smeared with dirt and grime, free of makeup, her mass of frizzy tendrils crammed under a scarf.

Chelsea enjoyed his company and tried always to treat him only as a brother. The whole experience was wonderful to her, and the Sorensen's were her new family. After a marvelous evening meal cooked by Thyra, she and Eric would clean the kitchen, then hurry back to work on the boat until midnight or so. Lafe remained with Thyra and handled business details by phone.

Rand Korbet arrived back from his two-week tow, dogged out and disgusted with the crew. They had found him ill-tempered and edgy for no apparent reason at all. News had reached him that Chelsea was rapidly becoming the toast of Biloxi–Ocean Springs. This was confirmed by the talk at Korbet Ship. Leslie Borba was no longer the shipyard workers' darling. Chelsea Norquist had their respect and admiration on every count.

On the pretext of helping out to hurry the project

along, Rand decided to drop by the Norquist yard as soon as he could.

It was after eight when Eric and Chelsea took their evening coffee break. She rested against the cockpit coaming, inhaling the fine fragrance from the fresh cup Eric had just placed in her hands. For the first time Eric started rubbing her shoulders and arm muscles. Chelsea didn't resist, still thinking of him as her surrogate brother, and slumped forward, moaning as she relaxed under his massage.

"These muscles have to be killing you, but you never complain. Feel good?" he queried as his hands found tender nerve centers.

"Uhmmmm," she groaned. "You're right. Don't stop," she mumbled, so relaxed she was about to spill her coffee.

That tiny bit of encouragement was all Eric needed. His hands hurried down her arms to allow his to enfold her while he lightly kissed her delicate throat, right under her ear.

Chelsea was shocked and immediately grew rigid and withdrew, but shrugged off his hands and advance with a humorous lilt in her voice. "Hey, come on now, Eric. I'm fine and time's awasting."

Neither said anything more as they went back to sanding on the topsides' raw wood. Eric's disappointment was quite evident, however, from the look on his face and from his drooping posture, which was considerable at his height. Chelsea was keenly aware for the first time of just how Eric felt toward her. All her energies and focus had been toward completion of *Triumph*. She had never noticed him as other than a facilitator to that goal.

Chelsea's mind contemplated how best to handle Eric as she huddled in the cockpit, sanding on the coaming, while he worked forward on the bow. Rand observed them both for a few minutes and remained unnoticed in the doorway. They looked so intent and were making so much noise sanding that he had to climb up the ladder and board the deck before either one looked up.

"Looks like you could use my help to expedite this launch. I just got in today, or I would have been here trying to get this finished all the faster. I need to buy this yard, remember?" He was trying to strike a friendly but businesslike tone, not wanting to give an inch in his original assessment of her inability to do what was now obviously going along quite well.

Chelsea was electrified by his presence, so sudden and unexpected. She tried not to look at his face but was irresistibly drawn to his amber-brown orbs, devilishly taunting to her sensual nature. He bestowed his breathtaking, deeply dimpled smile on her, and she could say nothing. Her sanding block was poised mid-air, and she remained crouched in position, as if in a still frame that had been taken from a motion picture.

Eric responded first. "Ah, that's okay, Rand. No sense you getting into a mess like this. A busy man like you don't need—"

Rand cut off Eric's diplomatic attempt to discourage him with a rude, "Eric, I decide how I spend my time best. Just get me the materials." He looked at Chelsea then back at Eric. "Sandpaper and a block. One more hand at work will surely get this thing finished that much faster and me ownership of the yard. I turn away money every day because I don't have the space," he pointed out in conclusion.

Eric glanced at Chelsea, who stood up and broke her stupor with a voice much calmer than it should have been. "Sure, Eric, get him some sandpaper. We haven't turned down any help yet, so why should we start now?" Her warm smile welcomed Rand to her side. Eric grumbled below his breath as he descended the ladder, reluctant to have Rand intrude on their evening alone, which was already off to a bad start.

"I hope your trip was as productive as our time

and effort here," she offered, turning back to her work, sanding on the coaming. For the first time since she had started all this, she wished she were well groomed—or at least was wearing a little eye makeup. He really bothered her, standing there, studying her appearance. The current between them sizzled. Eric felt it too as he produced the requested materials and shuffled back to his place at the bow.

She tried to sound businesslike as she broke the silence. "Eric will show you what to do," she said, hoping he would assign Rand to the stem and totally remove him from her presence on deck.

"I can see you need help right here," he proclaimed, defying her suggestion as he folded the sandpaper into thirds and attached it to the hard-rubber sanding block. As he worked across the cockpit from her, his conversation probed, "I hear this town has turned inside out for you and your *Triumph*," he taunted. "I'm surprised the boys from my yard been volunteering in their off time."

Eric glowered.

Chelsea struggled for control. Her voice sounded like a purr when she finally responded, "Is that right? I wouldn't know. We have had a great many people from all over in here, helping in every way they could, but I haven't left this place since I saw you at Pitalo's." She silently cursed the effect he had on her, realizing she couldn't stay angry with him no matter how arrogant he might be.

"Well, in that case I'll pick you up for lunch tomorrow." He stopped sanding, walked over, and whispered in her ear, "Wear, uh, something slightly more 'you,' or they won't let you in!" His warm breath was making her bonelessly fluid. It so distracted her, she took his insolent comment without insult.

The office phone begged attention. Eric saw to its needs, grumbling again as he descended the ladder about constant interruptions. When he finally answered it, he sounded off like a gleeful tattletale. "For you, Rand," he yelled from the office doorway. "Leslie Borba says you're late!" he added for Chelsea's benefit.

Rand took his time. His eyes lingered on Chelsea for the longest moment before he even moved. He betrayed no irritation with anyone as he softly bid her good-bye and said, "Twelve thirty tomorrow." He took the excitement and all her energy with him as he left. He had been there less than an hour.

She and Eric quit early at her suggestion. She tried not to think about what Leslie and Rand were doing as she fell, bone weary, into bed. It was awhile before the aspirin relaxed her muscles and even later before her mind let go of Rand.

A pristine sky of cobalt-blue painted the bay to match as Chelsea left the shed to dress for lunch. The winter sun, reaching for its zenith, shed a path of golden crystals everywhere her eyes traveled on the inland waterway. Work on the boat was progressing unusually well this morning, and she hated to quit in the middle of the day. On the other hand, she admitted, it would be great to smell and look like a woman for a change, to let her hair fly free from that scarf for a little while, and to have a friendly, civilized time alone with Rand.

She hurriedly showered and shampooed, wondering where all her intangible power went when he was around. Full of resolve to keep her strength and confidence, she applied her makeup quickly with a deft hand that redefined and enhanced her features. For a change she blew her hair dry, brushing it into a shining, squiggly mass that she pulled to her crown with a band and let long, tawny tendrils cascade near her temples, ears, and down her neck, needing all the femininity she could find today. Her tailored business suit of teal-blue worsted at least had a provocative side slit. She slipped the silk-lined matching jacket over her taupe silk shirt,

carefully leaving an extra button unfastened. A neck-
lace of cloisonné beads with matching drop earrings
was her final touch to please him.

Rand called her from the front door as she was taking an appraising look in the mirror, where she liked
what she saw. She was ready, confident, in control.
Nothing could go wrong this time.

Was it really an extra beautiful day, she wondered, or
was it just being with Rand that turned the ordinary
into a fantasy? The sky was a cerulean dome with the
sun, a golden sovereign, generously shimmering, skit-
tering, gleaming on the bay, a silver stage for the entire
performance. A profusion of variegated camellias had
burst forth along Highway 90 as they entered Ocean
Springs, proclaiming their time in that space with a
theme of rosy-pink blooms. How long have I been her-
metically sealed in that shed with the boat? Chelsea
puzzled. A little over two weeks, she mused, not caring
to get specific at the moment.

Rand had carefully directed the conversation toward
light, pleasant subjects from the moment he picked her
up. She was relaxed, her guard down, as they arrived at
the restaurant.

He was most gallant, playing at being a courtier,
when he opened the door of the Blazer to assist her
down from the high seat. Catching his mood, she deliberately swung her shapely legs around, crossed them,
and posed. *Games!!!* He watched with liquid enjoy-
ment. Her slender foot, clad in taupe pumps cut with a
vamp toe from Neiman's, she waved toward him. Rand
boldly encircled her finely chiseled ankle with his warm
fingers and daringly slid them up her perfectly tapered
calf. His touch sent chills that churned into inner fires
that matched his. To gain control she uncrossed her
legs to step down, unwittingly treating him to a glimpse
of nylon-covered inner thigh; her skirt hiked up, and
the slit fell open.

"Lovely," he murmured, taking both her arms in his strong hands to steady her as she stepped to the ground directly in front of him. He tightened his grip and molded her body to his while he whispered near her ear, "You are a most exquisite woman. I realize this more each time I see you. There's something special..." He stopped as she turned her head away.

She desperately wanted to believe all he had just said, but she doubted his sincerity at the moment. She lowered her lashes to hide her thoughts as he released her arms. He could be all business, then all lover, and she was learning his warm voice tone could be deceptive.

With a glance at the traffic she warily said, "Thank you," and adjusted her taupe kid-leather envelope purse under her arm as he took her hand in his. They crossed Robinson Street to enter Gallery Up from the Washington Street front door. "Didn't this used to be a bank of some kind?" she asked, trying for neutral ground.

"What a memory," he chuckled, his husky tones hot with honey. "Yes, until the architect, Bill Allen, Jr., bought it a few years back. He and his wife have slowly turned this into one of the most interesting places on the coast." Before he opened the ancient wood double doors he gazed for a long moment at her open face, sunny smile, and sparkling emerald eyes. The extra effort she had exerted to look her best was worth it. Hunger, appreciation, anticipation, announced themselves in his topaz-brown eyes, making her feel for a moment like a gift-wrapped package about to be opened.

"Oh, I agree. This I would expect in San Francisco!" she rhapsodized, gaping as they stopped, just inside. Soft music whispered in the background. The place was a feast to her senses. With a circling gaze she caught her breath at the aesthetic combinations on display. Here contemporary furnishings were for sale in a veritable art center of old-world charm. To her left Eames chairs were grouped around a Platner coffee table, almost dwarfed by giant potted palms that reached to the twenty-five foot ceiling. Her eyes lingered on the ceiling medallions. Rand followed her gaze and informed her they were the original intricate plaster, all white now, as were the walls. Oh, so tastefully, handsome paintings by living European artists displayed throughout the main floor, vied for attention.

A most delectable aroma pulled them through a doorway and into the small dining area, which held a few intimate tables for two and one low sofa with a long, rectangular coffee table. There they were seated by their hostess, Mrs. Allen, who it seemed personally made the soups fresh daily. Additionally she made and served each individual European cheese sandwich. The menu offered the usual drinks but specialized in fine imported wines and teas.

After meeting Mrs. Allen, Chelsea excused herself and left Rand to order lunch while she took a quick second look at the unconventional collection of art and furnishings. Within minutes Rand was beside her with two Bloody Marys and an announcement that their lunch awaited them. The subtle background music changed to an instrumental as she sat beside Rand on the low sofa and beheld food spread before them on the coffee table. She was quite surprised by how well he had pleased her palate without even consulting her: a simple tray of selected continental cheeses, a board of hot French bread, and two bowls of a delicately flavored, thick, rich soup, the exact ingredients to remain a mystery. When she asked, her hostess would only say the stock was a combination of beef, chicken, and pork.

She was further startled but pleased with Rand's knowledge and interest in the hand-thrown pottery on which their food was served. ''Each piece is a one of a kind from a young, undiscovered artisan deep in central Mississippi. I've wondered, but never asked, why they don't use our local Shearwater pottery of the Andersons?" He seemed like an entirely new person, totally comfortable in this atmosphere. She would never have guessed he could appreciate anything outside the realm of his boat business.

"I vaguely remember stories of Walter Anderson and of Shearwater Pottery. I guess it's just their choice," she agreed.

"Mayhaps, we human beings, foolish mortals be,'" he offered with a spoonful of soup poised above the bowl. He rolled his gorgeous amber-brown eyes in comical exaggeration, then dropped back to his unique accent to ask, "Is that the way Shakespeare said it?"

"I'm no expert on the great bard," she conceded, "but I got your message." Now she was thoroughly interested in exploring the many facets of this man. His physical appeal had blocked her ability to see beyond that one, magnificent aspect. Now she wanted to know more. "Do you read a lot, or watch TV, or see movies or plays or"—she tilted her head and shot him a knowing glance—"I know, you fish. I mean, being on the water so much, fishing must be your passionate pleasure!" Oh, why did I say *passionate*? "I meant," she stammered like an embarrassed schoolgirl, "what gives you the most pleasure...in your life, uh, other than Korbet Ship?" She fumbled with a slice of cheese, avoided his eyes, and wished her heart would quit hammering and her cheeks would cool down.

Rand very ably prepared a thin strip of cheese and fed it to her, locking into her gleaming emerald eyes. "Believe me when I say work—my plans for Korbet Ship—has been my all-consuming passion." His soft smile was replaced by a strangely serious look as he lowered his voice and added, "Until recently." His eyes and his voice held her speechless. She watched him take a drink and slowly lean back on the sofa.

Her voice cracked higher on the scales than usual when she responded, "I, uh, I can relate to that. But, uh, your bringing me here, a place I feel completely at home in, and seeing your appreciation for it, makes me realize just how little of Rand Korbet I know." She took a sip of her Bloody Mary and relaxed back on the sofa, a comfortable smile accompanying her statement. "I have considered you synonymous with your steel-ship empire."

He chuckled, and the warmth in her tummy spread all over everything on its way to her toes. "I like that, at least for now. But this lunch was meant for me to know you better—and to apologize for offending you at Mary Mahoney's and at Pitalo's." He reached across and touched the back of her hand, at rest on her thigh.

Though his fingers had been soft and gentle, she jumped as if shocked by electricity, and her heart raced again. Both his apology and his touch held tremendous promise.

If she had any defenses left, his double-dimpled smile took care of them. "Chelsea, you're the one full of surprises...." His statement drifted as their eyes locked; they stepped outside of time, mutually seeking the soul of the other. There they lingered until their hostess interrupted with a freshly brewed pot of special jasmine tea.

While Rand carefully strained the tea into the heavy pottery mugs, Chelsea took pleasure in his handsome ruggedness, his masculine scent, blended with that of his dove gray suede sport coat and aftershave. He handed her the mug of tea, neatly arranging his body so they sat touching on the small sofa. The heat in her hands was nothing compared to that where his thigh, covered in charcoal gray wool, burned hers, covered only in nylon, for her skirt's slit had pulled itself open again.

All her senses were momentarily aware of her exposed nylon thigh and the enticing friction occuring there as Rand shrugged out of his jacket and laid it over the arm of the couch. Then her focus switched to his powder-blue cashmere sweater, which she instinctively reached to stroke. She realized what she was doing and pulled her hand back, embarrassed this time at her seemingly brazen act.

"Go ahead. Don't stop," he coaxed pleasantly.

Her eyes caught at his open collar where a few sunbleached, matted curls beckoned her fingers also. She stomped on that impulse and instead brushed the chronically unruly lock of blond hair off his forehead. His hair defied any attempt to brush it into place.

"Did you enjoy your lunch?" Rand asked hypnotically. Chelsea only nodded yes, as she was still absorbing impressions of him, openly drinking in his uniqueness. His slightly crooked nose added to his strong profile. She could almost feel his full lips as they kissed the edge of his cup and sipped the hot tea. She again wanted to feel the slight scar on his upper lip, first with her finger, then with her lips, her tongue....

"Dessert?" his husky voice asked, drawing her into his eyes. Could he read her mind? She blushed and took a dainty sip of the amber liquid, but it was tasteless to her senses. The attraction, that awful, powerful magnetism, was building, exciting, distracting.

"No, thanks," she answered absently.

"In that case, if you're finished with your tea, come with me." His wicked dimples were more inviting than his husky words. He put his cup down, his voice urgent. "I, uh, have to show you the rest of Gallery Up."

She nodded, mesmerized. He placed her purse in her hands and grabbed his jacket, pointing out, "For this guided tour we go upstairs."

She hoped he couldn't tell how much her hand was shaking as he held it in his; then she realized his palm felt warm and moist. Perhaps he wasn't quite as in control as he appeared. At least, she didn't think his mind was fully on business. The more she thought of it, the more she realized she did not want to mix business with this pleasurable experience.

The strong, sensual bond between them enveloped them in a warm cocoon of silence. He led her through a back door and up a wooden stairway with a banister of intricately carved oak that led to a landing.

The Gallery Up held still more surprises for Chelsea. They ascended the next flight of stairs, then walked past a room Rand identified as Mr. Allen's office. She felt as if she had floated up the stairs and past that room when they entered a large area cluttered with construction. "This entire second floor is being turned into a bar and dance floor," he explained, leading her into the middle of the parquet dance area, just past the half-finished bar counter.

She stood, visibly shaking now and breathing heavily, but not from climbing stairs, she knew. Rand took her purse and put it with his jacket over a nearby bar stool, then, without breaking stride, returned to face her as the music from below filtered through an upstairs speaker. She idly thought it must be a tape, for again she heard, *Here, There and Everywhere* as he slipped his arms around her.

"This will be the dance floor soon." His hips were already swaying hers into motion as he added, "Let's initiate it."

Legs, don't fail me now, Chelsea begged as she practically swooned, easily moving into his body contours in rhythm with the music. That music, she vowed, would always have special meaning.

She got her wish and then some, as her downy cheeks snuggled on his cashmere shoulder, her frizzy tendrils gathering moisture as the two bodies increased in temperature. Only a few bars of the song later, his hot hands felt huge as they clasped her waist possessively. She let her head drop back, and they looked into each other's eyes. She delighted in the lazy look of sensuous pleasure narrowing his now smoky, amber-brown eyes. Her breath caught as his hand slipped down to press her hips against his hardened maleness;

her body knew what to do, and immediately softened to fit his. And they slowly, oh, so slowly, swayed in the same rhythm with the music.

She moved both her arms to circle his neck; the fullness of her breasts crushed against his chest. He lightly brushed his hot, moist lips against her forehead.

The music changed, and Rand huskily whispered the words with the song, reducing her to a puddle of honey right there on the spot. She couldn't move. He stopped dancing too and pulled her suit jacket back off her shoulders, which bound her arm and thrust her silk-covered breasts against the soft cashmere of his chest. One very hot, seeking hand covered her hips and pressed their bodies again into one form. She could feel her breasts swell, her nipples harden, and a wonderful moisture begin deep within.

She flashed on her daydream, then wondered if this was déjà vu as his husky voice in that crazy accent breathed her name. "Chelsea, I've wanted to hold you like this since I saw you at Fisherman's Wharf." His hand moved up her back, fondled her long, tendrilled mane of tawny brown hair, then tenderly followed the curve up her throat to her chin.

With parted lips she took his kiss, yielded to his demands, so much like her own, and allowed her desire to ignite with his. Her surrender set off a forest fire in Rand's loins. He pulled her jacket the rest of the way off and let it drop to the floor. To release some of his roaring libido he placed his strong hands around her waist, easily lifted her body high in the air, and inhaled her womanly scent. She braced her hands on his broad shoulders, locked as she was in his embrace, and enjoyed the long, crushing descent as her hips smoothly rode down his chest, his stomach, until she felt her hips slip past his waist. There he held her, as if to do so forever. She melted into his hardened body, his maleness. Her heart beat madly, as did his. She cupped his head in her hands, gazed into those heart-breaking

eyes, then lowered her lips to let the expertise of
Rand's mouth incite her passions even more. In unrestrained response she returned the play of his tongue
with her own and allowed him to deepen the lengthy
caress until he stopped himself.

"Rand!" she gasped, her eyelids heavy with longing.

He drew two deep breaths, then tenderly let her slide
until her feet rested on the floor. He backed away one
step. There in the dim light of the darkened upstairs
they stared at each other. Slowly they reentered reality.
He bent over, as if in slow motion, and picked up her
jacket from the floor, automatically brushing the dust
from it while his eyes bathed her in wonder, as if the
gift inside the wrapping had been more than he could
have imagined.

He didn't speak, nor did she, until he had assisted
her with the suit jacket, handed her her purse, and retrieved his sport coat. Then he took her hand, sought
the velvety green depths of her eyes, and murmured,
"I like what I'm allowed to know of the amazing
Miss—-uh, *Ms*—Norquist."

He paid their check, and, still in a wonderful, sensual
fog, they bade their hostess good-bye. Chelsea levi-
tated back across the street, aware only of his presence
and the imprint of his lips on hers.

As Rand pulled the Blazer up to the red light at Highway 90, his voice and manner were all business again,
friendly but definitely on business. "I meant to con-
gratulate you sooner. Your *Triumph* is looking good."
He leaned toward her to capture her eyes with his gaze.
The light changed, and he shifted into the traffic.

She put her hand on his thigh and smiled a modest
acceptance of his compliment, wanting to believe him
sincere, glad he had actually admitted, in so many
words, that she had done what he'd told her was impossible. She let her hand rest easily on his leg.

Rand continued, "Obviously some of the surprising
skills you used to build that boat have been used on the

people who helped you with it. When do you plan to launch? Another week?''

Enchanted as she had been with his touch and seductive attention, a moment passed before his question registered. A twinge of annoyance lurked. She wasn't certain, but she felt a double meaning trying to surface in his remarks. *Damn, was I just put down and set up to give him a firm sell date?* She pulled her hand away and looked out the window. A moment later she had to say it. ''Rand, are you accusing me of conniving, or practicing some trickery in my relationships with the many wonderful, talented people, *of all ages*,'' she emphasized, ''that have made, are making, the emergence of *Triumph* possible?'' She quickly turned back to see his reaction.

''Here we go again,'' he said, shaking his head in disbelief. ''I only meant it is a skill, a talent, to be able to commit other people to your personal goal. Your goal of completing your grandfather's dream has turned the entire community into a dedicated brotherhood of boat-building workmen.''

''How did you hear all this?'' she asked suspiciously, unsure of his explanation.

''The third degree?'' he snapped. A wickedly arched eyebrow evidenced his humor. ''I hear a lot at my yard—Korbet Ship has talked of little else—but I'm also in close radio contact when I'm at work, whether I'm delivering a vessel in the Gulf, or up river pushing a tow, or working a tug, docking a banana boat at Gulfport.... Come to think of it, you wanted to know more about me, so join me next trip out and see for yourself some of this life I live!'' he challenged, artfully rearranging the subject.

She had to admit he seemed reasonable and pleasant, so her suspicions were somewhat assuaged. His invitation was appealing.

Then he innocently asked again, ''Now, when do you plan to launch? Our deal was, if I remember correctly, I get the yard when you've launched that vessel, right?''

Chelsea was angry and confused. What to her had been an extremely personal, social, sensual experience, to him had been ''business'' as usual. Biting back tears of disappointment and pain and humiliation she responded in a tight steely voice. ''Sooner the better. Within the week, unless I waste more time with you than I have already.'' She scooted closer to her side of the car and demanded, ''Get me back to the yard—I'll show you how fast we can launch a Back Bay, Biloxi, schooner.''

The rest of the trip back Rand tried to make peace. He was honestly bewildered. ''What did I say that—that went down wrong?'' She remained silent. ''Wait a minute. Can't you mix a little pleasure with business?''

Was she wrong to feel one should be clearly defined from the other? She wavered but said nothing.

He reissued his invitation for her to take a turn on the tugs or pushboats with him. ''After all, you did say you wanted to know more about me, my work, my pleasure!'' he reminded her.

Fuming on her side of the seat, she refused to converse, and felt miserable. Chelsea wished she could get away from this man's influence. The heights were dizzying, but the pits weren't worth the trip.

Impatient with her furious silence, as they stopped at the Norquist Boatyard Rand popped off, ''What the hell, fast boats, fast women, and the money to support them—that's all I'm interested in!''

Chapter Six

By three o'clock Chelsea was back in the boatshed,
back in her dirty clothes, cutting through the remaining
work like a human buzz saw. No one could believe her
output. She herself was amazed at how much energy
her anger at Rand had tapped. She shouted encouragement to the others, cheering them to do more. When
the dust settled about eight, she briefed Lafe. He
agreed they could launch *Triumph* sooner if she skipped
some of the finishing work below deck. Their main
thrust would be the vessel's seaworthiness—no frills.

Late into the night, when all were gone but Eric,
Chelsea still slapped on primer. Eric worked beside her,
exhausted but delighted with her zealous spirit. He
wasn't aware of what had caused her frenzy, but somehow felt grateful to Rand.

With the purple and pinks of dawn, all primer was on
and dry enough in some places for the first coat of
paint. Chelsea was going strong, renewed with the
morning sun, but Eric was slumped over his knees, his
skinny bottom at rest on the loft steps.

"How do you do it, Chelsea?" he mumbled weakly.
"I know you want her finished—I do too—but you'll
kill us both at this rate. Anyway," he faltered, "I don't
want you to leave. I don't want you to go back to Houston when she's launched!" He looked sad and beaten.
"I can't help how I feel." His sheepish smile touched
her heart.

How perverse human nature, she mused, wishing she could feel more than she did for Eric. "Please, Eric. Don't say that. I like you, have from our first hello, but you've got to realize, my life was, is, centered happily in Houston." She went to him, tenderly touched his arm with her paint-smeared hand, and softly told him. "My time here with you has been a wonderful experience. I treasure our friendship; in fact, you're very special to me—like a brother. I wish you the best, and I hope all your dreams somehow come true, though building more wooden boats looks a little bleak right now." He turned his head, still resting in his palms, to cast a doleful, blue-eyed look at her. "But I will be going home as quickly as we launch, that's for certain," she concluded. Her voice was kind, but her words stung with honesty.

Eric got the message at last. He nodded and pulled himself up. Now more than tired, he was dejected, but resigned to his brotherly role. "I'll get us some fresh coffee," he pouted, "unless you're ready to break for breakfast?"

"Coffee would be great, thanks," she said, grateful for his acceptance. "Uh, before you go, do you know where that new can of thinner is? I think the forward area's dry enough to take the first coat of white."

When Eric returned with the coffee, Lafe was with him. Not one to interfere, Lafe merely asked her, "How you doin' this morning?"

As she stopped to accept the cup of hoped-for revitalization, she tried to sound more cheerful than she felt. "Fine, fine. She's looking more and more like the beautiful lady of Grandpa's design." She beamed in the direction of the painted starboard bow.

Lafe and Eric nodded silent agreement, then shuffled over and started to work, no more conversation offered or needed.

It was later in the morning, after several other volunteers had arrived and started to paint, that Dwight Con-

nors dropped by. He just observed the rather frenetic
activity for a while. To him, Chelsea looked like a be-
draggled and bent cattle prod. Everyone was moving
fast, but she was moving faster; a permanent scowl
pulled her lips down. He quietly signaled for her to
come with him. She put the paintbrush down and obediently followed him into the office and shut the door
behind her. Her weary but expectant green eyes looked
up at him as she plopped down on the wood bench,
stretching her tired legs in front, her hands crossed
over her lap, her back braced by the windowsill.

"Thyra called me. Said you worked all night!" He
paused for her response, but she only lowered her
lashes to hide her eyes. "'Tis the smile that makes the
face, child. Did you paint yours on that boat? She's
looking pretty, but you—you could use some rest."

"You're right." She sighed. "It's just that I'm running out of time," she alibied. At least it was half the
reason for her rush.

Connors raised a wiser-than-thou eyebrow, and she
could feel a platitude coming her way. "I feel a little
responsible for what you are doing; therefore I must
remind you that nothing in this life is worth missing the
present for a possible future—not even completion of
your grandfather's dream." He shook his head from
side to side and nervously tugged at his ear.

"Oh, Uncle Dee, I want to get this yard in Korbet
Ship's hands and get back to Houston as fast as I can,"
she confided.

"Oh, yes, how was yesterday's lunch with Rand, or
does your all-night effort answer that question?" He
absently rubbed his neck as he sat down beside her.

"That man! He is the most arrogant, smug, change-
able—does he always get what he wants?" she flared,
her energy picking up.

"Well, now, don't forget: stubborn, aggressive, ambitious: traits you both have in common—if you don't
mind my pointing it out." A tinge of humor played in

his eyes as he wisely excused himself on the pretext of having urgent business elsewhere.

Around noon most of the crew broke for lunch. Chelsea joined them for a brown-bag picnic near the water's edge, under the moss-laden live oaks. It was one of those fine Gulf Coast wintery days, crisp and cool but warm in the sun. The tranquil bay waters reflected a cloudless azure sky. Without even realizing it, Chelsea had begun to rely on the water to soothe her ailing spirit.

Eric had recovered his good nature and was sharing a joke with a laughing Chelsea when a pushboat roared by. It went so fast and came so close that it threw wake enough to wash the shores higher than usual, rocking the loose pilings under the dock. A few minutes later the pushboat returned in the same reckless manner. This time cursing comments from the other workmen made Chelsea look up in time to see the man at the helm. Rand Korbet waved, smiled, and throttled down, but his vessel's wake still created havoc.

"What's Korbet up to?" someone asked. "Crazy guy! Never seen him do nothing like that before," another added. "Who ever knows what's up at Korbet Ship?" remarked yet another.

Rand's actions had served their purpose. They had reminded Chelsea, as if she could forget, of this man who was the cause of more inner confusion for her than anyone or anything since her parent's death. For her own sanity, she wanted to be free of this Biloxi turmoil, away from a situation with Rand Korbet.

The sun was up early, along with everyone else, two days later. Dwight Connors and Thyra walked around the completed schooner, admiring the beauty of *Triumph*, which was ready for launch. "It's a miracle!" Connors declared.

"Like they say 'round here, 'when push comes to

shove,' that Chelsea puts some fire behind the shoving," Thyra pointed out.

An exhausted Lafe joined them, cleaning his hands of paint with a turpentined rag. "Bottom paint won't be dry, but she wants to put her in this afternoon," he decreed.

From the forward hatch where she was still at work varnishing, Chelsea called to Lafe as she acknowledged Thyra and Connors with a smile. "Remember, I'll call the Korbet Ship people to invite them for this afternoon's launch, but will you get the word out to the rest of the community and all the volunteers?" she asked, knowing the magnitude of her request. She added, "Puh-lease?" The freckles of white paint on her face added to her impish grin. What could her three friends do but say yes.

When Chelsea went to use the office phone, she sadly realized she had not been a good photojournalist. Some of the operation was well documented, but once she was deeply involved in the rush to finish sanding, priming, painting, and varnishing, she'd seldom remembered to get her camera. As she dialed Korbet Ship she promised herself this afternoon's momentous event would be thoroughly documented.

Mrs. Korbet answered and received Chelsea's announcement and invitation graciously. She turned around and repeated it to everyone in the office. Chelsea could hear Herschel Korbet whoop in exultation. His was the kind of reaction she felt herself. Mrs. Korbet's soft voice then inquired, "Would you like to speak with Rand, dear?"

"Why, uh, yes, if it's convenient." Convenient, hell, she was dying to gloat at him: *I've done the impossible, in record time, no less.*

Rand picked up the extension out on the drydock. "*Good* morning, Ms Norquist!" he crooned.

She swooned, then cursed inwardly at his damned appealing voice as she warmed to his husky tones invol-

untarily. It certainly took the cutting edge off her voice
as she began, "This is your official invitation to this
afternoon's launch of *Triumph*, the final Back Bay
schooner from Norquist Boatyard."

"Well, great! You did it, Chelsea. Think she'll
float?" he roared, daring to provoke her temper, as if
enough harsh words had not already passed between
them.

She bit her tongue to keep from slashing back and
rose above it with, "She goes in at three thirty. Please
tell the boys in the yard, all of Korbet Ship is invited."

"Yes, Ms Norquist, as you wish, Ms Norquist," he
mocked. "I'll pass the word." Then his little-boy giggle
both delighted and infuriated her. He caught his breath
and said, "Hey, Chels, how about a celebration dinner
tonight? Just the two of us, to show all is forgiven, all
right?"

She was shocked speechless. Three days ago they'd
parted in anger, and now, like a goose, each new day
was a whole new world. "All is forgiven" indeed, she
thought. Damn his unpredictability. Of course, all she
wanted since he answered the phone was to be in his
arms again. He took her silence as positive.

"And, Chels, dig into that seabag of yours for something kind of dressy. We're going to Trilby's, and the
owner likes boats and boat builders. In fact, he's a
likely customer for *Triumph* if he's there tonight. See
you at the great launch; then I'll pick you up at seven."
He hung up before she could utter a word. The
honeyed-up husky accent had done it again.

Chels echoed in her mind as she went back to varnishing. She reveled in the small endearment. But, she
vowed, tonight you'll be in control—of the situation as
well as your feelings. And tomorrow you head home to
Houston.

As early as two thirty Chelsea heard voices in the shed.
She stuck her head out of the great aft cabin hatchway

and saw the familiar faces of the men who had contributed to this "impossible" job. They waved and introduced some new faces as friends of theirs who had
come to share the historic moment.

Chelsea returned a white-freckled grin of joy and
bade them, "Welcome, ya'll, but excuse me while we
finish the last bit of paint and varnish. Just look her
over. Everything's dry out there." She backed down
the ladder, the last thing to be varnished, and went to
help Eric and a couple of his friends. They were madly
spreading a thin second coat of varnish on the mahogany trim of the port and starboard port lights. Chelsea
finished the trim on the beautiful paneled windows.
Lafe put the last brushstroke on the mahogany taffrail.
Though several more days were needed to give the ini-
tial six coats to all the mahogany, it was decided two
coats would be sufficient for the launch.

By three fifteen, when she ran to the house to clean
her hands and grab her camera, the crowd had spilled
out of the shed and into the yard. It looked like quite a
gathering. "There she is!" a voice shouted. "Hi, Chelsea." "Hey, Chelsea!" another shouted. "Let's throw
her in," a young man's voice threatened jokingly. She
waved in the direction of the voices, but kept going,
afraid that if she stopped for a minute, she would never
get her camera in time.

Her pulse rate went crazy; her breaths were short and
shallow; she felt light-headed and giddy. *Never in my
whole life have I experienced anything of this dimen-
sion,* she decided as she sat in the quiet house, fumbling with the film that obstinately refused to take its
place in her camera. The quiet tears of joy that blurred
her vision didn't help. Her emotional high reached out
and embraced her mom and dad, and her grandpa Norquist. Time lost its clout. Her head swirled with this
soulful reunion; the noise from the crowd in the yard
dimmed as her heart swelled with love. It had been a
long time since she had expressed these feelings, but

she atoned as she shouted to their memories in the still of the house, *"I love you—I love you."* Her mind carried the echo, as if her family had shouted in return. Leaping like a graceful gazelle, Chelsea was outside of herself, euphoric, radiant, free of any vain thoughts, as with camera and lenses she raced for the shed.

She embodied a tremendous excitement. She cut through the throng as if she were walking on water. People were so densely packed inside the shed, she had to climb up carefully on the band saw to gain a vantage point. Precariously balanced, her knees flexed, she took the overall shots to establish the event with her wide-angle lens. So intent was she on composition and angles, she saw only the mass of people, not individuals.

After she changed to her 50 mm lens, she saw for the first time pictures of individuals she would never forget: The enigmatic but always sexy Rand, with a beribboned bottle of Champagne in a net.... Next to him his mother, with an elaborate arrangement of ruby-red roses.... Then Herschel Korbet, an elderly giant chewing madly on a big, fat cigar.... Beside him, Thyra, still in her hospital uniform, dwarfed by an armful of beautiful long-stemmed yellow roses.... A chubby-cheeked Santa masquerading as Dwight Connors, wreathed in an elfish grin as he proudly displayed a brass nameplate inscribed *Triumph*.... Lafe, bent over the slipways, assisting some men as they tallowed the rails.... And finally, Eric with a friend, their backs to the camera as they finished the black letters on the beautiful tumblehome stern that read *Triumph,* and under her name, her homeport: *Back Bay, Biloxi.*

Chelsea jumped off the band saw, moved to a better position atop one of the tool shelves near the bows that pointed at the bay, and quickly documented more of this historic event, which she believed would never occur again.

Three rolls of 35 mm film preserved forever what

appeared to Chelsea as a totally ephemeral affair, but what might have been a destiny had her folks lived. She was on her fourth roll of film, having captured all the brightwork: the gleaming mahogany spoke wheel, sliding hatches, rail, companion ladders, port lights, and the golden luster of the brass cleats and chock. She was just about to pop on her telephoto lens to get a close-up of the plugged screws, so unobtrusive in their perfection in both the varnished and painted areas, when Rand shouted above the din, "Enough, enough! Come on, Chelsea." She obeyed.

Her hazy memory would recall little of the speeches rendered by the mayors of Biloxi and Ocean Springs, but she would keep forever the brass keys to their cities, strung on red, white, and blue ribbons. They slipped them around her neck as if she were a conquering heroine after she hurriedly pulled off the paint-smeared babushka she still wore.

She would remember Uncle Dee, misty-eyed, as he gave her a bear hug along with *Triumph*'s brass name-plate.

She would never forget Lafe as he told the funny story about Henry Norquist launching a vessel with rotten bananas smeared on the railways and of the vessel's unexpected speedy descent and its untimely resting place on the other side of the riverbank.

The memory that would burn brightest was of Rand and how she felt when he put his arms around her to help her swing the Champagne bottle, of his topaz-brown eyes, filled with mischief, and his warm, moist breath when he whispered so close to her ear she shivered with delight.

Eric, the thoughtful, was the one who picked up the Nikon and took the shots of Chelsea—*click*—standing among the dignitaries, clad in her well-worn, paint-saturated, shipyard gear, her hair wild and squiggly, two huge bouquets of roses filling her arms—*click*—Chelsea, assisted by Rand, breaking the Champagne on the vessel's stem, so intent her eyes were squeezed tightly shut, while her lips bit the tip of her tongue—*click*—the majestic *Triumph* break the red-satin ribbons as she descended to her baptismal immersion, bow first, down the building ways into her briny berth—*click*—*Triumph* beautifully waterborne.

The thought that the boat might sink never entered Chelsea's mind.

The rest of the afternoon was a jubilee. *Triumph* had provided an excuse for people to let loose, drink hard, laugh and shout. The yard was full of well-wishers who grinned, bragged, and toasted with everything from coffee and beer to Champagne provided by Korbet Ship. Friends and strangers talked, spouted, strutted, and thoroughly enjoyed their own good company. Chelsea thought she would explode with pride and the sheer tide of boundless joy reflected in all those around her.

Around five the Korbets left. Chelsea got a wave from them all after Rand yelled, "See you at seven!" She hated to leave and continued to circulate among the new friends of all ages who shared an appreciation for what had been accomplished.

She met some men from Pascagoula and some from Bayou Le Batre who had been active wooden boat builders until a few years ago. They had said many complimentary things about her grandfather and of what his *Triumph* would have meant to him had he lived to see her launched. They marveled that she had instigated the completion, and wondered why and how a slip of a girl could have done it. Many folks wanted to know when *Triumph* would be rigged and what the eventual plans were for the vessel. These were questions for which Chelsea had no answers—yet.

It was late when she finally pulled herself away from the last of the crowd. She wished for more time to leisurely bathe and dress as she hurriedly ran some bath water. As it turned out, she not only had little time, she lacked privacy also.

Eric had become morose after he learned she was having dinner with Rand. He sat, drinking beer, his feet propped on the kitchen table, his chair tilted precariously against the wall. She heard him while she bathed and while she dressed behind the heavy pine door in her grandfather's bedroom. Apparently he found it difficult to accept his new role as brother.

The door bell grated on Chelsea's jangled nerves. She knew it would be Rand. Desperate to keep him from hearing Eric's rambling monologue, she grabbed her black faille evening bag, her wool paisley shawl, and prepared to leave immediately, hoping to avoid a confrontation.

No such luck. As she opened the bedroom door, Eric was in view. She stopped, shocked at the emotional face from which his red-hued blue eyes, filled with hurt, greeted her. He looked pitiful. He tried to focus as his chair slammed its front legs on the floor, and he rose, then stumbled toward the hall after her.

Chelsea ran to open the front door for Rand and turned to say good-bye to Eric, only to have him brush past her and almost collide with Rand, who stepped aside in time.

Rand was in a great mood. He just shrugged off Eric's behavior without lessening his ear-to-ear dimples one whit. In an exaggerated bow he comically escorted Chelsea not to his utility Blazer but his sleek red 928S Porsche.

As she settled into the black leather bucket seats she saw several people still in the office and wondered if Lafe and Thyra were aware of Eric's plight. Poor Eric, she thought. At least he didn't utter a single sarcastic word to Rand, which could have been a major problem when he sobered up. She felt responsible and yet, damn! Hadn't she always treated him like a brother, a friend?

Rand settled under the steering wheel. Over the finely timed growl of the engine, Chelsea conceded,

"I'm glad it's finished. Now I can leave and none too soon. Eric has become a problem. Let's sign those papers first thing tomorrow." What she didn't say was what a problem Rand had become to her.

"Okay," Rand agreed. He quickly turned the conversation away from any further talk of business for fear the evening would be ruined before it even started. The powerful sports car crawled smoothly out of the ruts and onto the two-lane hard top of East Bay Road. They talked and laughed easily about the launch of *Triumph,* some of the people, some of the remarks Herschel had made, Mrs. Korbet's rapture with the beauty of the design. Chelsea silently observed how congenial, relaxed, and fun Rand was being.

She turned in the seat to admire his profile. He punched a button, and she was surrounded by the romantic piano of George Shearing from the tape deck. She relaxed even more. Shearing was one of Aunt Marianne's favorites. She would be glad to get home, but tonight was the night for a glittering celebration.

"When did you get this, uh"—she had been about to say, "expensive toy," but at the risk of his misunderstanding her humor, she chose instead—"luxury? I somehow felt the four-wheel-drive Blazer an appropriate car for a hardworking, hard-driving empire builder such as—"

"Ha! You're right," he cut in. "It's a toy, a luxury. I seldom drive it anymore. I bought it a couple of years back just to show—" He broke off. He glanced at Chelsea; his smile was gone, his jaws were clenched, and she felt more than saw a remote look in his eyes. They had stopped at a traffic light. His voice was hard and steely as he spoke. "Oh, hell, I had to have something, I thought," he glanced away as he said, "after my wife left me for that Philadelphia banker. I guess this was a symbol—of money, of power—to show my world, my friends, she'd left behind, that I had, uh, style, or whatever I imagined she found in him. I still don't really know why I bought it. For damn sure I didn't want *her*!"

Chelsea was touched by his sudden openness. His seeming honesty struck one more chord; for that, he was all the more dear to her. She was surprised to learn that he had been married. Somehow, in her weeks there she'd heard nothing about it from anyone. "I . . . guess, I mean I . . . didn't know you had been married. Who was she?"

He looked straight ahead and said nothing while he smoothly shifted gears. The powerful Porsche reflected the driver's needs as it glided, swiftly weaving in and out of the flow of traffic headed for Ocean Springs. His voice had softened when he spoke, but held little emotion. "I'll tell you about the joke they referred to as my marriage; then I don't ever want to hear about it again."

In a monotone he began, his eyes nervously flitting from rearview mirror to the road again. "Myrna Schaeffer had been a high school cheerleader after me most of my junior year." He ground his teeth, took a deep breath, and continued, as if he were reciting by rote something that held little interest to him. "We had two or three dates our senior year. You know, like the prom, valentine dance—dates girls could ask guys to if they're pushy, like Myrna was." He turned to Chelsea. "I know, I know. I didn't have to say yes." His eyes back on the road, he leaned forward over the wheel, steering with his arms resting on the top. "I wasn't interested enough in school or any girl there to bother with. Just as soon of skipped it all. I enjoyed being on my granddad's boats or working at the yard; that was where the real living was, not in that playpen called high school." While he talked, he nervously loosened his brown and beige silk tie and unfastened a collar button on his Champagne-beige dress shirt. "Anyway, she was after me, like I said. Hell, I was no fool. But then she announced she was pregnant." He shook his head in disbelief. "I was so damned naive, I asked my parents for advice. They agreed the 'proper thing to do' was marry her. To hell with whether I even liked her!" His voice had risen a couple of octaves.

Chelsea felt his discomfort and offered, "You don't have to tell me any more—"

His head snapped toward her. "Oh, no. You'll hear it all, and that will be it," he flared then went on. "My folks harped at me that things had a way of working out. We married. A couple of months later she announced she must have miscarried—and like a sucker I believed she had been pregnant by me in the first place. Finally, not long after that, I got her to admit she had tricked me. Our relationship was some joke. *Relationship!* What am I saying? The *marriage* was a joke on me. I felt betrayed more by my dad and mom than by her. She didn't mean anything to me." He shook his head again, "It sounds so damn dumb when I hear myself say that now." He flashed his golden-brown eyes and that crooked, dimpled smile at Chelsea. For that moment all was well with the world.

"Anyway, I left her alone after that. Completely. I stayed at the yard or on the boats. She played around, but she would have no part of a divorce—until a couple of years later. She met this guy here vacationing at a banker's conference. That was that. She had her chance to play in a bigger puddle with more money and social status. I got my freedom. Somewhere I also got the idea I was less than I should have been...." His voice dropped. He seemed embarrassed. A ponderous silence prevailed. His eyes stared straight ahead. Chelsea didn't know what to say. He regained a little humor and finished with, "I only drive this thing now when I want to impress a lady!" He leaned toward her, his amber-brown eyes twinkled wickedly, and his double-dimpled smile deepened outrageously. That smile and his candor impressed her far more than the Porche ever would.

Oh, she was drawn to Rand. Chelsea took a deep breath, unconsciously, as if with the expansion of her lungs, she could bring him a little closer. At that moment she compared the fascination she had with golden boxes of Neiman's chocolates to the infatuation she had for Rand—their quality was uncompromised; they tantalized; the closer she observed them, the more delectable they became. One sample was never enough, and right after the gush of epicurean sweetness came the inevitable, numerous pangs of regret.

Yet there he sat. His aura of strength, virility, power—all controlled—all the more appealing to her senses. She was convinced there was much more to this man than she had dared imagine.

Her eyes stroked his cinnamon-brown flight jacket; an Italian design in supple, shiny leather. She just had to touch it. Her hand, of its own volition, drew tiny circles on his shoulder before it came to rest on his thigh. His dress slacks, of a gray-beige hard-worsted wool, were apparently tailored by the same talented man who made the brown slacks he had worn at lunch a few days ago. His dark brown kidskin shoes applied the brakes as he slowed the car and turned left off Highway 90 into Trilby's parking lot.

Chapter Seven

Chelsea was dazzling at dinner. Rand was totally magnetized to her. She was aware of his stunned attention the moment she seductively dropped her long, wool paisley shawl while they waited in the lobby. Her longsleeved ivory shirtwaist was a simple, silky satin, designed and cut on the bias to define each slippery curve with every move of her body. She felt caressed, almost undressed, by Rand's stare as they followed the hostess through Trilby's main dining room to a place by the window. The lengthy walk to their table spotlighted her sensual motion, as did the click of her stiletto black suede heels on the highly polished hardwood floor. Gypsylike, her tawny brown mane of long tendrils was held carelessly on one side by an ivory comb. Goldchain earrings matched several lengths of gold chain around her neck that fell out of sight to be enveloped in cleavage, revealed by her habit of leaving a button or two casually undone.

She barely contained her inner excitement. Tonight she exuded an elusive, intangible power; it flowed from the happiness within her being as it had when she was working on *Triumph*. No disturbing thoughts of Leslie or anything intruded. She was wholly centered within the moment they were sharing, and never had she felt more alive....

As Rand seated her in the chair he murmured, "I would guess you have appealed to every man in this

room and, I believe, you're the envy of every woman."
Her cloud rose at least two inches higher.

Rand sat down across the crisp white-linen covered
table from her, and immediately a waiter appeared.
"The lady will have a Dubonnet cocktail—Chivas and
water here," he ordered without deliberation, and dismissed the man while riveting Chelsea with his piercing
gaze.

She was up to his game and sizzled as she leaned
toward him, then turned her head slightly away and cut
her eyes back slowly as she breathed, "Celebrating success agrees with me and tonight I feel great! Completely agreeable." A slow smile parted her glossy lips,
and the tip of her tongue outlined her upper lip. Her
meaning was unmistakable. Rand stared on, speechless.

The candlelight cast an intimate glow. Perfect. The
whole formal table setting was mirrored in the shiny
night-black of the window's reflecting glass. Periph-
erally Chelsea noted their partnered identical selves
and decided they looked the perfect couple. The
crowded restaurant's reflection remained unfocused as
she dwelled on the two look-a-likes beside them in the
window.

His voice brought her out of the ethereal reverie.
"You are lovely, Chels." His husky tones were golden,
couched in his soft Mississippi—Cajun accent, his eyes,
a slightly misty amber-brown. She felt as if they were
alone in a golden haze under a gossamer tent. He
placed his long, warm fingers lightly on top of her
hand. Her body tingled with his touch. The reverie
wove mystically around again, isolating them from the
world. They lingered in a rare mutual infatuation while
time forgot to exist. With unblinking delight they were
lost in each other's eyes.

The insensitive waiter rudely intruded as he placed
their drinks before them. Rand broke his gaze long
enough to tell the waiter they would order later.

"I would...." Rand's voice drifted as he looked again into her eyes.

"Yes?" Chelsea purred. "You would what?"

Rand drew back in his chair, dropped his eyes to his glass, paused as if deliberating, then finally allowed a crooked grin to play lightly across his face. The scar on his upper lip fascinated her as he said, "I, uh, was going to propose a toast." He lifted his glass across the table. "To Chelsea's personal *Triumph*." The candlelight electrified his golden-brown eyes as they lustily locked into hers.

Puff. Puff. Thoroughly enchanted in a rarefied atmosphere, Chelsea had, for a moment, forgotten the business reason for the dinner celebration. Therefore, she added, "Yes, with Rand Korbet!" and proceeded to lift her glass and capture his wrist by encircling it with her satin-covered forearm. "Yes, I'll drink to that," she declared, môre brazen than she'd ever been in her life. She leaned toward her drink, their arms still intertwined, and sipped the fiery liquid. "Ohhh, that is—nice!" She blinked as she swallowed and almost choked. "Th-thank you. I don't think I've ever had a—what do you call this?" she asked as she put the glass down and leaned back.

"Just a Dubonnet cocktail," he supplied innocently.

"Ooo wow, I think that will loosen up my sore muscles—along with everything else, I must add." She giggled, then wickedly enticed him with open lips and a raised eyebrow.

Rand chuckled low, took a drink of his Scotch whisky, and volunteered, "Good! Amazing what a little alcohol can do."

Suddenly repentant and uncomfortable with how bold she was being, Chelsea tried to change the subject. "This was a great idea," she smiled, casually indicating the restaurant.

"I have some other great ideas for you," he quipped, not straying one bit from her original intent.

Her sparkling emerald eyes shimmered with flecks of blue as she answered softly, "I'll bet you do...." She lowered her lashed, smoky crescents on her cheeks to hide her emotions as she admitted, "I must confess. I didn't want to see you again before leaving for Houston. I didn't want another...fight."

"Oh, no. No, you don't. No talk like that tonight. You haven't even seen my place," he reminded. Her heart thudded painfully in her chest, in her ears. "How about a tour of Korbet Ship after dinner?" he declared more than asked as he flashed a crooked smile, devilish with its double-dimpled message.

Chelsea fingered a golden earring nervously. "I, uh, ahhh, don't know," she blurted, automatically ready to say no. Yet she wanted to continue this evening forever.

"You will be introduced to the majestic world of steel ships," he pitched like a narrator, "through a Rand Korbet private tour." It was his turn to raise an eyebrow. "How about it?"

The aperitif made her even more agreeable than when they first were seated. She slowly nodded yes while wondering exactly what she was agreeing to.

That did it. Rand eagerly signaled the waiter. At his suggestion, he ordered the seafood casserole of Gulf shrimp and crabmeat in a delectable wine sauce for her and stuffed flounder for him. With their entrees came crisp salad greens, lavished with a special Roquefort, oil, and vinegar dressing, and a mushroom-filled rice pilaf.

Their oyster-on-the-half shell appetizer arrived almost immediately. Rand and Chelsea dined with sensual overtones to every bite. They read double meaning into every flick of their tongues, every swallow, each lick of their lips. All conversation remained on that level too; the meal was quite secondary to the evening ahead.

A white Bordeaux accompanied their dinner. Chelsea was delightfully numb as the dishes were cleared and she accepted a refill of the wine.

Her weeks of physical and mental punishment, of forcing herself and others to do her will, were momentarily forgotten. Neither she nor Rand noticed the scarred, bruised, and roughened skin of her otherwise delicate hands as she held her wineglass. She unconsciously mesmerized them both as she erotically stroked her wineglass, stem to bowl and down the stem again. As she repeated the Freudian stroke, up and down the glass, she broke the rhythm of the conversation between them by first touching the cool fullness of the glass to her lower lip, then languidly rolling the edge to her hot cheek and back to her lips, and slowly sipping the pale, potent liquid. This natural action on her part sent messages of fiery pleasure to the seat of Rand's desires.

In this satiated state they sat, two souls in harmony, brimming with anticipation as Rand paid the check. Then in a muted fog of tantalizing desire they left Trilby's, bound for...whatever fate decreed.

They drove languidly toward Biloxi. To Chelsea's euphoric eyes, the lights that lined the Highway 90 causeway wore diamond filters. The barge traffic under the bridge twinkled with the red and green lights of port and starboard as the multitows moved silently toward the Mississippi Sound. Rand slowed the car and stopped at the Biloxi Lighthouse to wait for the traffic light to change. She watched the gentle surf magically reflect red and white car lights as the traffic curved west to Mississippi City and Gulfport. When they turned north on Porter Avenue, she asked, "Where are we headed?" unconcerned, but willing to have conversation again.

"The best coffee ever"—Rand grinned—"for one thing."

She ignored the "for one thing" and innocently observed, "I don't seem to remember this street. I guess Biloxi's bigger than I recall."

"Biloxi's not an all bad place to live, you know, Chels," he challenged in that slow accent that was so sexy to her.

"That depends," she responded, reaching over and turning the radio on low. The romantic duet claimed her attention immediately.

Rand continued. "Biloxi has changed—who knows if it's better—since my boat-building great grandfather arrived from Germany, but with Korbet Ship set to expand, I think my great grandpap would still find it a good place to live and work."

With the last refrain of the love song, they arrived at Korbet Ship. "Diana Ross and Lionel Richie, night sounds on WQID," the announcer whispered soothingly just as the car engine was turned off. The music had continued the intoxicating spell for Chelsea. Rand opened her car door, and as she got out, she realized they had pulled up to the dock, where a tug was moored; the constant voices of its generators and pumps were muted slightly from where they stood.

Rand slipped his arm around her waist and hurried her up the wooden dock to the fifty-foot tug. "Chelsea, this is my old girl, *Sampson*." He beamed, his features painted with boyish joy. His happiness was contagious, and she felt giddy as they jumped aboard. They stopped between the pilot house and the galley as Rand grinned. "*Sampson,* meet my new girl, Chelsea." Before she could say a word, Rand enfolded her completely in his arms, steadying her on the sloping deck of the vibrating vessel. Her mind raced over the possibilities inherent in the phrase "new girl" while she lifted her mouth to meet his, and for a moment, or an eternity, he allowed her eyes to penetrate his soul. She was fathoms deep in joyous abandon, for there she saw love, tenderness, and blatant desire. Or was it only a reflection of what she felt for him?

He cupped one hand around her hip and pressed her compliant body to fit the sudden surge in his loins. The

other hand fondled her back, moving up to her shoulders and neck, then threaded through her long, tangled
hair. He held her a moment more, tantalizing her
senses as he slowly placed his warm lips on her forehead, then gently touched her temple and finally nibbled at the corner of her beckoning lips, parted to
respond to his—

"Well, hi, Cap'n!" a crewman called as he stepped
out of the galley, surprised to see them.

"Hey, Tim, how's it going?" Rand replied in an off-
hand manner, his arms still around Chelsea. "You met
Chelsea Norquist yet, Tim?" he asked, his eyes directly linked to hers. "I promised her a cup of your
famous coffee."

Blushing, Chelsea pulled away and acknowledged
Tim's presence. He nodded and mumbled "hullo" as
he headed forward. Rand sighed and took Chelsea's
hand. She followed him aft and into the midship's dining salon and galley.

The white light of the galley was blinding to Chelsea
in contrast to the muted night shadows of the dock. It
took her a moment to adjust, her hand still linked in
Rand's as he led her to the stainless-steel range. Compared to *Triumph*'s below-deck area, this was quite
large, she decided.

Rand poured two heavy mugs full of the always
ready hot coffee while he gave a narrative describing
various aspects of a working tug or pushboat. A man
who can do two things at once, she mused, taking the
fragrant, steaming liquid to her lips. Rand automatically replaced the lid of a sugar canister and wiped
up spilled coffee grounds from the gray formica counter while he amiably continued his pro-steel propa-
ganda.

"Obviously the galley is important," he began as
they took a seat at a formica-topped dining table, "so
the tour begins here. How's the coffee?" he asked,
studying her face for the answer.

"Just as you promised, possibly the best ever," she proclaimed with a charming flutter of lashes and another sip in confirmation.

He moved closer beside her on the bench, and their thighs touched; things were warming up, but his mind was on the promised tour. Enthusiastically he explained how important the generators were for keeping the galley in operation as well as providing for the electrical needs of the bilge pumps, running lights, radar, and interior lights. She tried to keep her mind on his words while distracted by his physical nearness.

"So, the boys call this the heart of the operation," he smiled. "Not me. The heart of this lady is below." He stood up. "Come on, I'll show you."

Dutifully Chelsea followed Rand out on deck and didn't point out that she was hardly dressed for a tour of the engine room. She balanced herself as best she could, hung on to the steel ladder, and descended into a hothouse of roaring confusion. The steel-grid plates forced her to walk on the balls of her feet lest her narrow heels slip through; one touch of the grease and oil essential for the engines would ruin her white satin dress. A wooden sailing vessel seemed ever so much nicer.

Smiling, she tried to read Rand's lips as he talked through the throbbing noise. She just shook her head yes at everything. She was relieved when they ascended into the fresh cool night air on deck.

He was elated. She rushed to keep up with him as he led her to the pilot house, explaining more of what she had just seen.

She protested, "Wait, Rand. My mechanical knowledge is limited to maintaining my little MG. I can handle some of what you're telling me about generators and twin screws and the diesel maneuvering ability of your 'well-designed' vessel"—she drew a deep breath—"but only *some*! I'm afraid you're assuming I know more than I do."

He simply grinned and continued, "This was my grandfather's design. Herschel is a fine marine architect, just like his dad and granddad. Seat-of-the-pants genius, I call it. Just took a stick and drew some lines in the mud and worked from pure instinct." He chuckled. "Anyway, I modified his design and built *Sampson* a couple years ago." They climbed up the ladder and into the pilot house. For a moment she felt like a princess in a tower.

"I'm proud of her electronics." He pointed out every inch of her controls once they stood by the helm. "We constantly update in here. Costly as hell, but necessary." Rand was in his element, she mused. "There's a duplicate wheel on the stern for some situations where a guy has to see what his stern tow line is doing in relation to the hull of the ship he's working." He stopped for a moment, looked into her intelligent green eyes, and decided she was a great audience.

"I have to tell you a story about my mom—you've met her."

"Yes," Chelsea acknowledged, "and I think you have her coloring, although I never saw a picture of your dad."

"Mom's Cajun, you know. I think she's beautiful. My dad.... Well, finding and marrying my mom was probably the only outstanding thing he ever did in his life."

Chelsea was puzzled and curious. "I'd love to know more about your dad, too."

"Nothing to tell," he said curtly, then rushed ahead. "This story is about mother. Oh, how my granddad laughs when he tells it." Rand was grinning as he continued. "Seems the first night here, after Mom and Dad married over in her own parish in South Louisiana, you know, off the main road on a back bayou not far from New Orleans. Well, Dad was driving in on old Highway 90 from Slidell, so naturally he stopped at the Port of Gulfport to let her watch some Korbet tugs working banana boats." Rand tilted his head at Chelsea confidentially. "You got to remember, this lady grew up fishing and gardening. She'd never even seen New Orleans." He shook his head. "Well, when she saw those tugs, one at the bow, the other at the stern, setting that big freighter against the dock in the dark of the night, she said, 'Why, that's a sight. Looks just like a couple of tomato worms huggin' on a tomato.'"

Chelsea didn't get the picture. "I don't understand. I'm not a gardener or a tug operator."

"Surely you know how the lights on the tugs look from a distance when they dock a ship!" he declared.

She meekly shook her head no.

Dismayed, he asked, "You haven't seen—I mean, the Port of Houston is a big, busy port, and you—"

"Hey, wait!" she cut in. "Remember me—advertising? I'm definitely not in the boat business in Houston." She was a tad indignant that he should see this lack as ignorance.

His enchanting eyes took on a special gleam. "In that case, the next call we take at Korbet Ship, you're going to be right here by my side. That is, if you still want to know more about my life," he challenged with a wink.

Chelsea returned a coquettish look. "You know I do. But that call better come tonight. As soon as we sign those papers in the morning, I'm on my way back to what's left of my job in Houston."

"We'll check the schedule right now," he announced quickly.

He displayed none of the arrogance that had infuriated her before, she noted happily as they walked arm in arm for the old two-story frame house that served as Korbet Ship's office. She was enjoying his company much too much; the thought of Houston and her life there lacked the original luster she had felt upon her arrival in this Mississippi coastal area.

"That's the floating dry dock; there are the cranes; those two big sheds serve as materials preparation and

some repair. Way over there's the electrical shop." He
was pointing into the inky darkness. All she could see
were vague outlines of what he suggested. As they
neared the lights at the edge of the drive near the office
she could see more distinctly boats being built on
cradles all over the yard, in various stages of completion from keels and frames to fully plated hulls of steel.
However, she decided, given the brevity of the tour
and the darkness, she remained somewhat uninformed
on the majesty of steel-ship production and construction.

"I really can't see much in the dark out there," she
admitted.

"Ordinarily we run a night shift or two, and this
place is bright as day. Things are—well, kind of off-
schedule what with the hold on acquisition of your
yard. So I let those that wanted go for Mardi Gras. This
whole coast is crazy for Mardi Gras, if you remember."
He stopped and looked her directly in the eye; the dim
lights cast intriguing shadows on his rugged features.
"They say the definition of a true Mobilian is a person
conceived under the azaleas during Mardi Gras, you
know."

For a moment she didn't realize he was teasing, then
she protested, "Oh, Rand." Before she could say more
he rushed her to the door.

"Come here, fast!" he urged, pulling her inside the
dark office. Instead of hitting the light switch, his
breath fanned her cheek, and he enfolded her in his
powerful warmth; then his mouth fastened on her full
lips. Immediately he made her body sing with sensations. Kissing him, that helpless, sinking feeling returned. How quickly the flimsy bonds of rationality
disappeared with his masterful, persuasive embrace,
she marveled briefly before losing herself in the emotions rioting through her body.

The telephone shrilled. It was insistent. "Let it
ring," Rand breathed as his lips left hers to nuzzle be-

hind her ear. The phone was distracting under the circumstances, and he gave up, flipped the light switch, and went to his mother's desk. The phone stopped ringing just as he reached for it.

Still somewhat removed from reality, Chelsea wandered toward a collection of faded photographs in dusty frames that filled the wall of the staircase. She glanced back at the man whose strong, virile magnetism held her spellbound. He was looking at something on the desk. She realized suddenly that he was more a mystery than ever now that he had begun to share his interests.

It was hard to connect him with the old pictures of men working on wooden boats. They looked similar to those pictures that hung in her grandfather's office. Here were old-timers with pride-filled postures, carrying the same tools, and dressed in those funny old clothes.

One picture especially intrigued her: a group of men, some young, some not so young, dressed in homespun, long-sleeve shirts and narrow ties, wearing slacks and hats and looking more like shopkeepers and bankers than boatyard workmen.

Rand came up behind her. She turned to ask him a question, but his hands hugged her waist and pressed her body to his while his face and voice confirmed the warmth in his topaz-brown eyes, so near she could see tiny flecks of copper in them. As if he read her mind, he answered, "Yes, yes, this is my mother's doing. She insists these pictures of my Korbet clan hang here as reminders of my Biloxi beginnings." He kissed her lightly on the tip of her nose, then turned her back to look at the photos as he continued, "This was my great grandfather and his father before he left Germany." He pointed out two men in a crew of ten as they stood in front of a wooden hull ready for launch. "That was my great grandmother, Herschel's mom, and that's Herschel at five." In the middle of the picture stood a lady in a multiskirted long dress with a pinched waist and leg-of-mutton sleeves; a small tyke sat on a large wooden frame joined to the keel of a hull under construction. "That's the Bay behind them. They were quite proud of the first vessel constructed here in Biloxi."

He turned her back to face him again. "Nowadays Korbet Ship runs a fleet of harbor tugs and pushboats. We tow barges everywhere. Of course, we build and repair—" He stopped, took her hand, and started leading her up the stairs. "We believe in the future."

When they reached the top, he turned on a wall switch that lighted another long wall, filled with color portraits of some of his prize modern steel-hull vessels. He leaned closer and looked her directly in the eyes again. "I also believe in this moment; who knows if we'll see tomorrow?" he whispered intimately. She had a feeling this was going to be a short tour. He continued to gaze into her liquid green eyes. For an endless moment, her hand held tightly in his, they communicated silently for mutual consent.

"I agree," she murmured, her heart pounding, her voice very soft.

He closed his eyes and kissed her, pressing hard, bruising her lips. It was pure rapture. The moment had returned. His kiss grew gentle for an instant while his arms crushed her to him; then his lips slanted hungrily over hers as his tongue sought to explore and taste her open mouth, so willing, so provocative.

Her knees were weakening; her hips wanted to begin the primitive rotation that came so naturally, instinctively....

The next thing she knew, he swept her up into his arms and cradled her satin-covered body to him while he carried her past the photo exhibit of his crew boats, pushboats, pilot boats, and tugs into a darkened room. There he gently laid her on a bed slashed with light from the hall.

"Where...are we?" she quivered, hypnotically

clinging to his leather-covered shoulders, strong and rippling, as he eased the length of his body down beside her.

"My bedroom, my bed," he breathed huskily, passion shortening his words as his warm hands found the pearl-smooth contours of her breasts, her waist, hips, thighs. His rugged silhouette, backlighted by the glaring fluorescents in the hall, gave an eerie, dreamlike quality to the longing he was creating in her.

He moaned as he moved to mold his loins to hers while his soft, moist lips found hers. She welcomed his exploring tongue, which swiftly fanned the flames of desire. She wanted to feel his naked body on hers, to be free of her confining clothes—until a wall speaker crackled to life somewhere in another room.

"Uh, Cap'n Korbet, call the *Sampson*—Cap'n Korbet, uh, call the *Sampson*. Come back."

Rand groaned and involuntarily jerked away as the voice jarred their overheated senses. "Damn," he cursed as he got up and headed out the door. "I checked the schedule. There's nothing! What can he want?" he finished with a shout that released his momentary anger.

Rand disappeared down the hall. From where she lay on his bed his distant voice betrayed impatience as he laconically answered, "This is Korbet. What is it, Tim?"

"Slight emergency with the pilotboat," Tim's voice squawked. "Cap'n Johnny just radioed for a tow."

Chelsea slowly followed the voice and found her way down the hall and into a large office that apparently had been two bedrooms before the dividing wall was removed. Rand sat hunched in a black leather contemporary desk chair, his elbows on his knees, a small microphone in the palm of his hand.

Tim's message continued. "They're at buoy four. Engine's out again."

She sat down on a black leather love seat across from

his desk to absorb impressions of Rand at work in his office. The totally Spartan contemporary decor contrasted starkly with the downstairs office, which looked right out of the 1920s. Rand's modern desk was a black leatherlike tabletop on stainless-steel legs with only two narrow single drawers on either side. It was uncluttered except for a small brass propeller paperweight beside a canister of pencils. His desk phone had a speaker and a multibutton call board. A green chalkboard dominated one side of the glaring white walls.

Rand noticed her and swiveled in his chair to face her while he gave her a slow, deliberate wink without a hint of a smile. He continued to listen to Tim's explanation.

"I, uh, thought I'd let you know, since you was here, but I got Warren on call. I can get him on it if you'd just as soon, uh, keep on, uh, workin'?"

Chelsea blushed at Tim's knowledgeable inference. Rand studied her face for a moment, then asked, "You want to go, Chels? The choice is yours. Either way, we get to know each other a little better. I can assure you my preference is to let Warren take this call, even though I promised the next call you'd be right by my side!" He shook his head, as if he wished he hadn't said it.

To Chelsea, the idea of Tim and who knew how many others being aware of she and Rand in his office, *workin'*, took the glow out of continuing where they were so rudely interrupted. She slowly nodded her head yes and unenthusiastically replied, "Let's go."

Rand keyed the switch. "We'll be right there. Tim, make sure Sam's in the engine room. Forget Warren." He replaced the microphone and pegged Chelsea with a smoldering accusation. "One of us loves to mix business with pleasure. Right now, I'm not real sure who it is!"

She squirmed uncomfortably at his insinuation, and

she recalled their anger as he drove her home after their heated luncheon date.

"I head a multimillion-dollar corporation that's getting bigger every day," he pointed out, spreading his arms to encompass the westward expansion to the Norquist yard. "I don't have to interrupt my personal pleasure to handle a call of this nature, but here I go anyway." His deeply dimpled smile melted her small misgivings as he came from behind the desk. He picked her up in his arms as if he were going to carry her back to the bed.

"Ra-and." She giggled.

At the top of the stairs he hesitated, then wisely put her on her feet and let her precede him as he switched off lights and followed her out the door.

Alert to all the proceedings, Chelsea stood beside Rand at the wheel as he backed *Sampson* away from the dock. Tim and Sam cast off and stowed the mooring lines in a neat coil on board. The powerful twin diesels vibrated the deck, roiled the black waters of the Bay, and thundered into the quiet winter night.

"What time is it?" she shouted in his direction.

Rand checked his watch, then widened his double-dimpled grin as he pulled her close enough to yell in her ear, "About eleven. We ought to be back in a couple of hours, if we're lucky."

With that news she suddenly realized how tired she was. It had been quite a day already, with *Triumph*'s launch. If he noticed her posture visibly droop with his report, he didn't show it. Oh, what the hell, she decided. I can always rest once I'm back in Houston. Again the thought of Houston didn't seem as glittering. She reminded herself to call Art Graham tomorrow and let him know she was heading home.

Chelsea pulled herself up onto the high stool near Rand. As she rested, she studied his wind-tanned face, so appealing, animated, and open to her tonight. What a night. The celebration dinner had been a most sensual experience, his office-bedroom had offered the promise of even greater pleasure, and now, he was all captain, in charge, in control. She was an attendant audience to his performance in this role. Although, she mused, he didn't look much like her idea of a boat captain. His dress casuals, for one thing, were much too elegant. However, his thick, untamed flaxen hair did indeed reflect his hours on the water, in salt air and sun.

Rand pointed ahead to the Highway 90 causeway as they cleared an old railroad span. "We were just crossing that bridge a while ago. Looks a little different from here, doesn't it?"

She nodded, then stepped out onto the starboard ladder to get a better view. She could feel Rand's eyes protectively watch as she leaned on the rail. Soon she forgot him, however, as a new perspective intrigued her, lulled her. All the lights on land appeared as if in a time warp. The vessel's smooth forward momentum through the barge channel at sea level bent shore lights in a visual arc that slowly, continuously changed like the flow of time; a densely lighted area seemed to pass more quickly than the darkened or sparsely lighted ones.

She could barely grasp how much time had elapsed when she felt chilled and pulled her wool shawl snug against the damp, cold salt air. The wind had whipped her mass of honey-brown hair into a more tangled, frizzy crown. Her face felt strangely clean but sticky as she went back inside the pilot house to join Rand again.

"Enjoy yourself?" he asked, his eyes aglow with affection or something very close to love. She didn't dare make the judgment for fear her interpretation would be wrong. He held one arm open, inviting her to his side.

She slid her arm around his waist, hugged him, and welcomed the warmth of his steel-hard body. "You must know I did," she responded dreamily, in spite of the engine's roar and a need to shout.

Sam and Tim appeared then with cups of coffee to take relief on the wheel.

As if they were playing out a well-rehearsed scene, Rand joked, "Yeah, she does look a little tired, now that you mention it, boys!" He chuckled and was joined in the laughter by his two well-meaning crewmen.

Tim handed her a cup of his "famous hot coffee," then took the helm. Sam opened the hatchway in a formica bulkhead, then handed a cup to Rand, who stepped through and invited Chelsea to follow. "Come on in, Chels. You can take your shoes off in here."

Puzzled but intrigued, she thanked the men and went through the oval hatch door, which Rand shut behind her. It was immediately quiet, she noticed. They could talk, not shout. "What is this?" she queried suspiciously, as the double bunk took up most of the cabin. A small mirror and sink took precious space at the foot of the bunk. A lipped, built-in desk with a hanging locker and a few drawers near the deck dominated the remaining space.

"Welcome to the infamous captain's cabin and my short-nap sea bunk," he quipped as he shrugged out of his Italian leather jacket and hung it on the port light, ensuring their privacy. She admired the muscles of his back as they rippled under the fine silk shirt when he took off his tie and opened his collar several buttons more. Then he walked toward her.

Chelsea looked as fantastic as she had at Trilby's, but she felt less like a preened and prowling tiger and more like a tired kitten. She warily sat down on the edge of the bunk. The smoothness with which the crew had set up their retirement to this cozy, relaxing scene nagged at her. It smacked of a conspiratorial setup, played out many times, with how many other women, she wondered. . . .

Rand bent down on one knee. "Allow me," he urged as he removed her shoes, a welcome relief for her poor tired feet but an added concern for her already anxious mind. He compounded her suspicions when he started a massage on the instep of her left foot using his thumb and the palm of his hand.

In delightful agony she moaned, "Ohhhh, ohhh, that feels great," aware for the first time of the nerve endings in her feet and how they affected the rest of her body. He continued the unexpected and sensational experience as he worked down the outside of her foot to the heel. "Oh, yes—ohhh." She melted, visibly relaxing. Before he started to massage the other foot, he took her coffee and set it out of the way, then invited her to lie back. She knew she should resist, but the opportunity to taste this new pleasure again was overwhelming. She complied with only an "Ummmmmm" of encouragement, which he didn't need, for he was a very determined lover—in her case.

"That's it, Chels...just relax," he said soothingly, watching her face as his hand practiced an expertise he really didn't know he had.

"Where did you, uh, learn...to do this?" she queried faintly as she slipped deeper into a weakened but erotic aura controlled by his hands.

"Instinct," he whispered.

He started a circular motion, widening his massage up the back of her ankle. When his hands reached her sore calves, he said casually, "You know, this would really work better if you had those clothes off."

For a long moment his words didn't register. Then she began to put together a picture she didn't like at all. She believed she was being seduced under the watchful eyes of two willing assistants, not five feet on the other side of a bulkhead, who apparently helped their captain with this routine so often it meant nothing...to any of them...least of all, Rand.

She raged as she bolted upright and tucked her feet protectively under her. "What—just what—do you think you're doing?" Her green eyes flashed and narrowed.

Rand was dumbstruck. "I—I, uh, thought I was relaxing you," he claimed innocently. He got off his knees and sat on the bed.

"Ha!" she slashed. "I don't know about your other 'friends,' but I've never been a—I mean, I'm not a—I'm not accustomed to well, being seduced with an audience in the pilot house," she finished in a hoarse, hissing whisper to avoid letting the "audience" hear, forgetting for a moment the noise outside the cabin.

A slow, infuriating smile spread across Rand's face, his dimples deepened, and he shrugged, "Suit yourself, Chels." He stood up, moved closer to her, and defiantly raked her body with a hungry glint in his gorgeous brown eyes.

"Don't do that! Don't smile at me like that, either!" she continued angrily while trying to contain her voice.

"I find it hard to believe I once thought you were a kinky-haired little boy," he said, and chuckled maddeningly.

She instinctively backed away from him as she shook her head defiantly, seething, "I would be much better off if I were. Since you entered my life, I've lost sight of who I am and why I'm here!"

Rand loved it. Loved what she had just said and the angry diamond sparkles in her jade-green eyes. He sat down on the bed again, a benevolent attitude in his posture but a wicked grin on his face.

"Don't—I told you—don't come any closer," she warned. "My God, do you realize I—I foolishly took your challenge and stayed here in Biloxi—to build a boat!" she screamed, her cheeks pinkening.

He could stand temptation no more. He leaned to kiss her, but she stood up, barefooted, on the corner of the bed. His arms encircled her. Wobbling, she tried to gain her balance, still hammering her point as he held her.

"Stop that! I should be back at my office, doing what

I'm trained to do, what I do best. Stop it! This is ridiculous and demeaning, and, and I'm—I—'' She struggled vainly in his arms. "I want to go home.''

Rand spoke not a word during her tirade, but he continued to hold her. For a moment Chelsea didn't know what else to say or do. She stopped struggling, suddenly emotionless—and speechless.

Her anger spent, she looked away from him to the brown-paneled walls. His powerful arms relaxed and momentarily her mind was empty; apparently a truce existed. Then the first thought that popped into her mind was a question of simple, childlike curiosity. Still, she did not look at him as she asked, "Did you get that scar on your lip and your crooked nose from 'fast cars and fast women'?''

Silence. Then she felt his palm, hot and moist, bridge the soft flesh between her hips and begin a sensual, undulating motion. "What do you want to believe?'' His voice was almost inaudible, while his hand produced a concerto in slow rhythm.

His voice quality was so unusual, she turned her head to look at him. His face betrayed pain, deep pain, finely masked. For a moment she forgot what she had asked—and there was that blissful distraction of his hand on her responsive, satin-topped flesh.

The the clouds cleared, and his sunny, teasing self grinned. "How about—a football injury?'' His hand inched up to her waist. "Or, I fell out of my baby bed?'' Warmth was spreading in all directions. "Or, I brawled with some woman, uh, make that *women*!'' He chuckled. She didn't care to stop his hand as it gently pressed against the lower fullness of her breasts, or as he deftly unbuttoned a couple of pearl buttons. He continued, "Or, I fell on a barge and was knocked out cold, broken and bleeding all over?''

Her breathing shallow, her voice soft, she replied, "Just the truth.'' Her imploring eyes widened. He noticed blue flecks colored the green to turquoise jewels ringed in black fringe. Her cheeks were pearlized apricots from the dim light cast across the cabin from the small desk lamp.

He removed his hand from her body and snuggled down beside her to stretch out on his back. "I was twelve," he began as he stared overhead and recalled the truth. "My dad was running a tow up the intercoastal. It was a moonless night like tonight when we crossed Mobile Bay. He could tell from the way she was steering, one of the barges was working loose. When he sent the crew out to secure it, I tagged along to help, as I always did." Rand shot her a knowing glance. "Things were kind of rough. The deck was wet and slippery. I somehow fell on a ratchet tool—you tighten tows with it," he explained. "When I fell, I managed to get all twisted in cable and..." He paused again with the freshness of the memory. "Damned if I didn't break a few bones. My face was a bloody mess, too. The only visible scars left are here," he said, touching his lip and nose. "My arm and foot don't show a thing, but hurt like hell with a weather change," he mumbled in a monotone.

"Worst part of the whole ordeal was my dad. He ordered me off the water for a year! Guess he was scared for me—but it was wrong. I hated him for being so... dumb!" Rand closed his eyes for a moment, then continued. "As soon as my casts were off, I talked my granddad into letting me back aboard—after school and on weekends, of course. My dad's word didn't count for much around the yard.

Chelsea had raised up on one elbow while he finished his story and was permanently etching his features in her mind. For the moment she had forgotten everything but this man who was open and sharing, willing to bare a part of his vulnerability. He was taking a risk, trusting her. His was a diamond-faceted soul; she wanted to examine it over and over...forever. There was no hiding the love in her eyes as she leaned

over and gently touched the scar on his lip. Or as she
trailed her fingers through his strawlike hair, across his
brow to see the wind-tanned skin relax and smooth instantly to her touch.

"Chelsea Norquist!" he said abruptly, and leaned up
on one elbow to face her. "You really know how to kill
a mood. Get me talking about my past—" Words
ceased as he rolled her onto her back. The top of her
dress had remained unbuttoned and fell open, revealing the fine French-vanilla silk camisole with dainty
lace ecru leaves appliqued on the cups.

Suddenly Chelsea noticed that the even, forward momentum of the vessel had started to change to a dip-
ping, slightly rolling motion. Gravity pulled them to
portside. She looked alarmed.

"No problem," he assured, searching her eyes.
"We're making the turn into the channel for buoy
four."

"How can you tell?" she asked, uncertain.

"Some things you learn by practice, and some you
know by instinct." She didn't have to ask which. His
full, soft lips widened over her mouth, enticingly
nursed its sweet moistness, and succored her con-
science from any possible doubts. She was anchored in
the moment, aware only of the need that threatened to
engulf her so easily. His touch—his kiss—she yearned
for them and more at the core of her being. She was
unaware he had unfastened the tiny pearl buttons of
her lingerie until his warm lips laved a wet, sensitive
path down her throat. His strong hands roamed under
her back, then arched her breasts high. Electrified
amber-brown eyes feasted for a long moment on her
firm breasts. Then he fastened his mouth on one rose
nipple as his rough fingers tenderly massaged the other,
which grew erect and hard and ached for equal attention from his honeyed tongue, lavishing a wet, tor-
menting warmth. His mouth, lips, tongue suckled...

teased... licked... the flames of desire that had smol-
dered—threatening to erupt—for three weeks now.

He raised his head; his eyes lowered and shut as he
whispered, "Chelsea... Chelsea." Then his lips re-
claimed hers in an embrace that became a crushing,
searing, plundering of her mouth. Her heart raced; a
tingle flooded her pulsating triangle like a current of
electricity in rhythm with the throbbing twin diesels.
His hand found its way to her inner thighs, too well
protected by a satiny dress, silk petticoat, and nylon
hose. Once again she wanted to be rid of those confining clothes.

"Rand," she breathed, his musky scent further
heightening her senses. Her hands on his silk-covered
shoulders kneaded the bands of muscle and sinew. His
lips left hers for a moment to speak. Gold danced in the
darkened depths of his amber-brown eyes.

The husky timbre in his voice crackled more as he
implored, "Chels, I want you naked under me." His
chest heaved rapidly. "I want to make love—to you,
with you. Chels, I need you tonight," he begged.

Her smoky green eyes searched his face as his words
set up an echo in her heated thoughts—*love... make
love... with you... need you.* She wanted to hear the
simple phrase, *I love you, Chelsea.* She needed to hear
what he felt for her.

Seeking clarification, she asked, "Rand?" her voice
erotic to his highly charged senses. Her naked breasts
could feel the matted hair through the silk of his shirt.

The expected but forgotten knock at the door jolted
her. The second knock caught Rand's attention. With
the third knock, louder still, he staggered toward the
door, his desire obvious in his now ill-fitting slacks. His
shirt pulled away at the waist and wild hair even more
unruly than usual, he yelled through the hatch, "Yeah,
just a minute." He swallowed, looked back at Chelsea,
and tried to tuck in his shirt. As he grabbed his jacket

off the port light and walked toward the door, he conceded in a hoarse whisper, "We talked too much."

He slipped through the hatch and held it open behind him so she could hear. "Pilot boat in sight, Cap'n," Tim reported.

"Thanks, Tim. I'll take over. You and Sam ready the lines." Rand stuck his head back inside the cabin and winked at her. For a moment he watched, appreciating the sight of her fumbling with the small buttons in her haste to get dressed and ready to meet the world again. "Join me when you, uh, get your *shoes*...on again." He chuckled. She realized that if the boys were listening, they could make more of that statement than actually needed to be.

A cold reality began to creep around her heart. The sensual dust settled. A stark truth gripped her stomach painfully as she admitted she had lost control one more time with this man. He melted her resolve, along with her heart, more and more easily each time they met. *Is it only his male sexuality that undermines my will, or have I totally gone to hell? No more control? No convictions to which I can adhere?*

She was so full of self-recrimination by the time she repaired her makeup and gave a stab at brushing her tangled mass of tawny brown hair, she didn't know whether to stay in the cabin and never show her face again or stomp forward to the bow to stay away from Rand and the boys.

Her mind jumped again to his statement in the heat of passion. Now it was quite clear to her that he had said the only place he wanted their relationship to go was to his bed. Making love...needing her tonight... clearly stated but misunderstood by her. No, not misunderstood; she had only hoped for more and had been crazy to think he might feel otherwise. She had fallen into his arms and into his seabunk like all the rest; how many numbers she could only let her imagination run wild. She was no better or worse in the eyes of Tim and Sam, and now the word would spread.

She felt a need to rush back to Houston, where her reputation was intact, and her dignity, too. Here in Biloxi it was now sullied, and she cursed, for nothing: incriminating circumstances and assumption. Ha! she thought. Chelsea Norquist—the toast of Ocean Springs, Biloxi—now snickered and gossiped about. For the past three weeks she had taken several steps forward for womanhood, and now, in one evening, set them back to where they had always been—at the mercy of men.

She began to whimper. "Why am I so eager to give myself to him?" She quailed, her throat constricting, her mind terribly confused. Fresh air, that's what I need, that will help, she told herself as she stepped into the pilot house and shut the hatch behind her. She lingered by the bulkhead, unnoticed by Rand, who was absorbed in the job at hand. She was surprised to see the pilotboat already secured alongside, still rocking in unison with *Sampson* while the boys finished tightening the big lines between the two hulls.

They were prepared to "tow her on the hip," as Rand had put it. The whole procedure was fascinating to Chelsea, who watched while staying out of the way. When all was ready, they started forward smoothly. The pilotboat, about the same size as the tug to which it was partnered, silently relied on the *Sampson*'s power.

Chelsea started to slip out on deck to go forward for the fresh air and some clear thinking on the long ride back, but Rand intercepted her and caught her hand. He pulled her to his side, kept one hand on the helm, and said tenderly, "You are very dear to me. Don't go out of my life tonight. Stay with me; when we get back we'll—" Rand looked up.

"How's it going?" asked the well-dressed, gray-haired gentleman, eating a sandwich as he stepped into the pilot house.

"Hey, Captain Johnny," Rand said in greeting. "I see the boys fed you."

"I'm surprised to see you at work tonight," Captain Johnny pointed out, still munching heartily. He glanced at Chelsea.

Rand hugged Chelsea to him as he started to introduce her, "Oh, John, I want you to meet—"

"Don't tell me," the well-intentioned pilot cut in as he took off his dark gray fedora and tipped it toward her. "You're Rand Korbet's lady. I've heard about this beauty," he said to Rand. "She's the talk of the coast hereabouts, you know." Then he beamed at Chelsea, "They all say, 'Rand's got the most beautiful woman, crazy 'bout him,'" He smiled a courtly smile. "They're right, too. Absolutely right. Pleased to meet you at last, Miss Leslie Borba!"

Chapter Eight

Chelsea jolted upright in bed, not quite awake, hoping it had been a dream, a nightmare, that she would be out of soon. *Surely I didn't; I—I wouldn't!*

Slowly she drew her body off the bed and dragged over to stand, wide awake, in front of her grandfather's old beveled mirror at his bureau. An awful-looking stranger stared at her. Dark circles from lack of sleep and an emotional merry-go-round lurked beneath the smeared black eye makeup that ringed her swollen eyelids and bloodshot eyes. She had cried herself to sleep, snuffling into her pillow for fear of disturbing the Sorensens after she'd slipped in quietly at 4 A.M.

With a heavy hand and a heavy heart she reached for the cleansing cream. Automatically she held her salt-air sleep-tangled mane of frizz with one hand while the other slowly massaged the softening, creamy cleanser into her sad face. She mentally ran the gamut of self-reproach. *How could you?* She glared at the image glaring back. *How could you be so—so out of control of your life, your plan?* She grabbed a handful of tissues and wiped at the shiny cream, still hoping against hope she would awaken from this nightmare.

What will I do? she asked the stranger staring at her in the mirror. I've really done it this time—I'm going to lose my job. My whole life is screwed up if I . . . Lafe—that's it! Of course. First I'll talk to Lafe.

She jumped into the nearest pair of jeans, forgetting underwear, and threw on the first sweater she found on top of a stack of dirty clothes. In her rush she half walked and half hopped down the hall calling for Lafe as she slopped into her deck shoes.

"Lafe. Lafe. *Lafe!*" she called, glancing at the old school clock on the living room wall. Nine o'clock! She hadn't slept till nine in years. She grabbed her down vest off the pegged coat rack near the door, grateful Thyra had cleaned it for her. Her mind was racing as she rushed out the door for the office still yelling, "*Lafe*. I've got to talk to you. *Lafe!*"

Eric opened the office door. Lafe was right behind him. They both looked alarmed.

"What is it, Chelsea?" Lafe implored.

"You all right?" Eric demanded suspiciously, concerned and obviously recovered from the night before.

Now that she had Lafe's attention, she wasn't sure where to begin. Lafe sat back down at the old desk. Eric remained standing near the door watching as Chelsea took up a sentrylike pace in front of the desk, her hands twisting nervously in front of her. Finally she blurted, "How fast do you think *Triumph* can sail?"

Both men looked astonished. Lafe quietly supplied, "Oh, she's not really a racer, you know. She's built for cruising."

Desperate, Chelsea demanded, "Well, how fast can she cruise? She's got to be...real fast! And"—she hesitated, looked at the ceiling as if in prayer and squeaked—"how many days before we can race her?" Then she slid her eyes sideways warily to wait for Lafe's answer.

Lafe shook his head as if to clear it of a misunderstanding. "Race?" his voice boomed. "She's not a racer." Then to substantiate his point he added, "She can't even sail. She's not rigged yet! How many days to—" he stopped himself, perplexed, drew a long breath and stood up. "Okay, now, Chelsea, what are you talking about?'' There was a sing-song calm to his voice.

''How *long*?'' she pleaded.

Eric responded to the urgency in her voice. ''A month, maybe more. Who knows. Sails will take awhile.''

''A month!'' she wailed, disbelief in her poor, tired green eyes. ''I've got to get back to work. It can't take a month,'' she cried.

Lafe slowly came from behind the desk, eased his gangly bones onto the front edge, and patiently asked her one more time, ''What is it? What is going on?''

Her voice trembled as she answered, ''I think we're in a challenge race—to Pensacola and back—against Rand Korbet.'' Her eyes widened in helplessness.

''What?'' Eric shouted.

''Wha'd you say?'' Lafe asked more slowly, then repeated her words. ''Challenge race, with what?'' He raised his eyebrows. ''A Korbet crew boat?''

She slumped down on the old wood bench, lowered her eyes, then sheepishly filled them in. ''No, his friend's sailboat—to prove steel hulls are superior to wooden hulls, even under sail.'' Silence, heavy silence, greeted this confession. ''Rand's friend has a forty-two-foot, uh, sloop or cutter, I think he said.''

''What friend? What cutter?'' Eric asked.

''A friend in Pensacola. Boat's name is *Starlight*,'' she added wearily.

With dread written all over his face, Lafe asked, ''Does it have a seven-foot draft on a cutaway fin keel?''

''Well, how do I know?'' she returned sharply. ''I mean, I was so angry, I didn't get details,'' she explained apologetically.

Lafe spoke with incredulity. ''The fastest, or at least, one of the fastest boats on the Gulf....''

Eric was appalled. ''How? Why? Uh, when?''

Chelsea leaned forward, elbows on knees, and held

her aching head in her hands. "Rand—uh we had an argument—a few heated words, and at the time I was hurt." She looked up at both men; her eyes begged understanding. "My pride. I got it all mixed up—"

Eric interrupted, "Did Rand hurt you? If he hurt you, I'll—"

Lafe stopped him. "Son, let's hear more of the story, see if we truly have a problem here." His calm logic prevailed.

Chelsea began, "I'm sorry, Eric. You shouldn't even be subjected to this. No, Rand didn't hurt me...physically. When Captain Johnny—"

"Cap'n Johnny hurt you?" Eric cut in, his blue eyes widening.

"No, no. When he met me...and thought I was... Leslie Borba, just because I was with Rand..." Remembering the humiliation, her lower lip started to quiver; tears were not far away.

"You? Leslie Borba? Ho, boy." Lafe smirked, then sobered quickly, sensitive to Chelsea's mood.

Eric remained discreetly quiet.

"Wait, now." Lafe continued. "How does it happen 'we' are in a challenge race with a boat that is not rigged or even built as a racer because you met Captain Johnny and he thought you were—Leslie Borba? How'd you come to meet Johnny, anyway?" he added.

Chelsea walked to the window and gazed into the yard. She didn't want them to see her misery as she tried to brief them on what sounded like, felt like, an illogical bad dream. She cleared her throat to steady her voice. "After dinner Rand took me for a tour of Korbet Ship. Shortly after we arrived, he got a call to tow the pilotboat in. I agreed to go with him 'to see that part of the business,' and that's how I met Captain Johnny." She paused to edit her thoughts before continuing. "While we were on the way to get the pilotboat..." She turned to her friends, who stood in rapt attention. She still couldn't face them and turned

back, propped her elbows on the window's wooden
sash, and continued. "Tim took the helm and Rand
gave me a massage—on my feet—and"—oh how she
wished Eric were not listening to this—"we enjoyed
each other's company, for the first time, really...."
She grew silent. Her cheeks flushed as she recalled
their passion. Then she realized her silence said more
than she intended and turned, her face revealing her
thoughts; she hastened to explain, "Nothing happened. Nothing!" she repeated, desperate for them to
believe her. "It's just that I had begun to—feel *special*
about Rand." She implored Lafe to understand, this
paternal figure from whom she expected a solution.
"Then to be confused with—just another woman—I
felt like nothing, less than nothing. Cheapened!" Her
voice broke as she finished. She fled to the wooden
bench and sobbed with the weight of the world on her
shoulders.

In spite of the knowledge that Rand and not he had
Chelsea's heart, Eric compassionately sat down beside
her, patted her hand softly, and tried to be of some
consolation.

Lafe, however, was not all that comforting. His objectivity led him to point out, "Chelsea, that man has
had a life of his own, a pretty complex one, from what I
hear, long before you showed up. You can't expect him
not to have had other women in his life."

"Plenty of one night stands from the talk around,"
Eric added.

"Son," Lafe quietly rebuked him. "Now, Chelsea,
can you recall how you came to—to discuss racing to
Pensacola?"

She sat up, wiped her eyes, more red-rimmed than
ever, and tried to stifle her weeping. "I—uh"—she
cleared her voice again—"I guess I lost my temper. I
called him a playboy, among a few other chosen insults
to his values and his damned obsession with steel."
She inhaled quickly and added, "He flung some equal-

ly unkind insults at my values, and somehow—the race was on.''

"To prove wood could outsail steel," Lafe pointed out, a bushy eyebrow arched in nonbelief.

In a tremulous voice she pleaded, "Lafe, we've got to *win* this race. Aside from my big mouth putting *Triumph* on the line, it really is the final step in giving Grandpa's dream a full life. If—I mean—*when* we bring *Triumph* back the winner, it will be a statement to the world for wooden boats—that may never be made again!" She finished with strength in her being, gathered from reaching beyond her problem to encompass a larger ideal.

Trying to stick to the facts, Lafe announced, "*Starlight* is long and fast—we don't have a prayer."

"Rand knew that, of course," Eric observed sarcastically. "And *Starlight*'s owners are about the best sailors on the Gulf. If they're going to crew, forget this race," he concluded mournfully.

"Uh, Chelsea," Lafe began quietly, his kind, ugly features suddenly full of compassion for this woman-child who had come to be like a daughter. "What will losing this race to Rand mean to you personally?"

She looked bereft. "I, uh, well, I haven't even thought of losing. I can't. We can't *lose!*" she wailed. "If I take time to stay here and see this—this last thing through—and I don't win, I may lose all the way around. I don't know if I'll still have a job," she muttered, dejected at the realization of just how encompassing this rash act of hers was going to be.

"Yes, well, there's that above all else. Money! Where do we go now for rigging and sails and hardware plus a little navigation equipment? Even at that, we'll be woefully under-equipped for a race with...that vessel," Lafe observed.

Chelsea looked dazed. Eric muttered something about, "Best sailors, fastest boat, ohhh," as he shook his head in disbelief. Lafe went back to his desk as each mind worked on the problem.

"Well," Chelsea began, a spark of life returning. She stood up and rubbed her aching temples. "I've got a partial answer, anyway. I'll sell my car! With my meager savings I should be able to at least get us to the starting line. My boss has wanted my car ever since I restored it. So, first I'll give him the good news before I admit I won't be back today or tomorrow," she moaned and headed for the door.

"You sure you want to do that, uh, before you think on it some more?" Lafe queried, caution in his tone.

Oblivious to Lafe's question, Chelsea wondered aloud as she went through the door, "How will I tell him it will still be a 'few' more days?"

Eric jumped up and shouted, "Better make that a week—maybe two!"

That stopped her. "Oh, no-oh!" she said, shaking her head. "We have to do this...in three days or better. Rand will be waiting for us at the Biloxi Yacht Club Harbor—Sunday!" Her green eyes widened in appeal.

"Chelsea," Eric bellowed, exasperated. "Don't you understand? After she's rigged out, a thousand things have to be checked. She'll need a trial run, her rigging tuned—"

Lafe interrupted with more negative remarks. "Suppose we work day and night again, and by some 'miracle' are ready on your timetable, who do you see as crew?"

"The three of us, of course. Then whoever else you decide on." She flipped and then started for the house again.

Lafe called after her, "How much actual sailing-racing have you done?"

She stopped again. A few steps farther, and she could make that call. "I—well, none to speak of. As a kid I was aboard with Mom and Dad but not on races."

"Ohhhh." Eric's low voice trailed away in hopelessness.

Then she recalled what her subconscious had tried to hide. "Uh, I—oh, I'll tell you something that may... help the odds. Uh, Rand won't have the use of his left thumb!" She bit the inside of her lower lip nervously watching their reactions. Both their faces registered shock as their eyebrows shot skyward. They awaited the rest of her story. "He, uh, caught it in the car door!" she threw over her shoulder and rushed to the house.

Her mind vividly recalled the blood as well as the reason she wasn't about to tell them.

After setting Captain Johnny straight on who she was, she had sulked at the port bow rail. When the *Sampson* docked at Korbet Ship, Rand tried to charm her out from under her black cloud and only succeeded in compounding her fury. She was seething inside, but didn't say a word until they were in the Porsche headed for home. Then venomous words spewed forth. She told him everything that had boiled within her during the long, cold, torturous trip back.

Rand finally lost his temper, and as they argued they challenged each other, sitting in the car in the driveway at Norquist Boatyard. How was she to know he was reaching for her when, in an attempt to end the shouting match, she angrily opened her car door, rushed out, and slammed it. In the process his thumb became the victim. He would probably never have a thumbnail again in his life.

She was flooded with guilt and sympathy when she turned at the sound of his *Damn* and saw him open the door to release his own mashed thumb. His face was a panoply of dark emotions.

Her "I'm sorry" fell on deaf ears. It had seemed as if he plugged his bitter wrath into the powerful Porsche, for it fairly exploded backward out of the dusty, rutted lane, then screamed east for Korbet Ship, laying an acrid trail of burned rubber half the way there. In the still, cold night, from where she stood, she could hear the roaring engine as it furiously convulsed when he killed the motor. She was numbed by the day, the night, and the final tragic event as she silently let herself in the old, dark house at 4 A.M.

From the kitchen window above the sink the warm sunlight splayed across the oak table, making a shadow-pattern of dancing magnolia leaves; it was as if the wind and the tree were joining forces to tease Chelsea into noticing the truly beautiful day.

Shakily she took another bite of the buttered toast, finished her coffee, and decided the phone call could wait no longer. Bolstered somewhat with the small breakfast, she was physically and mentally determined to have organized thoughts and a firm plan of action when she spoke with her boss.

Lafe was busy making calls on the office phone, ordering everything he thought they would need. Eric was off in his old pickup to locate three of the best sailors he knew from Gulfport to Ocean Springs, then talk them into this crazy, spur-of-the-moment, "love" match, as he sarcastically named it.

Try as she might, there was still a moistness in her palms as she listened to the ringing at the other end of the line and waited for Marge Blair, the receptionist, to answer. Then she heard the welcome greeting, "Good morning, Sherwood–Graham."

The familiar voice helped Chelsea make the mental transition. She was composed as she spoke. "Hi, Marge. This is Chelsea. Hope Art is in and can speak to me."

"Sure. Gee, Chelsea, where are you? When you comin' back? We got a stack waitin' for you, kid," Marge cheerfully warned.

"That's part of what I need to talk to Art about. As quickly as I can, in any case."

"Okay, kiddo. I'll see if I can get him. Hang on."

Chelsea's mind jumped ahead four days; they were bending on the sails, waiting at the Biloxi Yacht Harbor, set to win a race. A race carelessly challenged in the heat of angry confusion, now affecting lives in ever-widening circles. She decided right then that *Triumph* would belong to the Sorensens when she finally sold the yard. They were her life preserver for the moment and certainly deserved that reward for their devoted labor.

She was off winning the race when Art's voice startled her. "This's Art Graham," he crooned in his businesslike baritone.

"Art! Good morning. This is Chelsea," she chirped.

"Chelsea! Does this call mean you're coming back, or..." he queried hopefully.

"Sure does. In fact, I'm leaving in just a few minutes. I'll be there tonight. I'm, uh, bringing you my car as a peace offering." She rushed on, "I didn't think I could ever part with it. You know that, but something has come up. Does that standing offer of yours still hold?" She had spoken rapidly. Art couldn't comprehend.

"What offer?"

"To buy my MG."

"Oh! Well, sure—" he began.

"Perfect," she cut in, "I'll see you at the office in the morning, first thing. Oh, and Art—I won't be staying. I have to come back here for a few more days." She was rushing, trying to extend a positive attitude he couldn't counter. "I'll explain it all eventually, but in the meantime, can you have that check for my car in the morning?" she pitched assertively.

"Just a minute now, Chelsea. What is going on? Don't you hang up until you tell me why. What is so important that you are still not back at your desk? Things are so stacked up now, and we're waiting for you on certain clients that want you to—"

"Oh, Ar-rt. I'll explain when I'm back and we have

that dinner I promised you. I'm sorry I've put you and the office in a bind. I certainly didn't mean to. You know I'd never jeopardize a client. Please, just trust me on this one. It's too complex for a simple explanation."

"Is there a man involved?" he boomed.

How could she tell her boss a man was keeping her from her job. "Actually, it's a lady named *Triumph*. She's a beauty, Art. We finished the vessel for my grandfather just yesterday. It was quite a launch. Now we have to get her rigged out and set with sails. That's why I need the money." She took a breath, "I don't expect you to understand," she finished, a sweet challenge in her voice.

Silence punctuated with a sigh preceded. "You're right. I'll wait a little longer for that dinner and the full story then. Take good care of *my* car—and my most talented art director," he added.

With sincere appreciation she breathed, "You're a wonderful 'voice in the wilderness,' Art. Thanks for being there. See you in the morning."

"Well, it's about time you're coming home. I was afraid we had lost you to the mellow shores of Mississippi," Aunt Marianne teased. "Now, don't you try to make it by eight. My goodness. You just slow down and be here around nine or ten. Of course, I'll be up." As usual, Aunt Marianne was anticipating all questions and blathering on in excitement at Chelsea's immediate return.

"I need some girl talk, Aunt Marianne. May I stay the night with you? In the morning I have to catch a plane back here for some unfinished business before this whole 'sale of the yard' is complete."

"Still selling the yard? My, my. Oh, of course. What fun. I'll chill some Mountain Red and have a light supper waiting," she rhapsodized. "We'll talk till the talking's done. Lord, I've missed you." She sighed.

"I've missed you, too," Chelsea murmured softly. "Say, I better get in gear, or I won't see you in nine hours. Love ya."

As Chelsea replaced the receiver she enjoyed feeling a certain clarity of thought. Then she wondered why her life became turned around when Rand was involved.

These thoughts she pondered as she drove her little British sports car to Houston for the last time. The trip was effortless. The only stops were for gas and something to eat.

True to her word, Aunt Marianne had a hospitable table spread with hot, homemade vegetable soup, roast beef open-face sandwiches, and her Mountain Red wine with a twist of lime. She was set to listen. Her wisdom was in letting Chelsea find answers by herself, guiding her with the skill of a professional but within the framework of personal, loving concern.

By the next morning, when they said good-bye at the airport, Aunt Marianne was fully informed of Chelsea's love-hate relationship with Rand. Her parting anchor of wisdom for Chelsea was, "No matter what you choose to do, remember, there are no such things as mistakes."

Art had come through like a champ. He bought her MG, and his check had fattened her account by many thousands. Chelsea had waved hurriedly to her friends at the office and left for the airport before anyone or thing could detain her. Art was barely mollified.

She restlessly revved her mental engines in preparation for the upcoming race as she flew to New Orleans, changed planes, and landed in Gulfport. She deplaned to Connors's cheery face, beaming as he waved to catch her attention. He was brimming with excitement as he carried her small overnight bag to his car. Lafe had informed him of the challenge.

"Chelsea, child"—he smiled—"you know I want your *Triumph* to show her skirts to any steel-hull vessel, but I have some trepidation. That water can be dangerous.''

''I know, Uncle Dee, but I can't let that influence me. I—*we*—have to do it—to win. *Triumph* has to prove her rightful superiority!'' Then she lowered her voice to normal. ''According to the rules set up by that arrogant''—she faltered as she searched for the perfect word—''playboy,'' she snipped with vehemence.

Connors in his wisdom offered no comment. They rode in silence for a while. Chelsea gazed at the sights along Old Pass Road in a blur. She only vaguely noticed the small businesses, homes, huge ancient oaks, and modern shopping centers that passed every few miles.

The minute they arrived at the yard a smiling Eric welcomed her home with the news that her office had called. ''It was urgent, your boss said to tell you.''

The call took second place in her priorities; *Triumph*'s progress was first. ''What about the race?'' she asked, all business for the moment. ''What's going on? Tell me what's been done!''

''It's only been a day!'' Eric pointed out, slightly exasperated. ''Dad's got everything moving. I've got commitments from the three best sailors I could find.'' They were all walking around to the shed as he continued. ''We can count on them. We've already got our hollow spars in the shed. Boy, does Dad have a story on how we got them—how many more miracles are we allowed?''

They stepped through the door and the sight before her infused her with high energy. A clean maze of stainless steel wire rope snaked about from coil to coil as it found its way to collar fittings. The wood spars, astride sawhorses, had been sanded by Eric before she arrived.

Lafe rushed out of the office into the shed to inform her, ''Bobby's willing to drive his crane over. Just give him a little notice when we're ready to step these masts.'' Lafe hadn't even said hello, he was so intent on the job at hand. She informed him they had the money to cover the expenses other than the sails. He calmly announced he thought he had worked out where they could get sails.

"So, another day or two, and then what?" she asked, her emerald eyes flashing with happy anticipation.

Connors interrupted. "Chelsea, child," he reprimanded with a feather-light touch, "there you go, that infernal rush of yours. Lafe, here, and Eric too, are going about as fast as men can." He chuckled, trying to make his point with kindness.

Eric offered eagerly, "The very next thing we do, Chelsea, is bend the sails on, if we have them."

"That's the part I think I've got worked out," Lafe informed them abstractly. "I talked with Kurt a minute ago. He's offering us a used set for the race. Sounds like they'll do the job, but got to go to Fairhope, Alabama, tomorrow and get them. There's no way those in New Orleans would fit."

"What do you mean, used?" Chelsea asked. "Are we renting or buying or borrowing or—"

"Loan. They're on loan. If they work, we buy them."

"All right! Great! Sounds perfect," she said enthusiastically. "You've created miracles again, Lafe. Have you done this all your life?"

"Just since my association with the Norquist family," he joked, but it was true.

"Well, I'm hoping this is the last one you're called upon to perform. I promise the yard is Rand's as soon as we're back, celebrating our victorious win over steel," she proclaimed. "Oh, that reminds me. How long ago did my office call?" she asked Eric.

"Couple of hours or so."

She turned and gave a quick hug to Connors. "Thanks again, Uncle Dee. You're a great taxi, among other things. I'll be right back to help," she told Lafe, and headed for the house.

Thyra arrived home while Chelsea was talking with Art. She waved hello as she started to work in the kitchen, softly singing a perky little song.

Art's enthusiasm was barely contained. "One hour in Houston and everything breaks loose—what in the world are you doing over there, anyway?" he belted into the phone.

"Art, is this the, uh, urgent message?" She laughed. "They said you called right after I left your office."

"Honey, the important message is this: Right after you left this morning, we got a call from a new client," he crooned smugly. "At least we've got a good shot at landing them—with *your* help."

She was puzzled as to why this was so important that Art should need to make this call. "So, what else?"

"Ha! She says, ha!" He chortled in his excitement. "Chelsea, this is a brand-new account. A big one. I ran a D & B on them. And they asked for you to be in charge!" There, he felt supreme.

"Me, in charge?"

"You know, that puts you way up there, Ms Norquist." He was exultant. "We'll have to make you head of something. How about—Media Director. National media, since they're out of state."

"Head of Media? Oh, Art! You know that's been my goal since I joined the agency. And now maybe I won't start my own agency after all," she teased, momentarily back in her Houston life. *Triumph*, Rand, and the race were hidden behind this golden cloud of good news.

"Whatever, Chelsea. The point is, you've got to get the next plane back here. I covered for you, hedged about where you were. Give up the 'project' or whatever it is at that boatyard and come back today so we can plan strategy. This client's hot; I can feel it. They want you and you only. When can I expect you?" he asked with finality.

The golden cloud shimmered and turned to ashes.

Why was there never a clean deal? Always strings. She tensed, "I, uh, this is quite a shock. Of course I want it. I . . . just . . . I'll get back to you."

"But, but—Chelsea!" he stammered, disbelieving.

She was in the greatest state of confusion to date, other than the sensual fog that overcame her in Rand's arms. She muttered, "Thanks, Art. Bye."

Like a somnambulist, she went to her grandfather's bedroom so plagued with questions she didn't realize Thyra had followed her with a fresh cup of tea.

"Tea, dear?"

The kind, motherly voice startled Chelsea, who simply continued her thoughts aloud, oblivious to the tea or the listening post. "I can't leave yet—the race! I can't. That's just what Rand would love to have happen," she said, nodding her head. "Who from outside Texas would know anything about me? Or my agency?"

"We all know you, dear," Thyra gently volunteered.

"But no one *here* would qualify as a client." Chelsea shrugged as she accepted the teacup, which started to rattle in the saucer, her hands were shaking so. A seed of dread began to take root. "I'd better call Art back right now," she mumbled, chastising herself for not asking Art who the client was.

Her suspicion was too much to ignore. Chelsea phoned Art. *"Rand Korbet!!!"* she shouted into the receiver. "That arrogant—" Words failed her. "That—that—"

"Well, uh, Korbet Ship's the company. Yes? I wondered how you charmed him over there." Art was perplexed.

"He's despicable. I'll bury him."

"Wait a minute. He's a potential client. He was looking for—"

"I know what he was looking for. I've had it with him," Chelsea screamed, hearing only her own thoughts. Rand was manipulating her life one more time. "Thanks, Art. I'll get back to you," she murmured, suddenly as calm as water before a storm.

"But, Chelsea, when—" Art stammered as she hung up on him.

She was certain of Rand's intention. He had tried yet another ploy to be rid of her. He was totally guilty and already convicted in her mind long before she borrowed Eric's pickup and angrily raced down East Bay to Korbet Ship. She had no other concerns for the moment except a burning need to confront this man who seemed to stalk her life, godlike, thwarting her will at every turn.

Chelsea burst into Korbet Ship's office and immediately headed upstairs. She found Rand standing behind his desk, clipboard in hand, intent on the chalkboard filled with scheduling notes. His bandaged thumb was hard to ignore. So were the strong lines of his profile.

"Sorry about your thumb, but—" she started, short of breath from her rush up the stairs and her dominating wrath, which erupted past her apology. "You are an incredibly arrogant, insufferable— Just quit trying to run my life!" She had his attention completely as her eyes flashed with dark-green fire and smote the man of her dreams. "Quit manipulating me with your power and money." Her voice was losing volume; her angry heart thundered; she spoke more softly with a sharp intake of air. "You want me out of here fast so you don't have to race, to save face. You're so afraid of losing—you won't even compete!" Her voice grew lower, threatening. "That's a low trick—calling my boss and offering a phony client deal." Chelsea's body trembled with choked-back rage. "You knew how much it would mean to have my own client."

Rand ambled toward her slowly. Then he stopped, the tapered strength of his body within inches of her. He didn't smile. "Guilty," he sniped hotly. "But to start with, the only thing I'm guilty of is calling your agency. I called to talk to you; I wanted to...work things out... but I got your boss, and"—Rand shrugged—"he more or less 'assumed' I was a client. I'm sorry if things got out of hand." He crossed his arms; the sore thumb glared at her. "But while we're at it, there is nothing 'fast' about getting you out of here. We're a month late now on our acquisition deal. And you know why? Because you had to prove something—to yourself more than anyone else! I've been damn patient."

She held her ground. He was impaled on the green metallic shards in her eyes. His voice was brittle as he flared, "I really believe your hot temper got the best of you again the other night. Captain Johnny didn't mean to—" His amber-brown eyes matched fire with fire. He held her with a penetrating leer. "You can't possibly win this race against me," he scoffed. "You've got the mistaken idea that you can compete like a man in a man's world! Just back off; save us all some time. Drop this ridiculous challenge. Go 'do what you were trained to do,'" he mocked.

Shocked at his vituperative remarks, she felt sickened. Then he turned his back on her and in several long strides to the window, looked out at the Bay while one hand absently stroked his anguished brow. The wounded hand rested on his slim hip before he turned to address her mute fury, his words fanning the bitter flames higher. "You're right; this relationship can't go any further."

Her eyes stung with uncontrolled tears, the pain of his last words a knife in her heart.

He didn't quit; he goaded her: "I need that yard of yours a whole hell of a lot more than I need you or your body!" His eyes glinted with amber ice.

All the hold buttons were alight on the phone at his desk. The buzzer was insistent. He sarcastically dismissed her with, "Excuse me," as he picked up the receiver, then ordered with a shout, "Just have Connors send me those papers to sign." He turned away from her and took the first call, his voice normal as he answered, "Yeah, this's Korbet..."

She fled his office and down the steps, blinded by tears. The drive back to her yard was a blur. Unaware of space or time, she parked Eric's pickup and rushed to the privacy of her bedroom.

Chelsea fell onto the old-fashioned bed in an emotional shamble, heartbroken. Her inner turmoil swirled with love and hate.

After a half hour of listening to Chelsea weep great, rending sobs, Thyra left the kitchen and knocked timidly on the bedroom door. "May I come in?"

Though Chelsea was drowning in misery, the gentle voice pierced her clouded awareness. "Of course," she cried as she reached for a tissue from the nightstand by the bed.

Thyra exuded kindness and understanding as she took a seat on the bed. Chelsea greeted her with a smile that quivered, and she started crying again as she tried to explain, "It's no good...between us. Always... more anger. He...oh, Thyra, he said awful things, and looked at me like...he...hated me..." She tried in vain to stop the bitter tears.

Soothingly Thyra said, "Are you sure he meant those 'awful' things? People say things when they're angry they never would—we all do at one time or another. We have a saying back home that translated means—alienation is the stepchild of disagreement." Thyra's eyes shone with tender concern as she offered hope with this verbal Band-aid.

The words held a certain depth of meaning for Chelsea; she turned them over in her mind. A tiny voice somewhere admitted that she might have been hasty in her accusations, might have been a little bit wrong and jumped to conclusions....

"Let's try a fresh cup of tea again, dear." Thyra winked.

Calmed by Thyra's tea and understanding, Chelsea dialed Houston. "Art," she began.

"Chelsea!" he boomed. "I was just going to call you. Don't hang up," he commanded, exasperated. "Let me talk to you!"

"Please, Art, don't think for a minute I'm not vitally interested in the agency."

"I know that, Chelsea, but maybe we ought to at least talk about this new client. I'm not really sure he's a client at all, in fact," Art stammered. "I, uh, may have more or less jumped to some conclusions, now that I go back over the call. He was looking for you, though—"

"Oh, Art." She sniffled. "I'm sorry you got dragged into this. It's just—"

He sighed, "Affair of the heart, uh? No client."

What could she say? "It's a little complicated, but—I promise I'll call you in about four days." She tried to lighten things up. "Anyway, you have custody of my baby, and I want visitation privileges."

"Okay, Chelsea. Four days." The receiver clicked off. She wasn't sure now if she even had a job in Houston. But the race was on, and that was a fact she could cling to. Rand would rue the day he said those awful words.

Chelsea set the table and tossed the salad, then left Thyra to finish dinner preparations while she went to call Lafe and Eric from the shed.

As she stepped into the cold shed she apologized for not getting back to help as she had promised earlier. Connors was gone, and Lafe was almost ready for a break. Eric had finished one spar and was set to mount the collar and fittings after dinner.

There was a festive air to the delicious meal. Thyra whispered something to Lafe, and instantly a bottle of clear schnapps and four small glasses appeared on the table. Room-temperature beer accompanied the traditional Danish firewater. Three rosy-cheeked faces smiled and called out "skoal," initiating Chelsea as she followed their lead. She lost her breath completely, gasped, choked, and attempted a smile in response to their toast to friendship.

By the second and third toasts her throat was numb. The libation, loaded with dynamite, slid down smoothly, deceptively.

Lafe raised his glass to the mighty trees that lived in *Triumph*. Eric's toast saluted the power of a determined woman; his eyes applauded Chelsea. She proposed a fourth toast; her emerald eyes sparkling with excess sheen, she braced her elbow on the table to help steady that tiny, wobbling glass. "To...the wisdom"—she hiccuped—"of...clearrrthinking!" She giggled before draining her glass.

"Here, here!" responded three clear-headed hearty souls.

Between the potent drinks, Thyra's homemade, marinated herring went round the table. It was served on traditional brown bread imported from Canada and kept frozen by the Sorensen's for special occasions. Dinner was a rare repast, thoroughly enjoyed by four compatible souls, happily inebriated by the "skoals." A well-aged, thick beefsteak seared in butter and topped with a fresh mushroom gravy was served with buttery mashed potatoes and a tossed green salad, Chelsea's contribution. The dessert of fresh pears and a rare cheese was accompanied by a demitasse of strong coffee.

Lafe and Eric laced their coffee with a little brandy. But Chelsea almost tipped over her cup trying to shield it from the proffered liqueur in the hands of a radiant Thyra.

"Why—just tell me why—do you remind me of Mrs. Santa Claus?" Chelsea asked as her eyes slid sideways in an unsuccessful attempt to roll upward and focus, punctuated by another hiccup. "Oh, my." She giggled, then chuckled and chortled into an uncontrollable laughing spree.

The two men grinned, somewhat smug in their appraisal. But Thyra, with motherly compassion, understood. "You've had quite a day, dear," she pointed out, remembering the raw emotions Chelsea suffered earlier. "I'll help you to your bed. You just call it a night. The rest won't hurt you at all."

Chelsea tried to oblige the maternal authority, but found her body glued to the chair. She leaned to the left and then to the right. She could not will her body to stand up and panicked at this first experience. The floor, a mile away, pulled at her eyeballs; her head weighed a ton. She tried to look beyond the table, but sank lower in her chair, her nose level with her plate. From there the whole room began a slow swirl. "Ohhhh, uhmmmmmmm," she moaned, grabbing for security on the edge of the table.

Thyra understood instantly and was by her side in an attempt to assist. Eric responded too. With him on one side and mama Thyra on the other, they "walked" Chelsea toward the bedroom.

Just as they reached the hall, Chelsea was overcome with a dreadful nausea and leaned, desperate, in the direction of the bathroom. They quickly pulled her to the commode, where she lost her lovely dinner and all that had accompanied it.

Poor Eric, she thought as he tenderly handed her a wet wash cloth. He has seen me at my worst! A true friend; a brother indeed.

There was no floor under her feet as Eric carried her to her bed. He was reluctant to leave. Thyra shooed him away while she partially undressed an extremely troubled but relaxed young woman. Before she had the blanket over her, Chelsea had drifted into a merciful sleep.

Chapter Nine

Except for the relentless sledge hammer pounding on her brain and the reverberations stridently marching through the pit of her stomach, Chelsea felt great. She had awakened at 6 A.M., when Thyra tiptoed in to check on her before leaving for work. At Thyra's suggestion she drank a bicarbonate of soda immediately. It was now an hour later, and Chelsea was working on her first cup of coffee. She had dressed in her comfortable, faded blue warmups, wore no makeup, and her hair was still wet and squiggly from the life-renewing shower.

She dialed Dwight Connors's home. It was a call she'd meant to make last night before her evening was cut short. "Uncle Dee," she said weakly, still affected by last night's bad ice.

"Chelsea child, good morning." He sounded too bright and his voice much too loud.

She held the receiver away from her ear slightly as she replied, "No need to shout," then murmured, "Uh, I'm glad you're awake. I was wondering something." She paused. "Do we have any other buyers for the yard, other than Ra—Korbet Ship?" She couldn't bring herself to pronounce his name.

"What? Why, has Rand changed his mind?" he asked, incredulous.

"No. I have," she said softly.

"Why—why, Chelsea? I mean, it's been settled for

months, years actually,'' he questioned, still doubting what he had heard.

"I have my reasons, Uncle Dee,'' she said with quiet finality.

"But, Chelsea,'' he protested.

"Can you find another buyer?'' She paused, then added carefully, "If not, can you recommend someone who can?''

There was a long, heavy moment before he replied, "Can't say as I can, off the top of my head. However, I'll set about finding one.'' His old voice sounded tired.

Chelsea had perked up a little. "I knew I could count on you, Uncle Dee. Thanks. Talk to you later.''

There was something very hollow about vengeance, Chelsea decided with one more sip of the cold, bitter coffee. So Rand admitted he wanted my yard more than me or my body; it's natural that a woman scorned should deprive him of the yard, she mused. *Thanks for nothin', Rand Korbet!* The thought more than the coffee left a bitter aftertaste.

She dragged through the house and then went outside. What to do next? Her mind was whirling, but Eric solved her problem.

"Uh, pardon me. This bus is leaving for Fairhope in a very few minutes,'' Eric said tentatively. "You should come meet Kurt.''

"Oh, yeah.'' She chuckled, unwilling to leave the yard. "You go ahead. I'll stay and help Lafe.''

But Lafe thought differently. He concurred with Eric. It was extremely good public relations for Chelsea to go meet Kurt Pedersen, since he was virtually donating the sails for the race. Furthermore, he would probably sell them at an excellent used price if they decided to keep them.

Out of the grease and into the fire, she thought, let down that Lafe wasn't going to bail her out of being alone with Eric.

Gleefully Eric danced a little two-step as he hummed a snappy ditty on the way to the pickup. Grudgingly Chelsea let him open the pickup door and assist her up into the seat.

"What time you think we'll be back?" she asked, forlorn as they drove past Korbet Ship. Her heart yearned for a glimpse of Rand, in spite of the pain he'd inflicted just yesterday. Stubbornly her eyes looked straight ahead, but her peripheral vision strained for the sight of him.

"Oh, three or four hours, providing we take no side trips." He winked, his babe-in-the-woods-blue eyes twinkling. The look Chelsea returned was more eloquent in speech than a ten-minute tirade.

Nothing could deter Eric's joy in this rare experience. He flipped the radio to a country-music station, and soon the Blue Grass music worked its magic. By the time they had passed through Ocean Springs, Chelsea too was enjoying the moment, the warmth of the truck interior, and even Eric's good humor. She was, however, careful to keep a sisterly attitude and not mislead him for a moment.

The sights along Highway 90 were dim in Chelsea's memory, so Eric, the affable tour guide, reinformed her about the existence of Gautier, Mississippi, the Singing River Indian legend, and the massive Ingalls Shipyard at Pascagoula, off to the right just before they crossed the bridge.

"You know, to me this whole area from Gulfport to Pascagoula looks like a strip shopping center," she concluded as they left it behind and headed for Mobile.

"Serves the needs that be," he chimed.

Abruptly the truck tires changed songs as the highway became the property of the State of Alabama; pine trees and live oaks seemed a little more sparse atop slightly rolling terrain; a comfortable silence existed between Eric and Chelsea, and the country music played on.

With a quick, appraising glance, Chelsea noted Eric's head was just a breath away from the top of the cab interior. Why can't I find him appealing? she wondered. He certainly isn't ugly, though not handsome either. And he's infinitely less complicated than rotten Rand.

He interrupted her thoughts with a nod of his head. "The boys from Bayou Le Batre work off in that direction." He gestured south as they continued east for Mobile.

Eric's tour, she realized, was primarily boat oriented. He had also pointed out a couple of smaller yards to the left of the bridge in Pascagoula. Then, as they approached the freeway interchange at Mobile, he mentioned Bender Shipyard to the right, and as they crossed under the Mobile River and came up out of the tunnel, he spoke of the gigantic Alabama Dry Dock Corporation off to the right of the causeway that would take them east across the shallows of Mobile Bay.

The morning sun had cut through the earlier clouds and danced hypnotically on the brown, washboard mud flats, visible with the low tide. This glittering wintry beauty was new and pleasing to Chelsea's sense of esthetics.

The beautiful sight reminded her she had forgotten her camera in the confusion. A confusion she chose to blame on Rand.

By merely allowing his name in her mind, she flashed on his devilish dimples. From that vivid thought burgeoned a pyramid of coveted images: the kiss they shared in his office bed, his eyes, his electrifying eyes, his electrifying, topaz-brown eyes, the touch of his rough hands on her satin-smooth breasts, his full lips everywhere they explored, their first dinner, that lunch, the tug—oh, his slight scar! Reliving the memories, she was awash with a heat, a scalding flood that triggered a mysterious moisture deep within. For the first time ever she was aware that her blue warmups were uncomfortably tight.

Locked in her reverie with Rand, she didn't hear Eric's soft voice until he repeated, "It's just around the corner and up the next hill." He was staring at her while glancing back at the road. "You okay?"

"Sure, just a little sleepy," she prevaricated, and avoided his eyes by looking out the window. "Oh, this is lovely. I didn't know there was a hill on the whole Gulf Coast," she marveled as she viewed the rolling terrain with elevation high above the sea level.

"It's a well-kept secret," he confided, amused at her enthusiasm. "It's about the only 'hill' on the Gulf, that's true. A volcanic ridge or something like that. They say it runs all the way down from Georgia, I think."

At the top of the hill they turned left at the sign that read FAIRHOPE SAILMAKERS. The one-story concrete-block building surprised Chelsea. She had expected a sail loft to be an upstairs room over a barnlike structure with plenty of windows for light.

Eric backed the pickup into the driveway in preparation for loading sails. As they entered the front door Chelsea nearly stepped on the synthetic canvas rolled the width and breadth of the large room. The overhead fluorescents yielded a brilliant blue light that was augmented by warm sunlight from several tall, narrow windows across the front of the building. Her gaze quickly circled the room, which held a huge cutting table and several commercial-type sewing machines.

Then she saw Kurt walking toward them, barefoot on the laid-out sail he was marking. Intelligent blue eyes, a wide smile, and a simple "hello" introduced her to another blond Scandinavian. Mentally she noted he was about the same height and build as Rand. Kurt was obviously in good shape for a man in his early fifties, with a deep tan and white smile-lines of an outdoorsman. Then, as he spoke, she realized he sounded just like Lafe. She learned he grew up in Copenhagen.

"Hel-lo, Eric," he sang rhythmically, then looked at Chelsea. "And you must be Chelsea." He bobbed his head in acknowledgement. Chelsea automatically bobbed in response. "So, you gonna take on a forty-two-foot steel hull with your brand-new wooden *Triumph*!" he said, obviously well informed. "You know that *Starlight* is about the fastest thing in these waters? You got your work cut out, all right." He shook his head and raised his blond, bushy eyebrows to punctuate his judgment.

Before she could respond, Eric pointed out, "Chelsea's a very determined woman, Kurt. The launch of *Triumph* illustrates that," he defended.

"Thanks." She smiled at Eric. "Actually, Mr. Pedersen, I like to think the whole Norquist boatyard and some of the Biloxi community are taking on *Starlight*," she corrected. "Kind of looks like some of Fairhope, also," she teased, indicating Kurt and his sails.

"Sure, sure," he bobbed in amused agreement.

Eric volunteered, "You know, Chelsea, Kurt is also one of the best riggers and sailors in these parts. Don't suppose you could crew with us, could you, Kurt?" he invited.

Kurt was obviously intrigued, but professed no time as he helped them load the bagged sails into Eric's truck.

"Can we buy you lunch?" Chelsea offered.

"Thanks anyway. My wife just left to get us hamburgers about fifteen minutes ago." As an afterthought, he added, "Listen, call me from Pensacola. Let me know how these worked. If you have a problem, we'll exchange them. I can be there in forty-five minutes. Funny, we don't get many calls for schooner sails. Least of all not this type. Here you call and I hap-

pen to have two used sets. Just like they were kind a
waiting for you!"

Chelsea was impressed with his generosity and his
personal interest in the race. "Thanks, we certainly
will," she shouted as they drove away.

They rolled up two more hills south of Kurt's place,
and Eric turned the truck left off the main street. He
parked in front of a storefront café flanked by a shoe
shop and a dry cleaner.

"Thought we'd get a sandwich and a beer to drive
back on. They have great barbecue here. Okay?" he
asked, already out of the truck and halfway to the door.

"Sure," she called lazily. Then she snapped to,
hopped out, and hurried to join him inside. "This is my
treat," she whispered as she laid a five-dollar bill on top
of the register and smiled up at Eric. She was determined to keep out of his debt as much as possible, well
aware she could never repay him for the slave labor,
loyalty, and boat-building lessons he'd given so willingly, eagerly.

Before they left town, Eric gave her the once-
around-the-hill Fairhope quick-tour. They drove two
blocks south on the business-lined streets of Main,
turned right at Fels Avenue, and descended the tree-
lined, multilevel "hill" past houses out of the 1890s,
1920s and '30s. At the foot of the mile or so long hill,
the sun-dappled waters of the Bay dazzled them. Small
wharves and several homes fronted the Bay on the
other side of the small highway on which Eric turned
and drove north for several blocks. The area was truly
lovely, washed with serenity.

He pointed the old pickup east and set out up the
"hill." She saw nothing but cloudless azure sky before
them at the top of the village, and behind them, the
big, concrete public dock that stretched into the blue-
gray on Mobile Bay with dozens of bare-poled sailboats
nestled in their alloted berths.

Pervaded by a feeling of inexplicable nostalgia, she

murmured, "that was a treat. I'd like to spend some time here at a future time—like a date with *Brigadoon*."

"I hope I'm with you when you do," he rhapsodized. She let the remark stand without comment; they rode in silence finishing their lunch.

Soon the wooded hills swallowed *Brigadoon* as the old pickup rolled north on winding curves to Interstate 10 and home. The sandwiches and cold beer had been perfect. Hangover gone, Chelsea was feeling fine by the time they headed west on the causeway. She didn't mean to fall asleep, but the next thing she knew he was gently shaking her shoulder, saying, "Wake up, lazy. All you ever do is sleep anymore," he teased. He quickly opened her door, "I took time to bring you here. Hope you don't mind. I wanted to show you my fishing hole." His eyes glowed with a desire to please.

Groggily she looked around. Her vision blurred even more in the brilliance of the midday sun. There was something haunting and familiar about the place. For a moment she was spellbound by the shimmering spectrals from the great orb as they skipped across the old river. They held her suspended in a thought-free meditation. She wanted to prolong the pleasant experience, but could feel herself beginning to focus on a black silhouette. Regretfully she allowed the weathered plank walls of the old supply shack to claim her attention. Then she remembered the place.

"Eric. Is this Griffin Street Landing in Moss Point?" she wondered as she stepped down out of the truck. The cold breeze rudely sharpened her senses.

"You've been here?" he asked, disbelieving.

"I...It was a long time ago. My folks brought me here often." She walked closer to the cabin. "I don't remember so many trophies of happy times," she offered, indicating the skeletons of spoonbill catfish nailed to the weathered cabin exterior. "My parents never quit fishing until they had at least one spoonbill catfish—a delicious supper for me."

Eric followed her stroll to the edge of the quiet old Escatawpa River, also amazed that they had shared this special place.

Chelsea gazed over her shoulder at the oak-lined street behind her. Each ancient tree still hosted a wintry shrivel of epiphytic ferns, as they had when she was a child. She murmured, "I can't believe that in a world full of change, this place stayed the same. How many hurricanes later..." she drifted unwittingly. A deep melancholy pervaded her being. She was gripped by an unbearable longing for her parents, stronger than she had felt that day in the loft at the yard. She was overwhelmed with the cruelty of their early death, the deprivation of their love and the loss of the life they had shared here on the Mississippi Gulf Coast.

Vaguely she heard Eric speak to her, but his voice was only background noise to her poignant thoughts and waves of happy memories, too painful to bear right then. "Do you mind?" she pleaded softly. She started toward the pickup. "Too many reminders. We really should get back, anyway. But thanks—for showing me one of your favorite places." She smiled sadly as she settled up into the seat.

Always understanding, good-guy Eric took his place behind the wheel and quietly, without further conversation, drove them home.

Her mind turned over the options newly opened by her discoveries, traumatic as they had been, during the past few weeks. There was a tremendous pull toward staying, trying to run Norquist yard in spite of the facts against it, and settling into this area of the world that felt so very much like home. Her mind then countered with the logic of rushing back to her Houston life and the commitment to her career and future, so well planned until she arrived in Biloxi that rainy Sunday evening.

Eric had absorbed Chelsea's forlorn mood by the time the old truck chugged to a stop at Norquist Boatyard. As they headed for the office, Lafe met them at the door. "Chelsea, glad you're back. Rand came by. Had a notion the race was off." Lafe sipped his coffee.

"He what?" she shouted incredulously.

"Said you'd talked. Wanted to see you and straighten this out!"

"What'd you tell him?" she asked, gathering steam but still not ready to believe this news.

Lafe calmly shrugged. "Told him you and Eric went to Fairhope for sails. Didn't sound to me like you'd quit. I told him you'd call—"

"Eric," she interrupted, "may I borrow the pickup for a minute?"

"How dare you think this race is off!" she slashed, shouting at Rand from where she stood in the middle of Korbet Ship's main yard. He approached briskly from the direction of the dry dock. She yelled louder. "Nothing you had to say to me changed my mind about a thing—other than to *whom* I would sell my yard." The heat of her fury shone in her cheeks and burned at the roots of her frizzy hair. "You can bet it won't be *you*!"

He winced and stopped inches from her, much too close for her reeling emotions. The afternoon sun glinted off his white hard hat, hurting her eyes. She squinted up at him defiantly, though she hadn't missed a thing about his skin-tight, faded Levi's as he strode toward her. Not a thing from the rolled-up sleeves of the blue chambray work shirt that he wore over a black turtleneck sweater to his steel-toed work shoes, layered with paint and mud. Her heart melted at the sight of him, but she had kept her angry cool and given him a proper verbal lashing.

He stuck his hands in his back pockets, looked at her with a calm, friendly apology in his eyes, and said, "Chelsea, I'm sorry I called Houston. I'm sorry if

I... offended you yesterday," in his husky, honeyed tone.

"Ohhhh." She hadn't expected a real apology.

Then he looked away as he added, "Of course, you asked for it, coming at me, still angry from the other night."

Her eyes blazed again.

Then his voice regained its inherent warmth as he spoke, his dimples ear to ear. "Honestly, Chels, I'm a lover." He winked. "I don't like fighting with you." He reached for her arm, his eyes soft and inviting.

Not about to be taken in by his on and off charm, she stepped back. "You're afraid you'll lose. Right?" she taunted. Her voice trembled slightly from her uncontrollable, ambivalent feelings where this hunk of a man was concerned.

A few workmen stared from across the block-long yard. Rand leaned toward her; a long, exasperated sigh slowly escaped as he ground his teeth before he rasped, "I've got a business to run here—"

"An empire to build!" she sarcastically cut in to throw his words back at him for once.

Fury bolted from his fiery, amber-brown eyes. He clenched his jaws; a tiny muscle in his cheek tensed and twitched. He controlled everything except the cynicism in his voice. "I've no time—no interest—in proving to you what I, and the rest of the world, already know is fact!" He bent even closer to make his point. She could feel the heat of his breath on her face as he continued. "I have been extremely patient, like I said, while you wasted time—my time—building that damn, no good, wooden boat! Accept it lady, it *is* a man's world—and these days, steel is king."

She fired back, "You really can't stand the heat, can you?" She gloated, then thrust the gauntlet down again. "I'll be waiting for you in the Biloxi Yacht Harbor at noon day after tomorrow. If you're afraid to race, just don't show up. As for *Triumph,* my crew and myself, we'll be there!'' She glared at him for only a moment more before she gave him her back and flipped her trim hips all the way back to Eric's pickup truck, then sped for home.

Chapter Ten

In spite of the drab, gray sky streaked with angry, cold gusts, Chelsea felt like a giddy Kentucky Derby entrant. She leaped high in the air, then galloped across the yard to the dock, eager to board the beautiful *Triumph*. Her heart tripped with the thrill of the race bubbling in her veins. It was time to shove off.

Yesterday and all this morning had been filled with frantic last-minute preparations. Now Dwight Connors and a few of the faithful friends who helped launch and rig *Triumph* gathered around the old wharf to wish them well and wave good-bye. Thyra had risen extra early to prepare a special good-luck breakfast for them before leaving at dawn. She would be eager to celebrate their victory, she reminded, upon their return. Connors would foot the bill for a victory dinner.

They had borrowed a vast amount of gear. Chelsea was surrounded with equipment of unknown origin. She stood in the cockpit for a minute checking the list Eric handed her against the items at her feet. He assured her they had an accurate record of what belonged to whom.

Lafe, Russ, Chris, and Eric were bending on the sails as Dick Dustin, a sixty-seven-year-old, wisened yachtsman and veteran of many annual races to Pensacola, engaged the British Seagull engine.

The mighty midget motor was quick-rigged off the starboard side of the cockpit on a four-by-four oak plank that jutted from the rail about a foot; the small propeller just barely cleared the hull.

According to the rules, made in the heat of the great argument, engines were for docking and emergencies only. Short on time and money, this was certainly not much in terms of power, which made them very true to the spirit, as well as the letter, of the rule.

As *Triumph* glided smoothly away from the dock and into the Back Bay channel, Chelsea hurried below to help stow gear and food stores with Dale, the other woman aboard who was an experienced sailor.

They had met only an hour ago and had liked each other immediately. Dale Wilde was a pretty, dark-haired twenty-four-year-old who had sensitive brown eyes, a tall, slim figure, and kinky hair like Chelsea's. She was a schoolteacher who had managed at the last minute to get a three-day sick leave and was thrilled with the opportunity. Sailing was her number-one love, and she sailed anytime anyone would take her.

The guys in the crew had boarded yesterday to help and to familiarize themselves with *Triumph*. Strong and stocky, Russ Chaney, nineteen, crewed every chance he got. Full of enthusiasm, he was set to win.

Thirty-two-year-old Chris Landum was a male nurse at the hospital where Thyra worked. He sailed his own thirty-two-foot sloop out of Gulfport all year long when off duty. He spoke softly with a heavy, Mississippi-coast accent. His gentle manner enhanced his handsome face, Chelsea observed.

White-haired Dick Dustin was retired but active both in sailing-racing and with a musical combo that played club dates around the Gulf Coast. His high-pitched voice resonated with a natural laugh, enriching those around him. Thin and wiry, he was definitely the senior crew member with ranking expertise. Chelsea was impressed by the swift manner in which he slipped on his yachting gloves.

"Topsides, quick," Lafe shouted. Dale was up the

ladder first, and Chelsea right behind her. The men were setting the jib. Lafe handed Chelsea the tag end of a line he was pulling and said, "Training starts with the first sail. Haul away." She helped set the foresail and was taught how to cleat it down, how to stop a fast-running line with one hank under itself, take a "bite" in it, and to judge the best set of a sail by the way the wind filled it. She was told they would set the main later. From the first sound of snapping sailcloth as it caught the wind, Chelsea was awash in more childhood memories.

It was a crisp, cold day for early March. The winds were predominantly east-northeast. Warmed by her first pair of long underwear, though she found them strangely confining, Chelsea was grateful the Sorensen's had insisted she own some. She also wore several layers of cotton T-shirts under a sweat shirt topped with a waterproof parka to serve as her foul-weather gear. Extra turtlenecks, windbreakers, jeans, and warmups were stowed in a borrowed seabag. Her army-surplus rubber boots still made her feel clumsy and she held them in reserve while her old worn-out deck shoes tried in vain to grip. Her head was warmed with a black wool watch cap that threatened to pop off her frizzy mane.

It was just before noon as they made the turn for the Biloxi Yacht Club Harbor. There they saw, waiting for them, the sleek, silver hull of *Starlight*. Although Rand had never confirmed with Chelsea personally, he had sent word that he would indeed "lead" her to Pensacola.

Her silly heart stopped momentarily, only to begin racing. She knew the distant figure at the mainmast was unmistakably Rand. His thoughts loomed across the water at her. His brooding posture confirmed his lack of joy in this competition. She wondered why he was here at all. Pride? Or insecurity?

Dick maneuvered *Triumph* alongside *Starlight* while

Lafe and Eric handled small round bumpers to fender the two hulls as Chris threw a line to a tall, willowy blonde. She snubbed it off with ease. The two vessels, representatives of wood and steel, rocked companionably side by side while the crews were officially introduced and compared notes and race-rule understandings.

A sullen Rand greeted *Triumph*'s crew with a nod of his head, then said, "Ellie, George, Bill, Ted, and Craig—meet Chelsea Norquist, of wooden-boat fame," he added sarcastically.

She bit her tongue, smiled at his crew for a moment, then reciprocated. "Dale, Russ, Chris, Dick, Lafe, and Eric," she said, tilting her head toward *Starlight*, "meet the crew of the *Starlight*."

Briefly her eyes sought Rand's and were held by two amber-brown magnets while time stood still. Gulls screeched overhead in an upwind draft. He released her gaze as he muttered, "Time's awasting," and headed aft. "If there's no more questions, then let's settle the matter of how much handicap you want," he barked.

She leaned on the mainmast and laughed. "Seems to me we're about even," she said, indicating his thickly bandaged thumb.

Lafe quickly intervened. "Are you sure you don't want a handicap?"

"Yeah," Dick chimed in, "This is the smaller vessel. I—"

She tuned him out as Rand's eyes again riveted into her mind. She lingered in the past, reliving his persuasive lips, his embraces, his hard body next to hers... the old feeling rendered her legs useless, and she clung to the mast for support. All I really want is to be with you, she thought. A flicker in Rand's gaze acknowledged the message....

Ellie Danforth walked past him and broke the spell.

"No more discussion? So, follow us," Rand threw at

Chelsea. "I'll be waiting for you in Pensacola with your favorite white wine," he bragged as he tossed their line back aboard.

That was the signal. Both crews quickly scrambled to catch the wind and maneuver for the best position. Bumpers were stowed in a calm frenzy while headsails were set. Chelsea stole a glance at *Starlight* and had to admit the cutter rig was breathtaking. Her headsails were drawing beautifully as the main was going up. *Starlight*'s long hull parted the water like a knife and was in the channel long before lovely *Triumph* rounded up to head south for Dog Keys Pass.

Triumph was heeling well into West Channel. Full sail was set and drawing as it should. As soon as they could after going through the west end of Horn Island and east end of Ship Island passes, they would take their first tack for Pensacola. It was a pure sail race on the outside of the barrier islands. When they put *Triumph*'s seven-foot centerboard down, it helped a great deal. They plowed steadily into the deepening blue waters of the Gulf of Mexico.

Watches were assigned: Chelsea, Lafe, and Dick on the port watch; Dale, Eric, Chris, and Russ on the starboard watch. Chris and Dick were watch captains, but when it came to final decisions, Chelsea's race was in her own hands; she was skipper of her own fate. At least that's the way it was set up for the first leg of the race.

She was trying hard to learn everything at once as well as she could. Dick, the official navigator, explained the charts and their intended course with prevailing currents and wind patterns.

Lafe and Eric drilled her in the names of the various lines, as they had while she helped rig them yesterday. Now as she handled them she was at least sure of the difference between a halyard and a sheet line. Everyone in the crew was helpful in her education while doing their jobs. When it came to recalling terms for various parts of the sails, she was hazy on all but the clew and the foot. In time, they assured her, in time it would be second nature.

When she took her turn at the helm, she watched the orange-ribboned telltale tied on the port main standing-rigging. With one eye tending the ribbon for wind changes and the other minding her compass and set of the sails, she never felt busier. Eric hovered near in case she lost the course.

All she recalled from her childhood indoctrination was port from starboard, bow from stern, aloft, below, and topsides as well as such basic safety rules as always wear a lifejacket while on deck and keep a lifeline on in a storm.

Chelsea sat in on a hot discussion about how true *Triumph*'s design was, at least under the present conditions. Lafe, Eric, Chris, and Dick all agreed she was "showing her stuff." They were on a beam reach tacking southeast with a ten-to fifteen-knot breeze. According to them, she was married to the sea in a perfect union. This was probably her best heading. Chelsea understood only that the vessel was proving its unique design to be a fine one—so far.

Chelsea was much colder than she had imagined she would be even though she was well insulated. Her eyes teared from the wind. The ends of her long, tawny-brown hair whipped and bit her face. Dale offered some sound advice: she tucked her hair in a big scarf.

Chelsea loved the heel of the vessel. Even at that she was grateful for the high freeboard that kept the rails above the water. "Part of the comfort of the design," Lafe informed her. The big main was a constant concern to them, however. Chelsea didn't understand exactly, but it had something to do with the helmsman being too far forward to monitor it well.

They had lost sight of *Starlight* shortly after they rounded Horn Island and set their tack. Racing an invisible competitor made Chelsea more anxious than if she could see him.

After several more changes of tack, the crew was in sync. They were able to reset sail for the best speed with a fair amount of precision and efficiency. Chelsea had decided to take a few photographs of the last "ready about" rather than participate. Her photo-oriented mind needed to document this experience more than practice her amateur sailing skills.

And so it went. She gave some time to shooting pictures and some to acquiring more knowledge about the lovely *Triumph*. The boat behaved like a queen; Chelsea was treated like one. The whole crew deferred to her, she felt. They were patient and encouraging. No one laughed at her awkward attempts and mistakes.

"Here's your first cup of instant sea-coffee." Dale smiled. "Shall I go below and rattle some pots and pans for a late lunch?"

"Two of us can make it faster; I'll help," Chelsea replied, and followed Dale down the ladder to the makeshift galley.

"We're lucky to have a source for heating food, since this boat isn't completely out-fitted. This one alcohol stovetop will do for such a short voyage," Dale judged. It was temporarily secured but not permanently installed. "Since only one burner works, we can make instant soup, instant cocoa, coffee, tea, scrambled eggs. The main thing is to have enough water," she continued as she eyed the three ten-gallon spigoted Igloo coolers, lashed in place, that held their drinking water.

Chelsea unpacked Thyra's cold fried chicken and potato salad plus big chunks of buttered French bread. "I guess this is our big meal today," she ventured. She laid out paper plates and napkins and plastic forks and mentally thanked Thyra one more time.

Dale grinned. "Sure. We better enjoy it while we can. The rest of the time it's peanut-butter sandwiches, cheese and crackers, tuna, and sardines. But don't spill the oil in here or you'll have that memory below for years to come," she warned, automatically washing her hands in the bucket of seawater, their sink for the trip.

"That's it for now," Dale declared, drying her hands. "Other than the fresh fruit." She reached for some grocery sacks left untouched. "Yes. I thought so. Here: apples, oranges, bananas, pears," she enumerated as they poured from the bag into one of several mesh hammocks for gear strung along the overhead beam near the makeshift galley area.

There were sleeping hammocks slung around the aft cabin and the fo'c'sle too. No time or money was available to Lafe to install proper bunks. There was a Porta Potti to serve as a temporary head, partitioned for privacy by a flimsy curtain in the bow of the fo'c'sle. *Triumph* was virtually an empty racing shell except for her beamy design as a cruiser.

It was considerably quieter below, out of the wind and noise of the hissing waves. Of course, if you were inclined to be seasick, it was not a good place to be. Chelsea was surprised and pleased that she was experiencing no nausea.

Something startled Dale. "What's going on? Did you feel that?" she asked, holding the ladder for balance. The vessel's forward momentum had eased. *Triumph* had started to wallow. So had Chelsea.

They raced on deck to face an eerie sight. A wall of luminescent white fog enclosed *Triumph* except for a shaft of sunlight that pierced a small opening ahead of the starboard bow. Like magic, they had been transported from rough seas on a bleak, wintry horizon to a bright new calm world, as if they were suspended in a giant halo and being scrutinized for redeeming attributes. They were adrift with the current, sails slatting, starved of the wind. The only sounds were small waves patting the hull and its sighs and creaks as its wood worked naturally in the easy, rolling motion of the quiet sea.

The crew instinctively spoke in hushed tones, their voices echoing, while they discussed this crazy weather phenomena.

"Get on the foghorn—two blasts every minute," Dick ordered Russ, who was jumping about nervously. Dick's portable NOAA weather radio still had the same forecast as an hour earlier.

"What does it mean, other than losing time?" Chelsea asked Lafe as she peered into the sun-white cloud that seemed friendly enough to her.

"Well, number-one problem: Without visibility we may hit or be hit by something. Number two: We could lose our bearings if we keep this drift for long," he supplied, less calm than usual.

"Oh!" she squeaked. The bliss of ignorance began to fade.

"We're off Pascagoula right now. I wish I could tell how large this fog bank is," Dick reported, concern in his face. "This time of year you can expect anything on the Gulf!"

"That's for certain," Chris agreed.

The bow lookout shouted, "Off the starboard bow— something. Uh, like a silver flash." Everyone strained to see in the milky air, as they hung on to the shrouds and leaned out for a closer inspection.

Eric boomed, "*Ahoy...*" "Ahoyyyy," his voice echoed back.

"Hit that foghorn, Russ, and keep on it," Dick re-ordered, though Russ had faithfully been repeating it as directed.

The tense excitement held them all, pros and amateur Chelsea alike. "Anybody watching our stern?" barked Dick.

"I'll take it," Dale volunteered.

"It's *Starlight*! I saw a glimpse of silver," Eric boasted.

"Where?" asked Chelsea, and several others.

"Off starboard," Eric repeated. "No—it's gone now."

"Why don't they acknowledge with their horn?" Dick asked with irritation. "You're sure, Eric? Fog plays funny tricks, you know."

"I'm pretty sure. I mean, I think I saw it," he wavered.

"Only after a collision can you be sure," Chris added in frustration.

The mention of *Starlight* brought vivid thoughts of Rand to Chelsea's distracted mind. She walked aft, faced the direction of the sighted silvery ghost, sat down, put her elbows on her knees, her chin in her hands, and stared into a dream, a reoccuring dream with only she and Rand at center stage. Lazy sounds like the sails flapping gently, the gulf waters slapping at the becalmed hull, the regular bleat of the foghorn, the hushed crew, all lent to her hypnotic frame of mind.

The stillness had a greenhouse affect; the salt air was cloyingly warm. She felt overdressed and unconsciously removed her excess clothing. She stopped at her long-underwear top and blue jeans and stretched out comfortably on the deck.

Her eyes closed. She felt they were alone. As her fantasy continued, Rand stood at the helm, shirtless, in cutoffs. His bronzed chest glistened as he watched her swollen breasts beckon his touch. Desire blazed in his topaz-brown eyes, electric as they raked her body. He secured the wheel and came to her in slow motion while a scalding heaviness poured over her. His dimples deepened only slightly as his weight descended and their legs intertwined, her pearl-smooth skin brushed erotically by his hard body hair. His haunting eyes searched her face; then his demanding lips lowered to hers. They tasted the dew of salt air and fresh perspiration and basked in each other's scent. Her mouth opened eagerly to be tantalized by his tongue's explorations. His hands artfully spread her thighs; she fumbled with his zipper; the boat rocked in the sensual rhythm of their embrace.

Somehow everything seemed louder. Sails and lines banged; water splattered; voices shouted all around her; people were running; sheet lines screeched as the sails began to fill.

She opened her eyes and realized the fog had thinned. Light winds gamboled with the headsails while the foresail shivered with delight. Chelsea hurried to her feet to escape a crew gone mad.

"Catch it! Boy, it's light."

"It's coming and going."

"Okay. Everybody assigned?" Chris asked.

"What's the current? Can you get a fix?" Lafe asked Dick.

"Trim it now, and let's stay on it. Let's work every ounce of wind we can find and get to Pensacola," Chris, now watch captain, ordered.

Lafe looked at Chelsea. "I hope that *Starlight* was caught in it, too. If that's the case, we've still got us a race."

"I'll bet they headed further out," Eric speculated.

"I know it was *Starlight*. I just know it."

"I know it too. I could feel it," Chelsea added, then decided to keep the rest of her thoughts to herself. *I know his essence walked across the water and lay with me.* She shivered at the thought.

Eric noticed. "You need your jacket," he advised.

The three-hour watches went quickly. Chelsea was on duty when a brilliant russet sunset burnished the sky to purple hues off the stern, while a full moon rose over the bow and hung, like a single giant pearl, close enough to touch. She alternated her gaze through the rigging, forward then aft, breathless, while the fragile, changing panorama slipped through her fingers, like many of life's greatest moments.

Too late she remembered her camera. Her mind's eye would hold the image forever, but a print would have been more enduring.

She puzzled over how so much of what had been

Chelsea Norquist seemed to be changing and slipping away like the rare sunset she had just observed. Was she being reshaped by the will of Rand Korbet?

At 3 A.M., sipping an eye-opening cup of hot tea, she had more time to reflect. Lafe and Dick were good about leaving her alone with her thoughts. Everyone else was asleep.

The wind was asleep too. When Chelsea came on watch, Dick had informed her of their relative position and put her on bow lookout. They had just past the entrance to Mobile Bay. Lights on the beach seven miles off the port beam glimmered through the shifting mist. Stars peeked through holes in the dark gray wall at the horizon, looking like beacon lights where none should be. The dark water sloshed against the new, planked hull. *Triumph,* like a true mother-of-the-sea, cradled her crew and rocked them gently toward their destination.

Dried apricots, dates, and raisins gave stamina to Chelsea's shocked system, which was unaccustomed to short naps in swinging hammocks and constantly changing weather conditions. To get warm, she wore everything she could and still be able to bend. The parka was wonderful. She shifted her weight from one numb hip to the other while the cold, hard deck under her failed to yield any softness as her watch continued. Like a compass needle her mind turned back to the cold, hard facts of Rand Korbet—her true north. *Why can't I just be me with Rand? Why do I lose perspective, my temper?*

Her mind played imaging games: Chelsea Norquist as Mrs. Rand Korbet; that didn't allow for her Houston career, her creative goals. Was creativity so important? What about Chelsea and Rand as equals—sharing thoughts, the same bed. *Equals?* Are you kidding? her inner voice said. Rand Korbet? He's got his own problems to work through, not the least of which is being a southern male chauvinist. A sexy southern male chauvinist, she added.

Her mind drifted to a replay of his voice—on the phone, in person. Honey or velvet? she debated. She flashed on their last couple of shouting matches and then chastised herself. He'd insulted her. He needed the yard more than her body. Ohhh, she fumed silently. But why is he racing me? Why did he show up at all? Rand, Rand, Rand. Get out of my mind; get out of my life!

"Wanna grab this line? We gonna change tacks now." Lafe's quiet question surprised her. "Why is it I feel we have only part of Ms Norquist with us on this sail?" he teased, chuckling as he handed her the lines for the call "hard alee" from Dick at the helm.

Quickly alert, Chelsea replied, "I, uh, what do you mean? This whole experience is—uplifting! *Triumph* is wonderful. You have my full attention," she added, fibbing only a little to the smiling Lafe.

Soon all sails were trimmed in the windless night, and she was again alone with her thoughts.

What if I do lose this race, this challenge? Did I really do that or did he? she wondered, trying to sort through those angry moments in his Porsche. Her jumbled thoughts came back to losing the race. *I would be defeated in every way. I could never break through his arrogance, his accusations. He would relegate me to a woman's role for life. In his mind, I would be no different from all women who have disappointed and hurt him. I would disappear from his life!*

Her inner voice challenged: *So, don't you want to be rid of this emotional roller coaster, to be centered in Houston with your own agency eventually, and financially, emotionally, secure...?*

Chelsea went off watch and nearly missed the exquisitely patterned sunrise. Dale called it to her attention as she came topside.

This time Chelsea got her camera and was able to capture a symphonic array of colored hues, from blues, red, and orange to mauve and pink. They met in a striking crescendo that preceded the great orb's appearance at the horizon. Lyrical cloud handmaidens reclined in gossamer designs, choreographed by the subtle whimsy of the Gulf winds.

She braced herself as she snapped the 35 mm still shots, for *Triumph* began to frolic gracefully, climbing the mounting waves as the seas picked up in the renewed energy of dawn and a new day.

Weary from her vigil and incessant thoughts, she left nature's one-of-a-kind spectacle at last to fall asleep instantly in her hammock.

Chelsea felt as though she had just closed her eyes when she was awakened by the halyards, shrouds, and sails shrieking a soprano harmony while *Triumph*'s wooden hull creaked out the rhythm. The increased tempo was orchestrated by wind and seas, which kicked up even more now. As she came on deck *Triumph* was on a port tack with reduced sail on, but she was still showing them her stuff. The little vessel galloped until the seventh wave, then took a breathless leap and glided smoothly into the valleys between the salt-water mountains. The climbing and diving in the confused seas put everyone aboard in a crouched stance with a tight-fisted grip on anything that was stable.

"We're making our last tack for the Pensacola sea buoy," Lafe explained, shouting over the screaming sails and rigging and hissing seas as he wrestled the helm. It was almost 10 A.M.

Chelsea came closer and shouted toward his ear, "I really slept! Now I feel drugged or something." She looked around through half-opened eyes, then shouted again. "What happened to our beautiful day?" A low, ominous cloud cover was dark and menacing.

"The one thing that's constant is the changing

weather at sea," Dick supplied, coming forward to the cockpit from a sheet adjustment on the main. "You have to be alert to the least sign of change or you'll get a knock-down right out of the blue, or gray, today. Come on, let's trim the headsails, then the fore, it's backwinding." She followed him forward and managed to help without a single mistake. She was proud of her newly acquired skills. She had natural "sea legs" and was grateful she still remained free from nausea.

"A lot of commercial traffic this morning," Dale observed. "Look at the freighters waiting. See, way over there? That's a fairway anchorage."

Chelsea could see a dim outline of a darker gray against a lighter gray horizon, but would not have known a freighter from an oil tanker had Dale not differentiated for her.

Dick called everyone together near the wheel to make certain the crew was organized as they neared the pass to Pensacola Bay. "We need Eric and Chris on the centerboard. Lafe'll make the call to roller from the bow. Chelsea, Dale, Russ—you move smartly when I call for change of tack. If we can't synchronize this move, we'll ground. If we make it over Caucus Shoals, we'll be at buoy number nine and have thirty minutes shaved off our time," Dick instructed, still exuding energy in the final stage of the first half of the race.

It worked. Within five minutes, board up, board down, and several tacks later, with the helpful incoming tide *Triumph* was through the cut and on a beam reach. After much minute trimming of sail, she ghosted past the Port of Pensacola's east warehouse into the narrow eight-foot channel to the scenic harbor near Preservation Square.

It had been rough crossing the deep-water bay, and the crew was tired. It had taken them a little over twenty-four hours from Biloxi, but the last two and a half were a frenzy of effort as they still hoped to be the first in.

Chelsea thought she heard *Triumph* join the crew in a simultaneous groan at the sight of *Starlight*'s silver hull resting alongside the one small pier.

Chapter Eleven

Distant hoots and cheers from *Starlight*'s crew greeted them as *Triumph* edged closer. Country music drifted across the water from a portable radio somewhere on *Starlight*.

There was no mistaking the elation aboard *Starlight* and the valiant effort to be good sports aboard *Triumph* as the various crew members exchanged questions: "How long you been here?" "Did you get caught in that fog?" "Boy, we did." "We caught a little rain, but then we were further out." "Been waiting a couple hours, I guess."

As they secured their lines on the narrow dock, Chelsea saw Rand seated cross-legged on the stern, like a wild, flaxen-haired prince. True to his word, he extended a chilled bottle of white wine in one hand and two stemmed glasses in the other.

She could no longer ignore him, though she had been keenly aware of his presence since spotting *Starlight*. She stared back at him.

"Glad to see you finally found us," he crowed. "Sorry you got lost. We should have given you a tow." He hooted at his own humor. His eyes grew friendlier; his smile deepened his devilish dimples.

Her hands on her hips defiantly, she took the bait. "We would have been here waiting for you had the fog not reached out and grabbed us." She looked away quickly to avoid his smug, victorious mug. Then she noticed the beautiful restored eighteenth-century village homes surrounding the old-fashioned, parklike square in front of them.

George and Ellie Danforth were the first to jump aboard and officially welcome *Triumph* and her crew to Pensacola. George explained that they were docked at the newly dredged harbor near Historic Pensacola Preservation Society's Seville Square. The dock, channel, and harbor had been one of his personal achievements as a participating member of the Society.

Soon both crews had stowed gear and were stretching their legs on the dock and taking part in good-natured discussion. They made a unanimous decision to have a midrace dinner and dance at Phineas Phoggs.

Rand caught up with Chelsea aboard *Triumph* and steered her to a more private conversation on the far side of the stern. He poured both of them a glass of the white Bordeaux. He handed her a glass and then, as if to make a toast, leaned close and whispered, "If you can inconspicuously throw a change of clothes in a bag, you and I are joining the Danforths for dinner at their place on Perdido Bay!"

She caught her breath, shocked at his audacity. The wineglass trembled in her hands. That artful charm of his once again beguiled her as he continued, smiling, "We can spend the night alone, away from the crew, if you're ready to let tonight belong to us." His husky, velvety tones caressed her, weakening whatever resolve she might have had. He added, whispering in her ear, "I am."

The dew from his hot breath cooling on her ear was just one of the disturbing things beginning to happen to her. She managed a faintly indignant, "What? This isn't logical. We're...enemies." She needed time. "Winning certainly makes you magnanimous," she breathed. Her legs were getting weak; her heart pounded; her breath was short; her palms were moist, but not from salt air. She knew it was triggered by his closeness. She glanced away, tried to concentrate on the bay waters, only to feel his eyes and thoughts penetrating her being. She considered: a night alone, together, uninterrupted.

She took a deep breath, leveled her gaze directly into his enchanting eyes, and turned to face his lean body, so close she could feel the warmth from his thighs. "You do get right to the point," she murmured. A slight thaw in her emerald eyes told him she was acquiescing. She lifted her glass. He followed suit. "I just lost the first half of this race to you. I should feel a competitive need to keep you at arm's length," she said insolently, jutting her chin up at him. Then she added confidently, "Of course, I'll take the race tomorrow." She naively believed she would too.

Rand leaned against the rail and shook his head. "This is some crazy race. Thoughts of you consumed my mind, awake or asleep. Thank God George and Ellie were along. I'd still be adrift, somewhere in the Gulf of Mexico, wondering why we fight—" He stopped his intimate whisper and looked away, as if gathering strength. He looked back, and his eyes held hers in an unwavering gaze as he implored, "I'm sorry." His throaty accent choked. He tried again: "For what I said. Let's give ourselves another chance."

He was offering a new beginning. To her, "free of the world" meant free from all that had gone wrong between them. "I, uh, I need a minute... to adjust. I'll think about it while I change clothes."

Rand wasn't about to take anything less than yes for an answer. "Come on, Chels. It'll be great! We're going to throw net for our supper. We'll have to start early if we intend to get enough mullet for six of us!" he pitched enthusiastically.

"Six! I thought you said 'alone'?"

"We will be alone—for the night. Peggy and John Glass are good friends of the Danforths—and our ride!" He indicated the powder-blue Mercedes waiting near the circular walkway to the harbor. "I know you. If you liked the Gallery Up, you'll love the Danforth's hexagonal home. It's an architect's experiment. It's great."

His enthusiastic description did intrigue her. He *was* offering what she wanted: to be with him, alone, free of conflict. "Sold. Say no more," she agreed with a crooked grin and a sparkle in her soft green eyes. I'll meet you at their car." She disappeared down the ladder.

She found Lafe in the aft cabin, changing shoes. "How do you think we'll do tomorrow?" she asked, quietly sitting down beside him.

"Fine, fine." He nodded in his sing-song Danish accent. "If we follow through on some ideas Chris and Dick and I were tossing around. You have to make the decision, though."

"Why sure. Let's hear it." She was thrilled with his optimism.

"Hear what?" Eric asked brightly as he walked up.

"We think Kurt ought to bring that other suit of sails over tonight. If he does and sticks around to sail back with us, we can pull a few tricks out of our old sea bag," Lafe calmly informed them.

"I'm for whatever it takes now. Losing the first half won't be so bad if we take the last," Chelsea declared.

"So, we'll bend on the new sails tonight?" Eric asked.

"Soon as Kurt arrives. But you run along now and have a little fun. Kurt probably won't make it, oh, till after seven," Lafe pointed out. "Just bring us back something to eat that's hot. Hard to take more peanut butter when we're in port," he joked.

"You're staying here, then?" Chelsea queried. "Don't you need my help? What are you going to do till Kurt arrives?"

"Soon as everyone's gone, I'll remove the sails." He chuckled.

Chelsea wished Eric were not always in the audience. She needed to discuss Rand's invitation with Lafe. "Eric, would you mind checking on Dale? I think she needs an escort," Chelsea suggested, her big eyes growing bigger as she added, "Please?"

"Really," Eric responded quickly. "But what about you?"

"Oh, I've made other plans," she said simply. "You go ahead. I'll see you there." Eric shrugged and ambled slowly to the ladder. Once he was gone, Chelsea turned to Lafe. "I don't want to shirk my duty. If I can be of any real help, I'll stay, but . . . I want to consort with the enemy!" she admitted, slightly embarrassed. "Do you mind? If nothing else, perhaps I can give him matching thumbs!"

Lafe grinned at her black humor. "Go, enjoy," he assured her.

She leaned close and said softly, "Don't worry about me if I'm late." She glanced over her shoulder. "We'll be at the Danforths' fishing for supper. Call if you need me for anything."

"Sure, sure." He nodded and picked up his ditty bag, more interested in his own schemes for the race back to Biloxi.

As Chelsea descended the ladder into the fo'c'sle she found Dale half-dressed and liberally applying baby powder to her neck and arms. "Hi. What a great idea," Chelsea said in greeting.

"Only in lieu of a hot shower." Dale smiled and handed the baby powder to her. "See you at Rosie's or The Patio, or Phoggs. Just stick the powder in my bag when you're finished.

Dale was dressed and gone before Chelsea had peeled off her final layers. She pulled a pair of blue jeans and a green turtleneck cashmere sweater from her sea bag. Her wardrobe had not included anything for an evening with Rand. So what? He'd invited the "real" girl, not the carefully put together version she usually presented the world. She gave up on her hair and twisted it into a knot. With a few pins, the hair perched precariously on top of her head; a few tendrils slipped out and framed her face and tickled her neck. A few sundries in her handbag and the parka over her shoulder, and she was off, skipping lighthearted down the dock.

Rand waited, propped against the Mercedes, in conversation with the Danforths and the other couple as she approached. His smiling eyes watched possessively as she smiled in return. She felt enveloped in his warmth, though she was still five feet away.

She marveled as she went into his arms. How can he be so—so wonderful and then turn around and infuriate me?

"Chelsea Norquist, meet Peggy and John Glass, and, of course, you've met Ellie and George Danforth, masters of *Starlight* and now our good hosts."

*Hello*s were friendly all around. Chelsea felt secure with Rand in this group. No Captain Johnny here. They all knew she was his choice—tonight, anyway, her inner voice meowed.

"Let's go! Time's awasting. Besides, it's cold out here." Rand chuckled as he pulled her to him in a bear hug. "Get in," he ordered with a grin as he opened the door and pulled her into his lap. "Do we have time for a drink before we start fishing?" Rand asked without taking his eyes off Chelsea. She held his gaze, loving the close warmth of his body and his scent, a mixture of salt air, his special woodsy aftershave, and his own unique maleness.

"Sure," George answered as everyone piled in. John Glass was behind the wheel and his Peggy, beside Chelsea and Rand in the back.

As the powerful Mercedes pulled away Chelsea found herself thrown even closer to Rand. She hardly noticed the brightly painted Victorian mansions and cottages as the car maneuvered around the scenic square. In what seemed like only a couple of blocks, they stopped in front of a block-long, red-brick building of some vintage.

Though it was only midafternoon, the gray winter sky was cold and somber. She hated to leave the cozy warmth of Rand's arms and body, but once inside the building she was delighted. Both Rosie O'Grady's bar and restaurant on the right and Phineas Phoggs bar and disco on the left were jumping. She spotted some of the crew from both *Starlight* and *Triumph* among the crowds.

Chelsea urged Rand toward the sounds of country bluegrass played by a band at Phoggs. As they entered, couples were circling the dance floor with adaptations of the two-step. She was reminded of Gilley's back home.

They found a table near the tall-windowed front and ordered a round of beer, but before it arrived, Rand pulled Chelsea onto the crowded dance floor as the music changed to a slow waltz. Oblivious to everyone and everything else, they locked into each other's gaze. They missed the hot-air balloon suspended overhead, and the musically synchronized slide and film show playing the full height and width of the back wall with breathtaking sights: majestic mountains, rolling seas, beautiful people dancing in grassy meadows.

The music segued and they felt a mutual need to merge bodies. She rested her arm higher on his shoulder; her fingers caressed the back of his neck. Her body sensuously fit Rand's, and they moved as one. Without words she lay against him, their minds in harmony.

Rand wore a double-layered cotton turtleneck under a finely woven red-and-gray plaid wool shirt. With all that padding she wondered if he could feel her breasts swell and her nipples harden as he crushed her to him. Then his hands dropped lower to cup her hips against his thighs and obvious maleness as they moved to the slow rhythm. They shared a residue of salt air on skin and hair, evoking an earthy, almost primitive response in each other. An onslaught of emotions rioted through her body; she caught the look in his smoky-amber eyes, of sensual pleasure anticipated.

His dimples deepened as his mouth teased her brow before lowering to nibble, then softly kiss, her full lips. Her mouth parted eagerly.

Still shaken by his kiss and the whole pleasurable experience, Chelsea blurted, "I vote we go fishing." Rand nodded, wickedly agreeing as he led her from the floor, then from the building.

Cuddled against Rand, his strong arm around her, Chelsea was supremely happy as they again rode three in the backseat to the Danforths' home. In rhythm with the jazz that played softly on the car tape deck, Rand's hands played a hypnotic concerto on her erotically aroused senses; his rough fingers had only to stroke softly here or gently touch there...on her arm...or hand...or neck....

Once, when the harshness of his bandaged thumb accidentaly touched her sensitized skin, she felt a terrible, spell-breaking remorse.

When George sang out, "Home again, home again," Chelsea became vaguely aware of the tall pines that lined the narrow highway before the tires crunched onto a graveled road. About a half mile later he parked the car next to the back door of the strange, barn-red structure they called home. It was secluded, surrounded by wild acreage and fronting on the sandy shores of Perdido Bay.

Chelsea and Rand participated in the preparations for the evening, but were linked on a different level of being a part of, yet apart from the others. They were spiraling toward a mutual goal as they helped unload the car, start the charcoal fire, mix daiquiris, then shoulder throw nets as the whole group paraded to the beach a hundred yards or so from the house.

When they passed a couple of catamarans and an old beat up trimaran pulled high off the beach into their yard, Ellie explained they had a passion for refurbishing old boats. It was relaxing for George on weekends, while Ellie taught sailing with their good catamaran.

The three men rolled up their pant legs when they reached the sun-warmed sandy beach, then waded into ankle-deep water. George expertly threw his net first; it circled high overhead. They all watched it fill with air like a dancer's skirt before the weights took it plunk, plunk, plunk, into the frothy water and out of sight to capture what it could on the shallow bottom. Everyone hoped it was full of mullet when they worked as a team to pull the net to shore.

By the time John and Rand had exhibited their expertise with the throw net, the sun had started to set across the Bay and behind the tall pines on the Alabama shore.

The winds died with the sun, but it was still very cold. Even with the parka, it was a reluctant Chelsea who waded, at Rand's urging, into ankle-deep water after him. She squealed involuntarily and backed out quickly to burrow her bare feet into the residue of warmth left in the shore sand. From there she continued to watch him perform with the net again and again and wondered how much she would be privileged to learn about him in the process of losing her heart forever.

Surely, she thought, what I see in his searching eyes and hear in his velvety voice is more than lust, surely...

Ellie and Peggy arrived back from the house with daiquiri refills for their enormous, pint-size crystal stemware. "Thanks," Chelsea stammered. "Is there anything I can do to help?"

Both women had long since gathered that Chelsea and Rand were inseparable. "We're dining on paper plates with paper napkins." Ellie giggled. "Or else I would let you set the table."

Peggy shouted at the men, dragging the net, "How many by now?"

"Twelve at last count," George hollered back.

"We'll be eating at midnight, folks." Ellie shrugged, resigned.

Another hour passed, during which Chelsea divided her time between watching Rand with the men and listening to Peggy tell of her designer boutique newly opened near Seville Square. As the last sweet ice of Chelsea's third daiquiri trickled smoothly down her throat, she wondered if it had finished her, instead. She sat slumped against a driftwood log, trying to find the elusive warmth remaining in the sand when the women announced they were going for ice just up the road and invited her to join them.

"She's got other, more important things, to do," Rand instructed as he appeared from out of the dark shore water and sat down beside her. She was all softness and smiles as she tried to focus on the face from which the mesmerizing voice came. She loved the wonderful, unique voice that could hold her powerless to speak, or move, or counter his will.

The two women gestured you two are hopeless and walked to the car.

Rand's warm lips gently sought her receptive mouth. The longing he found there fired the embers of his desire. His arms surrounded her in a full embrace as his body's weight settled the length of hers, nicely pinning her to the powder-fine sand. Their daiquiri fog provided an ethereal framework for their spellbound bond, stronger than any Cupid's flower juice Puck might have sprinkled about them in this midwinter night's dream.

"Dinner in an hour, lovers!" George's faint announcement trailed off in the distance toward the house. Rand got to his feet and pulled her up. She felt no gravity; she was all fluttery, weightless sensations. His rough embrace crushed her to him. Delicately poised, her sandy bare feet on top of his, she felt a throbbing throughout her body and the wonderful, mysterious moistness central to wanton readiness.

"Let's explore George's trimaran." Passion slurred his words as he lifted her easily and carried her the short distance. Effortlessly he set her down inside the trimaran's cockpit. He descended the ladder into the center cabin, found a flashlight, and checked the area. He extended his hand, and carefully she descended the ladder to him. "Welcome to my web," he whispered. "Said the spider to the fly."

She naturally wondered which of them was the fly. I guess this is about as alone as we'll ever be, she decided, and quickly wrapped her legs around his hips, clinging to him where he stood at the foot of the ladder. Suspended thus in space, their kiss went out of control. His lips savagely bruised her equally hungry mouth. He momentarily ravaged her lips, her cheeks, her eyes, chin, neck, ears, with his ravenous, exploring caress. Locked in his embrace, she was oblivious to being transported until he placed her on the bunk, and gravity pulled at her compliant legs, which were grasped around his waist. Then she positioned herself to receive his full weight upon her.

They were set to soar outward to the far reaches of their universe; to orbit in the immense vacuum of their magnetic attraction. They lay in the dark on the cold Naugahyde cover of the double bunk. Rand gasped, "Chelsea, Chelsea," in a voice filled with emotion. "This is ours alone, our time." There was no world outside.

A slice of moonlight spilled through the hatchway, outlining Rand's rugged features from where she lay, looking up at the face she would know if she were blind.

Silently he removed her jacket and his and laid them

on the bunk as an Eskimo might prepare his bed against the cold. She heard not a sound, not the breeze in the pines, nor the gentle washing of the Bay on the sandy shore, nor the night creatures' rapturous chorus. All were mute to Chelsea's senses, which were highly tuned and heated toward only Rand Korbet and their mutual secrets, yielding to the pleasure about to unfold within them.

Unself-consciously the lovers performed a slow-motion ballet of smooth, uninterrupted movements as they undressed each other silently. When Rand stood naked before Chelsea, still resting on her knees on the bunk, he reverently slipped his rough hands inside her pink lace bikini briefs and slowly lowered them, then impulsively pulled her upper thighs to him. Her arms remained at her sides, her hands holding his, while the tips of her breasts brushed against the wiry blond curls on his broad chest.

The very touch was electric. Sparks shocked them in the dark cold. She raised her arms and clasped the nape of his neck; her breasts gloried in the feel of his hair-roughened skin. Her entire body quivered as he parted her lips, his tongue searching hers in wild erotic flicks. He groaned breathlessly for a moment, "I wish there were more light to see your body."

In one move he swept her up into his arms and placed her on the jacketed bunk again; her bikini fell to her ankles. As she stretched out, a wedge of moonlight played across her face and the top of her full breasts. "Come to me, Rand...now!" she pleaded huskily as she traced featherlight strokes around his corded stomach and up his chest, gently tweeking two brown points with her forefinger and thumb.

She felt his bandaged thumb follow his four fingers as they started a tantalizing trail around the mounds and valleys of her breasts. Again she wished his thumb could have been spared during their argument. "I'm so sorry about your thumb," she gasped as his warm tongue suckled her aching nipples, fulfilling a need for both of them.

"Shhh, don't speak. Don't think," he ordered as he eased his naked body down beside her, pinning her with one warm, hairy leg between her silky thighs. He leaned on one elbow and let his hand reacquaint him with her flat stomach, narrow waist, and for the first time his contoured palm found her warm, moist triangle, ready and waiting. She instinctively arched against his hand.

Her thoughts joined her body in seeking a release from this all-consuming burning need deep within. Caught in the overpowering urge for physical release, she aggressively thrust her hips, trying to envelope his body. Though he wanted to prolong the merging of their bodies, he gathered her to him as he covered her hips with his and took her lips in long, drugging kisses. Quite naturally, as if they'd been born for each other, his full masculinity found a home berth between her thighs, eager to receive him.

"Chelsea," he gasped. "You're like...no other." His words were disjointed with spasmodic breathing building with every touch, each passing, heated second. Her only response was to capture his lips and arch her hips further, inviting his entry to mutual fulfillment. Her hands clung to his head, her fingers in his unruly hair; she held her body against his. She'd never climbed these dizzying heights before.

She tasted a thin, salty film of perspiration from his shoulders as he raised his fully aroused body and cupped her firm hips in his hot hands. She spontaneously loved the male-female scent that invaded her nostrils, erotically stimulating her further to center with him.

"Now, Rand," she cried, feeling warm tears of joy. Her voice was erratic as her undulating hips sought release.

"Yes, Chelsea..." She felt his touch, then his throbbing strength filled her deep within. "Yes," he gasped, his voice engulfed with passion.

Her fingers kneaded and scratched his back, hips, spine—everything in reflexive rhythm with their long, encompassing tumult.

"Rand..." she breathed, reaching for the stars that smiled through the portlight at this coupling of bodies and merging of souls.

His thrusting power exploded inside her as he spoke her name, a heartbeat before she melted in the heat at the pinnacle, then slipped over the brink and twinkled...twinkled...twinkled....

There was no past, no future, only the eternal present. Their mutual need had defied man's calendral concepts. Oh, so slowly, they returned to sea level in the protective womb of the trimaran cabin. Cradled by Rand's body, her head on his shoulder, their ragged breathing regulated. As the heat of their passion dissipated their bodies began to feel the chill. Night sounds intruded.

For Rand and Chelsea, time began again where they had left it—on the beach. They started for the house as the clanging ship's bell announced dinner. Rand's arm surrounded her waist possessively as they walked. She slipped her arm around his hips.

Her thoughts bombarded the mental walls she had erected to avoid analyzing the experience she knew was inevitable. One persistent thought slipped through to prick at her euphoric balloon—though "love" had never been mentioned, even as they silently redressed each other, if what they had just experienced wasn't based in a rare blending of souls, what was "love" after all?

Rand's rough hands and fingers had been tender and caring. She lovingly kissed his fingers and bandaged thumb. He gently slipped her sweater over her breasts, helped her step into her panties, and finally, reluctantly, zipped her jeans. The silent pas de deux was not finished until the last button was fastened and they were both warmly jacketed.

Just before they reached the house, the distant laughter and the aroma of frying fish brought the curtain closed on their idyll. Rand turned her to him. She knew she would never forget his face by moonlight; it fully reflected what she felt. They studied each other's eyes. Then Rand slowly lowered his head and laid his cheek on hers to softly whisper, "You're one of a kind, Chels." His voice choked with emotion.

She waited, ready to hear, "I love you," but instead he swallowed and in a hoarse voice, declared, "I—can't let you go. What we just shared will never be quite the same, but I want it to always be—great!" His dimples deepened wickedly while he paused. "The Danforths guest bedroom is ours for the night." His lips closed on hers, a promise of new heights to soar. She found herself easily able to slip back into the veiled aura where only she and Rand existed. After all, she thought, he had offered the whole night. As long as they were free from misunderstanding, from abusive shouting matches, it could continue to be heaven. Her fantasies could never compare. She pulled away from his persuasive embrace to reconfirm her decision. "Okay," she stammered. "This night is ours."

She turned in his arms to face the full moon above Perdido Bay. He held her around the waist as they lingered together—lovers, not enemies—his chin nestled in her hair at her temple.

Moments later he said, "I know you think—" He changed his sentence. "I mean, tonight can be the first of many—for us." His strong arms squeezed her closer. "We can work it out, if you really want to," he finished, his eyes questioning.

The ship's bell clanged again, more insistent this time. With a sigh they joined the party.

The hearty laughter from the raucous foursome seated at the great rectangular oak dining table was in-

consequential to the lovers as they joined them. Rand
and Chelsea were still linked and attuned. A lingering
smile, a soft glance, a dreamy gaze isolated them from
the group and kept them on their own plateau, no matter the conversation.

After the informal meal of deep-fried mullet, fried potatoes, spinach salad, and fresh biscuits, Ellie brought
out her dessert coup: cheesecake tarts.

Peggy and Ellie relished the dessert, but the men and
Chelsea declined. Chelsea still savored the sensual feast
so recently shared with Rand—the most erotic pleasure
she'd ever known. Her appetite was awakened for the
delights yet to come. Mere food could not compare.

She helped clear the table before Rand pulled her out
of the kitchen for a stroll through the unique house,
though they were more in a world of their own making.
They held hands, eager for the moment they could
again be alone to soar among the stars.

Her attention was divided between looking at Rand
and listening to him as he explained the architect's concept. The walls were built with louvered glass and
screened to allow a breeze from any direction of each
hexagonal room, and the house was roofed with a plastic dome that allowed natural light. Steel girder beams
raised the house four feet off the ground. The furnishings were a contrast in values: outstanding antiques,
clothing hung on rods in lieu of closets. There were no
doors except to the bathroom. Each room opened on to
the main living-dining area. No privacy. The bedroom
Rand and Chelsea would share had a tall ceiling, a black
antique room divider gaily painted with an Oriental array of aubergine and orchid pansies. The idea of no
door bothered Chelsea. She wanted to be alone with
Rand. Sound carried so easily throughout the house
that whispers from the kitchen were heard in the bathroom.

Her delicious expectation of the night ahead was
faltering when a bright, staccato knock at the front door

was followed by a lilting, "Hellooo. Anybody home?" The door opened with a theatrical flourish to reveal the cover of *Harper's Bazaar*, perfectly posed and extremely alive.

Crimson lips pouted, then parted in a smile. "Hi, ya'll. I'm Leslie Borba." She paused a beat. The girl had timing. "The crew of *Starlight* told me I might find my beau, Mr. Rand Korbet, at dinner here." Her drawl fairly dripped with breathy sexuality. Her entry, however would have made royalty envious. With her hips in a high-fashion runway swivel, she carelessly removed and dropped her full-length sable coat and Hermes handbag on a chair near the dining table while gliding to the center of the room. There, assured of the spotlight, she fell into an *S*-pose to continue her one-woman show, "Fortunately, I used to live in Pensacola, or I'd never found this place."

Peggy and Ellie exchanged a glance as if to say, "What can we do?"

If Chelsea had felt insecure and jealous before, she now found renewed basis for even more irrational feelings; Leslie Gorgeous looked better than ever. Her stunning features, framed by that radiant crown of shoulder-length burnished copper, needed little makeup. Eyelashes thick as three pairs of false lashes, fringed doe-gray eyes that widened as they sighted her goal. With a slink designed to dazzle, she headed straight for Rand.

Leslie wore a strapless sheath of nubby-textured black wool with a top of long-sleeved black chiffon. Green with jealousy, Chelsea had to admit Leslie's dress was perfectly fitted and sexy as hell. However, she noted, the see-through chiffon revealed no cleavage; in fact, Leslie's chest was practically concave; a wonderful flaw. *If she were in Houston, I would hire her as a fashion model with her height, her flat top, size twelve shoulders and size eight hips and that aloof air, so right for haute couture* Chelsea mused; then she remembered that this presumptuous woman was not her employee but her rival.

Immediately diminished by her competition's presence, Chelsea felt like Cinderella as the clock struck twelve. Her green sweater and blue jeans turned to rags as she stood barefoot beside the prince who still looked more like a king to her.

Chelsea's fingers self-consciously stroked under her eyes for any stray mascara. She tried to smooth her hair, which was a total mass of salt-laden tangles. She longed for a hot shower and shampoo and a fighting chance to compete with Leslie, though she knew on her best day she wouldn't stand a chance.

Leslie stopped in front of Rand, smiling, beguiling, and breathed, "Here you are, my li'l honey." She held open her arms to receive him as John and George watched, speechless, from their chairs near the fireplace.

"What the hell are you doing here?" Rand growled, and glowered.

"My little surprise!" Leslie sang sweetly, rocking her hips, her arms extended with confidence. She knew exactly what she was doing—baiting Chelsea, shamefully. And it worked!

Rand took Chelsea by the hand and led her past Leslie to the sofa near the fireplace. He pulled her down beside him as he slumped back, closed his eyes, and ran his fingers through his wild blond hair. He sounded tired as he spoke without even looking at her. "I didn't invite you, Leslie! Did you just assume I would want you?" To Chelsea it seemed the rest of the room had stopped breathing.

Undaunted, Leslie slinked some more, as if invited by Rand, and paused near the sofa, commanding an audience from the men, her back to Peggy and Ellie, who still leaned on the kitchen counter. "You're even more irresistible when you pout, darlin'," she fluted. A seductive laugh followed, emphasized by a swing of her

head that allowed her sparkling red hair to circle and
fall again to one side of her head. "You don't like my
little surprise?" she whined as she eased down into a
chair in front of the coffee table, crossed her long legs
elaborately, and gathered a look of approval from
George and John with a subtle, sidewise glance.

Rand sat straight up. "You're damn right, I don't!"
he uttered like an oath, his eyes blazing.

Chelsea looked from Rand to Leslie, who didn't look
the least bit affected. Playing the game, Leslie lowered
her luxuriant, thick lashes in mock repentance, then
opened her gray eyes, waiflike, toward the other men.
She blinked slowly. George and John waited on the
edge of their seats. "Well, let's see, now," she tinkled
in a little girl's voice while crimson fringernails toyed
with her Dresden-peach cheek. "Ya'll suppose I could
have a little drink of water before I find my way back to
civilization? That's such a long, dark road back...."

Though she had looked at Rand, John and George
simultaneously shouted, "Sure! Certainly!" George as-
serted himself, "How about something more refresh-
ing?" Then he yelled to Peggy, "Any more daiquiris in
the blender?" while his eyes hungrily devoured sweet
Leslie.

Ellie's response was akin to that which all sisters feel
when their territorial imperative is threatened. "I'll
check," she fired back, teeth clenched. She looked
over her shoulder at the blender on the kitchen
counter, paused briefly, then replied sourly, "Nope!"

Leslie's mere presence brought out the worst in
people, Chelsea decided. Then things went from bad to
worse. Ellie's remark brought a few choice ones down
on her head from George. Then Peggy and John had a
word or two. Suddenly angry, battling spouses had the
spotlight. Chelsea, shocked, sat planted beside Rand.

Rand took command and announced to Leslie,
"Even though I sure as hell didn't invite you, I'm getting you out of here. You've caused enough trouble in

paradise for one evening. Get in your car, *now*. Wait for us, we'll be right there," he snarled. Leslie obeyed happily, as if she were a woman who'd got what she came for.

Rand pulled Chelsea after him to the room they would have shared. "Get your gear. We'll ride back with her. I'm sorry. It appears this whole mess is my fault. I've got to get her out of here fast. Have you seen my shoes?" he asked, glowering while he ducked down to look under the bed. "Damn." He bumped his head as he raised up too soon, shoes in hand.

Chelsea tried to speak but found she barely had a voice, "*No!* No, thanks. I'm not going anywhere with her!" Now that she had her voice, her mouth ran away with her blue jeans again. She grew angrier and angrier as she thought of Rand's concern for Leslie's welfare. "*I* can call a cab," she hissed. "I can see to my own safe return 'down that long, dark road,'" she finished, with more sarcasm than she had intended.

Rand grabbed her wrist in a tight grip, his anger at Leslie and the whole out-of-hand situation getting the best of him. "Don't you give me trouble too!" he said seethingly, trying to hide his anger with a smile, but his dimples held no charm; his eyes glinted with glass shards of amber-brown. "You will ride with me. I invited you and I will see to your safe return also," he bellowed.

Except for the pain in her wrist, she couldn't believe this was happening. She succeeded in twisting her wrist free from his grip and rubbed it involuntarily.

"Hey, Chels, I'm sorry," he apologized, his voice tender. "I didn't mean to hurt you of all people," he added, his eyes soft and warm again.

"Look, Rand," Chelsea started, but felt anger rising as she continued, "I know a woman who can take care of herself when I see one. That's a clichéd act. She'd be safe in a den of tigers. She doesn't need you or anyone else to squire her to safety!" she challenged.

"Ah, hell. I told you I feel respons— Don't argue with me!" He glowered then inhaled impatiently. "Now, come on," he demanded through grinding teeth, his eyes threatening.

A raging battle was being fought in the kitchen, the war zone for the four antagonized mates. Screaming accusations were answered with a volley of breaking plates. Chelsea felt no hope in getting a ride back with the feuding couples. Even getting directions from any of the warring partners to inform a cab of her location seemed a little unlikely. All she knew was that she was on the Florida side of Perdido Bay. Damn, she declared to herself. One more time I'm dependent on Rand Damn Korbet.

She found one of her shoes and maintained an icy silence while she set about looking for the other shoe, lost earlier in the euphoric haze.

Impatiently Rand shouted, "Chelsea!" his hands defiantly on his hips, his canvas bag slung over his shoulder. He looked like a grizzly bear full of hornet stings.

The environment in that house at that moment was conducive to radical thinking. Chelsea wasn't afraid of bears. "Listen to me, you, you—two-timing lothario!" she screamed. He blanched. "I'll walk back to Pensacola before I get in the same car with that—that—that person!" she hammered, shaking her shoe which had magically appeared from out of her bag. She stuffed her foot into it and raked past him, pulling her parka together, oblivious to the flying kitchenware schrapnel of the domestic upheaval.

Of course I can walk back, she told herself, stomping back tears with every step she took, tears of frustration, anger, disappointment, and hate for the man she loved—whom she would have stayed in bed with for the rest of her life. She fled past the gold Jaguar, vaguely aware of Leslie on the passenger side in the front seat.

Suddenly she heard Rand behind her, running, panting. "You stubborn, irrational little—" He stopped as he swept her off her feet and into his arms. "I am responsible for you, like it or not," he snapped. "You are riding back with me!" he huffed as he carried her back to the car and none too carefully plopped her in the backseat.

Frantically she fumbled with the door handle, it opened, and she escaped toward the highway, her bag bouncing on her back as she ran.

She could hear the throaty car engine start, race shrilly, then slowly approach like a menacing monster. The car lights threw some light on an otherwise totally dark gravel road. A half mile later her angry strides brought her to the two-lane highway. The Jaguar still slowly followed. Rand kept pace as she stumbled along the graveled shoulder of the road, seething. She felt stupid. But what could she do? Her pride wasn't about to let her get back in that car. Then she had a horrible thought. What if he left her on that dark highway? She was confused; she couldn't go back; she couldn't get in the car.

Rand made the decision for her. He pulled ahead and off on the shoulder. He got out and ran back to get her. "Enough of this crap; get in the car," he ordered. Well, at least the decision had been made.

The forty minutes back to the dock were completely humiliating for Chelsea, seated in the back, listening to Leslie glibly recall fond memories of Rand's courtship of her in Pensacola. Rand drove the car like a stone chauffeur. No matter, Leslie carried the conversation for all of them. Some of her stories were extremely informative, even though Chelsea tried not to listen. She found out Rand had been stationed aboard the *Lexington* when he met Leslie. Chelsea didn't even know he had been in the navy.

When the car stopped at Seville Square, the stone chauffeur growled, jaws locked, at Leslie, "Shut up!

Just shut up!" Then he turned to look at Chelsea in the far corner of the backseat. His voice kinder, he pleaded, "Chelsea, we've got to talk. You've got to understand—"

But Leslie interrupted—nothing stops Leslie. She pouted her lips prettily and cooed, "Is my li'l darlin' tired and ready for bed?"

That did it. There was nothing Rand could say that would hold her in Leslie's presence another second. Chelsea flew out the car door and raced down the dock for a safe berth aboard mama *Triumph*. With trembling legs and aching heart, she found her way into the dark fo'c'sle. She could hear their approaching footsteps through the open portlight. Not a word came from Rand, but Leslie called a syrupy, "Good night, Miss Norquist, wherever you are," her voice trailing as she stepped aboard *Starlight* behind Rand.

Bedded down next to Dale, Chelsea's sleeping bag refused to cushion her bones. The hammock was only good sleeping at sea. Tired as she was, sleep eluded her. Her tormented mind questioned over and over how Rand could have invited Leslie aboard *Starlight* for the night. Chelsea tossed and turned the rest of the night away, reliving their precious moments in the trimaran while feeling hurt, confused, angry, and keenly alert to any sounds of Leslie leaving the good ship *Starlight*.

Chapter Twelve

Chelsea greeted the sullen gray dawn without the healing benefit of sleep, though *Triumph*'s maternal womb had gently rocked her troubled soul through the early morning hours. She had lain in the dark, reordering her priorities, aware her foundations were shattered with the love match of her lifetime. She could no longer treat her feelings with any objectivity. In the past she had built her personal life to include relationships, but never to be dominated by them. No one could compare; her heart would belong to that one man.

I...I felt so complete in his arms. Surely he found me to be more than...something casual? she thought in anguish. Her thoughts returned to their lovemaking. Did he really change when Leslie showed up, or did I? Why did he feel responsible for her "safety" and—

Footsteps thudded overhead, distracting her introspection. It was 6:30 A.M. The crew was getting up. She heard Lafe's voice drift through the open portlight, followed by the fragrance of coffee.

She pulled on her blue sweat pants and gray sweat shirt, captured her hair under a scarf and sun visor, and quickly cleansed her face. She finished her toilette with a dab of skin freshener and skipped eye makeup. Toothbrush in hand, she went in search of a glass of water to finish her ritual. As she climbed out of the fo'c'sle and into the cockpit, careful not to awaken Dale, she greeted Lafe with a quiet nod. "Morning."

Then she saw Kurt on the stern. "Kurt, welcome," she called. "I'm so glad you could make it."

"Yaa." He waved, still busily involved in some work on the sail. She leaned against the bulkhead close to Lafe and asked in a low voice, "Does this mean we've activated Plan B?"

Lafe smiled and confided quietly, "Ya. We gonna defy gravity and fly home on *big* wings. Bent on the new sails last night."

"Is Kurt going with us?" she whispered.

"That's the best part of Plan B," Lafe chuckled. "Kurt loves the tradition *Triumph* represents. He wants to help her win this leg at all costs—using tricks we've never heard of."

Chelsea needed this news. Her competitive drums slowly started to beat, numbing her inner emotional pain and confusion.

Just then Eric and Dale, hand in hand, came up the ladder from the main cabin and joined them in the cockpit. Dale gave a cup of coffee to Chelsea with an understanding wink, which Chelsea returned. "Thought you might need this," Dale said quietly.

"I just saw you asleep in your sleeping bag!"

Dale laughed. "You are in bad shape. I walked past you a minute ago to get this coffee. Eric had it ready and waiting." She smiled at Eric happily before she descended the ladder into the cabin.

Eric looked at Dale wistfully, and Chelsea hoped a romance might be blossoming.

Lafe chuckled and lithely stepped to the dock. "Okay, crew, up and at 'em; we got us a race to win," he shouted, loud enough to challenge the *Starlight* crew, yet to come topside.

Chelsea hurried below to join Dale for a sandwich called breakfast.

She was finally ready to brush her teeth, glass of water in hand as she climbed back into the cockpit, when she saw them: Leslie in jeans and jacket, apparently borrowed from Rand, lazily brushing her silky hair while standing possessively near Rand at work at the helm.

Chelsea's autonomic nervous system went to work: Pain stabbed at her chest and stomach.

She turned away, leaned over the cockpit rail, and tried to brush her teeth. She felt devoid of vital energy—the simple act of spitting could not be accomplished. An awful, burning lead seared her stomach.

She slipped down the ladder into the fo'c'sle and shut the hatch behind her in hopes of being alone. On a boat there was no hiding from the crew. Confined quarters made one unit of the individuals aboard. Right now she needed privacy in which she could cry aloud and sob a healing, cathartic release of her raw emotions. Instead, she rolled her sleeping bag into a tight coil and pounded it relentlessly into submission. Exhausted, for some reason she felt better. She leaned back, but her thoughts were interrupted.

"Hey, skipper. It's time to shove off," Chris yelled down the hatch to her, cutting through the buzz of conversations on the deck.

"I'm going to win this race," she told herself grimly. "I don't care how I do it." She cast aside her sleeping bag and went topside.

The crew of the *Starlight* faced off the crew of the *Triumph* and parameters were adjusted for the run back to Biloxi. Both skippers acknowledged crew changes while avoiding each other's eyes. Rand curtly announced that Leslie Borba had replaced George Danforth, who had sudden "urgent" business. A bag-eyed Ellie had made it back, however.

Ha! Chelsea mused, then realized the irony of how much and how many lives had been affected by their domestic squabble.

Chelsea calmly announced that Kurt Pedersen had joined *Triumph* but deleted any discussion of the new, larger sails. There was a mumbled mention that the race was no longer just an "outside" race. This from Lafe and Dick, intended for Rand's ears. He didn't seem to care one way or the other about anything from the tone of his voice, the distant look in his eyes, and the droop of his shoulders.

As *Triumph* headed up into the main channel out of Pensacola Bay, the scuttlebutt had it that Leslie Borba was certainly no sailor and no replacement at all for George Danforth. Though Ellie was a good hand and sailor, she was no navigator. Everyone agreed *Starlight* would have a tough time now, in spite of her long hull, classic racing lines, and lighter steel construction.

Chelsea remembered with a twinge of guilt and a little glee the matter of Rand's sore, smashed thumb.

Straight down the middle of Pensacola Bay *Triumph* trailed *Starlight,* pushed by a strong north-northeast wind as they headed for the exit to the Gulf. With sails set wing and wing, Lafe, Kurt, and Dick nervously tended the lines lest a shift of wind or the wheel cause a sail to jibe.

They were setting *Triumph*'s hull speed at around six knots, and the three excited experts guessed *Starlight* was making good her true hull speed, too, somewhere around nine knots.

Both watches worked tirelessly reducing sail when needed and efficiently changing tacks. Everyone was fine-tuned for an efficient maneuver as they angled out with the tide and across Caucus Shoals, centerboard up, then down. The successful team work again cut off several minutes. For the first time *Triumph* screamed ahead of *Starlight.*

Chelsea was all smiles, tremendously elated, as was the rest of the crew. Even Kurt allowed a small expression of joy to cross his otherwise inscrutable countenance. Chelsea's renewed competitive spirit fed on the exhilaration of the moment like food for a starving soul.

Watches were ignored as the entire crew eagerly

checked wind direction and trimmed sail to guarantee
their lead. All went well for another twenty minutes
before the winds shifted and became erratic. The seas
grew confused, and so did the crew. *Triumph* rolled and
pitched and soon lost the distance gained.

The chiefs held a powwow, and Chelsea listened.
They decided to set a greater angle on their sea-
ward tack, and within minutes the vessel was under
control again on a steady run. With everything working
smoothly, the chiefs counseled the Indians on "the
plan."

Dick began. "Though sailing 'by committee' isn't
usually done, and our 'skipper' is admittedly inexperi-
enced"—he smiled at Chelsea, who nodded cheerfully—"she's proved the community spirit can build,
launch, and rig a perfect boat. Now we're going to
prove that same team spirit can win a race sailing that
boat!" he finished in his high-pitched voice, then
handed the speaker's platform to Kurt.

Kurt shouted above the wind. "We have to utilize
the offshore current this side of Mobile Channel, then
make a sharp cut inside just west of Dauphin Island. If
all goes well, we should beat *Starlight* to the Pascagoula
Channel by jumping shoals, centerboard up and down,
as we did through Caucus Shoals. We'll be moving
sandbag ballast foreward and aft as we straddle those
shoals, and you're gonna get mighty tired, fast!" he
warned, his sing-song Danish accent emphasizing certain words. He let a slight grin crease his cheeks. "We
hope to entice Rand inside the barrier islands. If he
bites, we further hope to lead him over the horseshoe.
With any luck, he'll go aground; then we can pick our
way through the rest of the shoals and leisurely go
home, winners. Right now, the larger sail area is gonna
get us there just that much faster, *but*," he shouted,
"they need constant attention!"

Chelsea understood the plan. It sounded like a dirty
trick. Her words came back to haunt her: "I'm all for

whatever it takes." A victory by default didn't have a satisfying flavor. But a lot depended on Rand taking the bait, since George wasn't aboard. Rand was not a racing yachtsman. If he were dumb enough to jump inside at Horn Island Pass, they would know the race was theirs by buoy nineteen or twenty.

Angry and hurt, disappointed and confused, Chelsea's ambivalence kept her from altering "the plan."

Triumph had left the dock at Seville Square around 7:45 A.M. By noon they were losing their off-shore current and rapidly approaching the time when the game-plan maneuvers would begin in earnest. *Starlight* was in sight. Russ, Dale, and Chris were poised to spring.

Once again a meeting was called. Both watches were ordered to get some rest and proper nourishment. They would need stamina to remain on alert for the all-hands-on-deck call that would come frequently during the rest of the twenty-four-hour race back to Biloxi.

The crew came through. Everyone but Chelsea was inspired. *Triumph* won according to the plan, in spite of shifting winds, a squall or two at midnight, and sheer exhaustion from lack of sleep, working the ballast bags and the centerboard. Rand had followed like a programmed computer and grounded on the horseshoe in six feet of water. It was dawn. Though there was some distance between the vessels, Lafe used a loud-hailer to call to Rand. "You want us to send the Coast Guard?" A ripple of chuckles rolled through *Triumph*'s crew.

Rand's disgust was obvious in his voice, which carried easily across the water. "Hell, no. We'll work the tide." He paused, then with biting sarcasm offered: "Congratulations."

They left him in the dinghy, rowing the anchor out to deep water so he could kedge *Starlight* off with the arrival of the one-and-a-half-foot tide. Instinctively Chelsea felt compassion for him. Ellie drooped around a forestay. Several crewmen were busy on deck, but

there was no sign of Leslie. A forlorn gray mist hung
around *Starlight* for company.

With Rand stuck for a while, the crew had little interest in running into the Biloxi Yacht Club to celebrate.
Triumph headed on around to Back Bay and her berth at
the Norquist yard.

Bobby McClellan spotted *Triumph* between the Highway 90 causeway and the railroad bridge. He had
spread the word so fast that Connors and Thyra and
several others were waiting when the tried and true
little schooner docked triumphantly. The well-wishers
jumped aboard with arms full of Champagne. Everyone
downed a fair portion before showering each other with
the bottled bubbly, which flowed like fountains.

For Chelsea it was a terribly hollow victory. To have
deliberately resorted to trickery to win galled her. It was
an illogical race; that was perfectly obvious to her now.
Rand had been right. She felt grossly immature as she
recalled his angry words: Call off the race. But she had
not because of her pride—damn, ruffled pride, she admonished herself. No, she argued, you did it because
you thought your cause was just! Then her know-it-all
inner voice told her to go ahead and be brutally hon-
est—to admit the real reason she felt so miserable, was
one Leslie Borba. And that was a fact.

Miraculously, near the end of the victory celebration,
even while slightly inebriated, everyone managed to
pitch in and clean up the inevitable human mess. *Triumph* was left only slightly broken-in and a wiser girl by
far.

The group dispersed around three in the afternoon
with plans to meet at the Old French House at nine.
Lafe and Kurt headed for the showers.

Before Connors left, he managed to get Chelsea aside
and give her the news. "Uh, as you asked, I've investi-
gated the possibility of another buyer for the yard." He
smiled. "I'm quite sure it can be sold to someone else."

"Great," she responded brightly.

"But Chelsea, child," he continued, "another buyer might be just as unacceptable to you as Korbet Ship." He reached for her hand to emphasize his counsel. "Of course, I don't know the nature of your problems with Rand, but I do know you are both alike in many ways." Chelsea smiled tremulously as she obediently gazed into Santa's sweet face. "You are both outstanding youngsters: strong-willed, proud, ambitious, and, yes, you both have suffered some personal losses. Kind of like you want to make up for it in business." They walked toward Conners's car. "Rand looked at you mighty proud the day you launched *Triumph*. I can't speak for him, but I saw his eyes were full of appreciation, admiration, and something else mighty tender."

"But Uncle Dee."

"No, hear me out. Someone a great deal wiser than I am once said, 'Wind from the land seeks the coolness of the ocean; so, too, does the ocean seek the heat of the land.'" They had reached his car, parked near the office. He got in and rolled down the window. "I hope I'm not out of line, speaking as I have, but—you're both such fine young people and I care for you dearly."

She swallowed hard, held the lump down, then replied, "I think it would be best if I get on back to Houston as fast as I can. I've had one too many encounters with Rand." Her misty green eyes matched her quavering voice. "I don't feel like this dinner tonight, at all. But I'll be there." She leaned in and gave him a soft peck on the cheek. "Thanks for everything," she said as she backed away, "and for caring." She waved. "See you tonight."

The Sorensens and Kurt were having a great time, reminiscing in Danish over beer and schnapps at the kitchen table. Chelsea could hardly hear the reservation information as she used the phone in the hall to check the airport for flight times.

When the jovial friends moved to the living room,

Chelsea called Art Graham. "Hello, boss. If I still have a job, you can pick me up at Hobby Airport tomorrow afternoon at four thirty. Sorry about the time, but old 'sometimes' airlines doesn't give us many choices here in the hinterlands," she joked. Loaded with misgivings, she waited for his response.

The slight pause seemed like an eternity; then Art chuckled. "Of course you still have a job!" he blurted.

"I'm eager to get back, Art. I've missed my Houston life."

"And we've missed you," he returned. "We need your ideas, your talent. And since you promised me a dinner and a long story—let's go right from the airport!"

In no mood to press her luck, she agreed. "Fine. I'll just unload and unpack later." She finished the conversation and hung up the receiver with a sense of dread. How could she tell anyone the real story of her experience in Biloxi?

Though her body was under the shower in the old-fashioned bathroom of her childhood, Chelsea's mind was back in the trimaran, where just forty-eight hours earlier she and Rand had loved in perfect harmony out there under the stars. *Flawed as our relationship was, it surpassed any Cinderella expectations I might ever have entertained.*

She felt low on energy as she slipped into her silk dress. It was the first time she had worn the bias-cut outfit, but even a new dress didn't help. All she could think of as she zipped the diagonally-striped black, white, and mauve tunic, was how attractive Leslie's red hair was. That was depressing.

Ummmm, I wonder what a little red in my hair would look like? she pondered, gazing in the old mirror at her grandfather's bureau. There was a knock at the door. The Sorensens were ready to go to the restaurant. Who needed red hair, anyway?

In a warm cocoon of filial affection, Chelsea and the Sorensens and Kurt Pedersen arrived at Mary Mahoney's one big happy family. Lafe and Kurt tried to teach her a Danish song which sounded like, "Real-lee Reel-lee-ronk-ka, Het-and-het-ter-blan-ka." They said it was a lullaby. They all laughed at her pronunciation.

As they entered a dining room like the one in which she had dined with Rand that first time, memories flashed as clearly as if she still sat across the candlelit table from him—just prior to their first misunderstanding and the inevitable challenge.

"Hey, here we are—over here!" Dick Dustin yelled from the large rectangular table assembled to seat *Triumph*'s victorious crew. Kurt and Lafe took seats near Dick, and Eric placed himself between his mother and Chelsea.

"Ya, looks like we better order more Champagne already," Kurt proclaimed with a huge grin, spreading his arms to include the rest of the tippling crew, already seated and well into their celebration.

Connors, the host-in-fact for the affair, was already in conference with the waitress. He caught Kurt's message and indicated it was being handled, his in-charge dignity supremely competent.

Chelsea waved at Dale at the far corner between Russ and Chris. She noticed how fragile and lovely Dale looked as she smiled in return. It was hard to believe that a fine sailor lurked beneath that genteel manner. Eric took note of Dale, too, for he excused himself and went to her corner. Chelsea was happy for him, and Dale, too.

The dark walls and candlelight gave the impression of an old-world castle where a conspiratorial gathering of well-heeled musketeers was about to be held. However, the stark white linens and formal table settings gave an elegance to what might otherwise have felt like a rank orgy.

As the food arrived, everyone agreed Connors had ordered well. Crab claws and broiled shrimp were piled high on platters with side dishes of hot red sauce. Champagne was still in abundance, but a fine Beaujolais was served with the prime rib dinner. A fragrant, strong coffee accompanied the pecan pie dessert.

Just before dessert was served, Lafe felt the need to make a statement. He tapped his spoon on his water glass for everyone's attention. He towered above the table and bellowed from his toes, "I just want to say, I think this is one fine get-together." He picked up his Champagne glass—refilled, as all the others had been— and saluted Connors. "I thank Mr. Dwight Connors."

Between the booze and the praise the only thing of Connors's that didn't rosy-up was his white hair as he impishly eyed those friends gathered around the table saluting his honor.

Lafe then turned to Chelsea. "And the bright spot in our midst, the inspiration for getting us off the dime and giving *Triumph* life—and a chance to show her stuff—Henry's granddaughter, Chelsea." The table of supporters joined Lafe in the toast and chanted together, "To Chelsea's *Triumph*." Lafe added, quite seriously, "Thanks, Chelsea Norquist. I'm sure your granddad and your mother and father would be very, very proud of you."

Ohhhh. Now it was Chelsea's turn to blush. She certainly did not feel very deserving of this praise, the facts being what they were, but those joyful faces were anticipating her response. She let her gaze travel around the table; the candlelight glistened in her happy eyes. In the spirit of the celebration, she stood up, lifted her glass, and toasted them all. "The thanks really belongs to each of you: Lafe, Dick, Kurt, Chris, Eric, Russ, and Dale. Thanks for caring enough to give your all, without sleep, and bringing *Triumph* home from Pensacola—a one-leg-winner."

Chelsea was distracted by a vision in gold lamé

moving majestically past their table. Rand was right behind Leslie. His eyes were steely as he caught Chelsea's gaze; she felt an iron curtain had dropped on their relationship. With a slight nod of his head, he acknowledged the table in general and moved Leslie out of sight into another room.

Chelsea's heart stopped. Churning in their wake, she tried to pick up the threads of her tribute. "For s-some, this race would have been a draw, but we know this was a victory for the lovely wooden boats *Triumph* represented, a victory for her designer, a victory—" An awful leaden weight permeated her body. There was no preparing herself for the extreme emotional reaction she had had to Rand's arrival, to the effect of his presence somewhere in the same building. She realized she had drifted again, brought her glass up in a gesture of "salute," and shakily sat back down.

Muttered thoughts circled the table: "What's wrong with Rand?" "Yeah, we beat him but—" "Not too fair and square, however." "But by the rules he agreed to in Pensacola." Someone laughed.

Connors looked slightly uncomfortable.

"He's a sore loser," Dick complained. "After all, he got there first agoin'."

"But we had Kurt and his bag of tricks coming back," Russ let out with no thought of decorum, pointing at Kurt, who kept a straight, dignified face at the well-intentioned compliment.

Chelsea was desperate to leave. The sight of Rand with Leslie had just ground coarse salt in a fresh wound. She endured a little longer; she played her fork through the now tasteless remains of her meal, responded when spoken to, but felt her source of being was totally severed. She had to get away, leave the problem of Rand behind, hide from the constant confrontation.

She slipped out of her chair to talk with Connors. "Uncle Dee," she whispered near his ear, "I hate to leave a great party, and I don't want to break this one up. I just wanted to say 'thanks,' then slip out the door after excusing myself for the ladies' room. I can get a cab and bother no one."

"Oh, I'm sorry," Connors said comfortingly. "I'll take you home."

"No, no. This is your party," she pleaded. "Please, stay. I'll be fine," she insisted. "I'll phone you in the morning." She took her purse and casually pulled her coat from off the back of her chair, covering her exit with, "Brrr, it's cold."

Luck was with her. A pay phone was in the ladies' room. "It will only be a few minutes," the cab dispatcher said. "Would you mind waiting outside?"

So far so good. Chelsea opened the ladies' room door. There loomed Eric, like a bodyguard, his arms folded across his chest. She tried for humor. "Eric, are you lost? The men's room is across the hall." Her joke went unappreciated.

His dear blue eyes were completely serious as he replied, "Dale and I will see you home. You shouldn't have to take a cab. Connors told me what was up."

This was exactly what she didn't want or need. "Please," she shrilled, "I will be just fine alone. You and Dale just enjoy the party. I need to be alone." Her eyes pleaded with him to understand.

Eric wavered, but at that precise moment Rand Korbet appeared, without Leslie and apparently in search of Chelsea. She looked at him, unable to ignore his presence, though she desperately wished she could.

"Pardon me, Eric. I need to speak with Ms Norquist—in private, if you don't mind. This will only take a minute," he assured with an authority that assumed Eric would immediately leave them alone.

Wrong. "No!" Eric began with a low threat. "You hurt her—"

Chelsea cut in with a hopeless wail. "Eric—Rand—don't do this. I can take care of myself." She stomped to emphasize her point, then ducked quickly away to escape to the front door.

They both followed her to the sidewalk, where she impatiently hoped the cab would be waiting. Eric accused Rand of playing with her affections. Rand ignored the young knight and yelled at Chelsea, "Wait, Chelsea. We've got to talk. Damn it, wait!" he ordered. "There's so much we have to settle. Talk to me!" he demanded as he pulled her arm and turned her around to face him.

The taxi arrived. For a moment all three just stood there.

Then quiet tears made liquid emeralds in Chelsea's eyes. Her throat and stomach and mind constricted in confusing pain. If only Eric would leave, perhaps—

At the sight of the tears, Eric answered the call to arms, though unasked. He fell into that role for lack of encouragement in any other area. "You made her cry," he shouted at Rand.

Chelsea was conscious only of Rand's amber-brown eyes, more smoky than she'd ever seen them before. His anguished voice rasped in half sentences, "Where can we talk? We've got to straighten out some misunderstandings." His pleading voice was piercing her defenses until he mentioned they also needed to "settle on the yard." All she could perceive was his need for the shipyard—to do business. All that he said before was blocked; she was blinded to his feelings for her.

She flared, anger the only emotion she could single out from the whorling maelstrom within. "You and your gilt-edged soul—get on back to Leslie and leave me alone. You're not buying my yard! I told you that the last time we argued!"

She moved so quickly both Rand and Eric failed to stop her. Through angry tears she opened the cab door and threw herself in and quickly pulled the door shut, weeping and sobbing. "Hurry," she cried at the driver.

He pulled away just as Rand's hand was reaching for the door handle.

"*Triumph* is a dubious gift," Chelsea acknowledged, a faint smile on her tired face, a small reminder of a night spent tossing and turning, sleepless in her grandfather's bedroom. Thank goodness no one had tried to talk to her. Now she had at least some direction. She continued: "However, under the circumstances, she is all I have to pay you with right now." Her voice cracked from underlying tension as she spoke to Lafe, Thyra, and Eric. Kurt had left for Fairhope, and they were all gathered around the kitchen table having their coffee after a late breakfast. She cleared her throat to say something else.

Lafe leaned back in his chair and shook his head, "Oh, no, no. You just forget talk like that, now. You don't pay friends for work they loved, especially when it was something they should have already had the gumption to do themselves." He pulled himself forward and took a quick drink from his mug of coffee, then added, "We'll be all right when you sell the yard to Rand. We'll be working for him then. Don't you worry about us anymore." Thyra nodded her agreement with Lafe's sentiments, as did Eric, a beat behind the others.

Chelsea took a long appreciative survey of the three faces she had grown to depend on and love, each in a special way. Feeling the weight of their world on her shoulders, she sighed, leaned her elbow on the table, supported her head with her hand, and told them, "You don't know, do you? I had thought Uncle Dee would have told you by now." She paused again, then blurted, "I'm not selling the yard to Rand! I asked Dee to find another buyer before we made the race to Pensacola. He told me he'd thought he could, but I don't know when the yard will actually sell." The three Sorensens nodded, resigned.

Speaking rapidly, Chelsea tried to reassure them. "I guess you and Eric could work for Rand anyway, Lafe. But you see why I won't have the money right away. That's why *Triumph* will have to be an interim kind of payment to you," she said, her voice tight from the effort.

"But *Triumph*—that's like a member of your...family," Lafe protested. "Ya, Henry worked and dreamed and, you too. You put yourself into debt for it. We can't accept it!" he declared with finality.

"You, of all people, can," Chelsea reiterated. "You three are my—Biloxi family. Surely you know that by now. Also, I know you will certainly appreciate and enjoy *Triumph* far more than even I would. However, like I said, I don't know whether she'll cost you money or make you money. You're free to do with her as you wish. I can only hope she's not a problem for you." She rose from her chair, placed her cup on the sink, and concluded, "I'm going to try to sell the yard as quickly as I can to get money to you, as Grandpa promised. She smiled mistily at her adopted family, then headed for her room to finish packing. She stopped at the doorway as she remembered something. "If Rand calls, I'm already gone. Uncle Dee is taking me to the airport and should be here in about fifteen minutes."

The memories flooded her again, old ones, new ones, too. Shakily she snapped the locks on her suitcases when she finished packing. She brushed her hair carelessly and had just pulled it back with two combs when Connors arrived. She gave her grandfather's room the once-over and told it good-bye forever. The pain wrenched.

Chelsea hugged Lafe, a solemn Eric, and Thyra with pangs of regret and misty eyes and what had become a permanent lump in her throat. Connors, jolly as ever, took her bags to the car. She could only wave good-bye. No words would form.

She didn't look back. The photographs she had taken

during the past six weeks would serve to help her remember all of what she had so thoroughly blocked for the last twelve years.

Connors's high spirits kept him in a storytelling mood. Chelsea listened with only half her mind as they drove the now-familiar road to the Gulfport Airport.

Much to her surprise, the plane was on time, and they barely had time to check her bags before she was in line to board; then, too soon, they were airborne; the ground below became an increasingly distant tiny land of make believe or never was. How fleeting were the moments of life, agonized over when they happened, then wistfully remembered. All of it gone forever.

Chapter Thirteen

Chelsea was exhausted, but her mind would not shut down and let her lapse into a nap. By the time her flight landed at Hobby in Houston, she had played out the future a thousand ways. There was a certain savor missing.

Now life in Houston begins again, for a sadder but wiser girl, as the old saw goes, she told herself in the colorful, noisy terminal.

"Chelsea. Here!" she heard Art call, but couldn't see him. Another "Chelsea," and he was right behind her. They exchanged a hug, then hurried to get her baggage. Art eagerly asked a thousand questions and elaborated on things at the office all at the same time. He had driven her old MG. She felt alternately happy and sad as she took a seat opposite the driver, who used to be her.

Life in the hinterlands, though filled with emotional trauma, had certainly been led at a more natural tempo, she quickly observed. Tires screeched, horns blared, rankled drivers sat in exhaust fumes and good old pollution as Art and Chelsea made their way into town and off the freeway to the restaurant parking lot.

Even as they waited to be seated at Brennan's, there was an urgency about the place, from the patrons to the maître d', who hurried the busboys and in hushed tones barked commands at the waiters and waitresses.

The beautiful old courtyard with the New Orleans atmosphere and huge palms was designed to reflect the lazy, southern flow of life. Instead, Chelsea felt the uptight attitude that seemed to hurry even the diners along. Perhaps it was only her view of it.

Once they were seated at the table that looked out upon the palmed courtyard, Art stopped his genial prattle and became serious. "You look great. Welcome back," he crooned warmly.

"Thanks. I feel as if I've been gone a long, long time. It's great to be back."

For the next two hours they discussed it all, business, boat-building, and even the abortive call that Rand had made to try and find Chelsea that fateful day. Surprisingly, Art was not only sensitive to the fact that he had presumed Rand's interest was professional, but he had actually read a "future client" relationship into every word Rand had uttered. Chelsea couldn't help but laugh in spite of the pain it caused. Good old business-first-last-and-always Art. It had never occured to him that Rand had romantic inclinations toward Chelsea.

When they arrived back at her apartment, he dutifully carried her luggage to her door. He placed it on the porch and bowed low. "Your bags, ma'am," he joked.

"Thanks, Art." Chelsea sighed. "Thanks for being more than a boss—a friend." She continued: "Thanks also for the ride, delightful dinner, good company, and vote of confidence." Art followed her in bringing her luggage with him.

"Get a good-night's sleep," he admonished, straightening his elegant tweed sport coat and tightening his tie, the proper business executive to the end. "I want you there bright and early—and as rested as you can be. I'll pick you up at seven forty-five."

"What can I say?" Chelsea acknowledged. "You think of everything. I was going to ride my ten speed."

"Not a good idea for our new Head of Media."

"Oh, Art."

"Shush. Not another word. You've earned it." He sprang out the door, closing it firmly behind him.

Chelsea should have felt great. Back in Houston, job secure, Head of Media. Oh, well. Before doing another thing, she opened all the windows of her tiny one-bedroom apartment. The place aired out quickly in the cool March night. By ten she was unpacked, organized, bathed, and snug in bed with a promise to call Aunt Marianne tomorrow. At eleven she was still wide awake. At midnight she was ready to turn her mind off Rand Korbet, but couldn't. At 3 A.M. sleep finally came. Once more she found fulfillment in her dreams.

True to his word and punctual nature, Art picked her up at 7:45. KIKK radio blared country music as he negotiated the snarled traffic that snaked the few blocks to their office. Yes, sir, Chelsea told herself. It's great to be home. I'll forget him in no time at all.

"I think you'll like your new executive office," Art teased as they rode up in the elevator. He wouldn't tell her another thing about it. Marge, the receptionist, was talking intimately into her headset as they walked in. She smiled and waved, indicating welcome, then announced, "Yes, Miss Norquist is in. One moment, please." She put the caller on hold. "A Mr. Korbet in Biloxi, Mississippi, is dying to speak to *Miss* Norquist," Marge emphasized, raising her eyebrows and pursing her lips.

Chelsea was so shocked by the entrance of Rand once more into her life, she hardly noticed Art leading her to a small room with a full wall window that overlooked the Westheimer traffic. She automatically dropped her briefcase and camera bag on what she accepted as her new—unearned—desk; her unseeing eyes were directed at Lord & Taylor, the Westin Oaks hotel, and the Galleria parking lot across the street. Her thoughts were scrambling for words with which to handle Rand. Why was he calling?

Art stood with a broad grin lighting his face in anticipation of her reaction to the evidence of her promotion. In a daze, she waited for him to leave her in privacy before she picked up the phone.

Impatiently Art put his hands on his hips and spewed, "Chelsea, is this so commonplace it doesn't even rate an 'ah' or and 'oh' from you? What do you think?" he prompted.

She snapped out of her fog. "Oh, Art, no. I mean, this is great. Terrific. Forgive me. It's just this call that's holding. I'll look around after I take it. I'm sorry." Her mind raced with thoughts of Rand. "Do you mind?" she asked delicately.

"Ohhh." He nodded. The fog clearing. "Korbet! It's him!" He held up his hands in recognition. "Certainly. Certainly." He backed out, closing the door quietly behind him.

Her heart beat unevenly as she picked up the receiver. "Chelsea Norquist," she announced breathlessly.

An extremely heavy silence greeted her ears before he exhaled. "You really are there this time," he confirmed in disbelief. His husky-honeyed voice melted her resolve right there. Rand continued, "I...find it hard to...believe...you really left." His words stumbled out, erratically. "You left without—we never talked! We have so much...unfinished business," he murmured in anguish.

Chelsea closed her mind to his anguish. The word *business* drowned out everything else. She wanted words of love. "Business" talk only triggered the same old angry emotions. "Oh, Rand Korbet," she snapped. "You're still not listening to me. We have no further business. I'm selling the yard to someone else."

"Chelsea," Rand implored. "I—I—" He stopped. She could hear his deep intake of air and picture his lips, his eyes.... "This is really messing me up," he blurted, his voice tight.

"Rand, I've got to get to work. I just walked in when you called—" Her throat constricted as tears threatened.

"Come back, Chelsea," he pleaded with just a hint of demand.

Quiet tears began to find a path down her cheeks. The knife in her voice nearly gave away her lack of composure. "Talk to Uncle Dee. He...handles the yard business." Her voice quavered.

"Chels, are you crying?" She didn't hear his tender concern.

In an inaudible whisper she cried, "Good-bye." She dropped the receiver into its cradle and fell into her chair, then fumbled for some tissue while her heart thundered in her chest from suppressed spasms of pain-filled weeping. She sat dabbing at ruined eye makeup when Art knocked.

"May I come in now?" he called through the door.

What could she do? Her first day back had hardly begun. "Sure," she squeaked as she turned her chair to face the window to avoid his eyes. She mastered a weak smile that was too broad for her still-glistening blue-green eyes. "I love it, Art," she offered. "Talk about a dream come true...I—I—don't deserve it. I—"

"Chelsea, Chelsea." Art sighed. He ran his hand through his graying brown hair. "Anything I can do?" He stood on the other side of her desk like a helpless little boy.

"Hey, Art. It's—it's nothing. I'm back. I'm going to do a great job. Now, where were we when we were so rudely interrupted? A tour, I believe," she ventured, rising from her chair and heading for the door.

Art followed. "Okay, tough guy. Whatever you say." He took great pride in all the details of how he had rearranged the office to accomodate her new needs as Head of Media. It was a vote of confidence after all she had put him through. The production area was larger and included spacious rooms for her art and layout departments as well as a fair-size product photography studio and dark room. Even the conference room had been updated and now included the latest in multimedia screening capabilities. The writers, account executives, bookkeepers, secretaries—everyone was there, and they greeted Chelsea with a warm welcome back. But Chelsea wasn't happy at all. She knew she desperately needed time without contact with Rand to heal her wounded soul. She threw herself eagerly into her job.

During the following week she refused a dozen calls from "That Mr. Korbet with the wonderful Mississippi voice."

"Tell him I've gone for the day, and do not under any circumstances give him my unlisted home phone number," she cautioned Marge.

With a determination that bordered on fanaticism, Chelsea whirled through the production schedules with client after client, working until 2 and 3 A.M. at times at the various taping sessions at the local television stations. She wouldn't allow herself to stop long enough to ask why. Why was she so miserable?

When she returned from her latest all-day-and-half-the-night session Saturday night at midnight, she was thoroughly exhausted. She considered calling Aunt Marianne, whose messages she had been collecting on her desk all week, but decided it was too late and chose a hot, soaking bath instead.

What a luxury, she pondered, chin high in soothing bubbles that relaxed her body as well as her brittled spirit. She slid deeper into the tub, laid her head to rest at the back, and slowly reflected on the last time she had enjoyed this rare experience—at the Ocean Springs motel, after her muddy encounter with—with—him.

Certainly the frenetic week had helped block most

thoughts of Rand, but now salty tears mingled freely with the sweet steam on her cheeks. With no need to suppress her feelings, she cried it all out. The cathartic cry only rearranged some cobwebs in her head. She showered the soap from her body and stepped from the tub feeling greatly relaxed, but no less confused. Wrapped in her orange bathtowel, everything reminded her of Rand, of Biloxi, of—Ocean Springs, Pensaçola. Damn—I love him!

She slipped between cool sheets, but sleep eluded her. Surely, with enough time, memories of him would disappear. Eventually, in the wee morning hours, nature provided fulfillment in her dreams once more. There she and Rand, free from misunderstandings, loved in total harmony.

Chelsea blissfully slept through Sunday, woke up in the evening, turned over, and went back to sleep for the rest of Sunday night.

The shrill bell jangled her sleep-numbed nerves! She begged the fates, Please, where is that button? She strugged to find the clock. *When did I set that alarm, anyway? It was so cozy in bed.* Chelsea groaned. One leaden eyelid reluctantly parted to allow a squint at the gray-black dawn; a typical spring rain poured on the Monday blues.

Listlessly she dressed, uninterested in life. Dread weighed a ton. If only I can get through today at the office. . . . Good-bye, bed.

The soggy weather mired the taxi in more than its usual share of traffic snarls. It was after nine thirty when the driver extended a hand and assisted her from the backseat. She paid him automatically, then remained under the skyscraper's protective canopy a long moment after he drove away. Her attaché case seemed intolerably heavy and bumped her thigh out of rhythm with her shoulder-strap handbag as she made her way through the lobby toward the elevators.

On the ninth floor she moved off with a wave of

bodies that exited the cramped elevator. The sleek glass and chrome double doors that announced Sherwood–Graham in gold letters seemed heavier than ever as she leaned against one to gain entry.

"Morning, kiddo," a much too energetic Marge greeted her, handing Chelsea a stack of pink messages with one hand while holding a cup of fragrant coffee in the other.

"Thanks," she muttered like a robot, offering a nod in return. She flipped through the pink call-backs, checking the names for one in particualr that wasn't there. *I guess he gave up.*

The dove-gray utility carpet cushioned her dragging footsteps as she ambled to her office, half-aware of acknowledging others as they said good morning. The door closed itself behind her as she dropped her attaché case and handbag on top of the paper mountain that loomed on her desk. Ah, yes, the pinnacle of success.

She was drawn to the all-glass wall. Water trickled down the window, then at the command of the wind, marched sideways, shimmered, and slid downward, distorting her view. She was lost in thoughts; Rand's face, his eyes, their last embrace, Biloxi.

The phone buzzed and brought her to the edge of her reverie as she reached for the receiver. It took a great effort for her not to sound tired. "Chelsea Norquist."

"Chelsea, child, how are you?"

"Uncle Dee. God, it's good to hear your voice." She was sincere. "I had you on my list to call!"

"Good. I have some news. I have found a new buyer. A large northern corporation wishes to put in a public boat ramp and a bait camp and one of their fast-food stores. I can't say I—"

"Uncle Dee." Chelsea sighed, her voice sagging. "I can't accept that offer. I want you to give the papers to Rand just as they were originally. He can have the yard." She took a deep breath and realized her adrenaline was pumping well again. "At least he'll continue to build some kind of boats." Her energy was rising. "He'll carry on some type of maritime tradition."

"Well, I'll be—" Connors paused only a moment. "That's wonderful news. You are sure... you want to sell to Korbet Ship?"

"Definitely!"

Connors chuckled. "For what it's worth, I think it's at least a step in the right direction."

Curious at the vote of confidence, she asked, "Why?"

"Oh, well. Rand's been on a tirade ever since you went back to Houston. He called me, determined I would give him your home phone number. He was so upset, I had to tell him about the codicil then—but I don't think it helped much."

"What codicil? To what?"

"Oh, I just found it myself."

"Found what?" she insisted, her voice louder with impatience.

"The codicil your granddad handwrote and attached to the original design on your *Triumph.* I was in the loft, trying again to get some of that stuff thrown out, and I came across a strongbox just almost buried in that mess."

Chelsea wished he wouldn't digress so.

As if he could read her thoughts, he said, "Your granddad was not the designer, child. Karl Korbet was."

"Wait. I don't understand. What are you saying?"

"Just that. Rand's father designed your thirty-six-footer. His genius was in wood design. He offered it to Henry in a poker game shortly before he... just gave up on this life. His was a thwarted human spirit that died young."

"I... still..." She stopped, confused. Then asked softly, "You mean Grandpa Norquist lied all these years?"

"Well, now, not exactly. Sort of on purpose. It was

part of the deal. Rand's dad made Henry promise not to reveal this information as long as Herschel still lived. And Karl's dad is going strong at eighty-six.

She was shocked, unable to comprehend what she was being told.

Connors continued, "Uh, may I give Rand your home number, now?"

She closed her weary eyes. "He won't need it now I've agreed to sell. That's all he wanted. Just handle it all. There's no need for further contact. Take care of Lafe and family first and let me know when it's done." Her voice had dropped to a whisper.

She hung up, then sleepwalked through the rest of the day. What a strange turn. She was curious as to how Rand had taken the news. She pondered again why he had rejected his dad at every turn.

Slowly the reality of Rand's father being the designer of *Triumph* seeped through her own numbed senses. Then she realized she had completed a dream for both men: Karl Korbet and Henry Norquist.

As four o'clock rolled around, Chelsea absentmindedly dialed Aunt Marianne—the source, the pillar upon whom she had leaned since age fourteen. "This is Chelsea, Aunt M."

"Of course it is. Haven't I been expecting your call for days? Must have been some week! When can we get together?" the throaty, non-stop conversationalist asked, warming Chelsea's leaden spirit immediately.

"How about an hour from now?"

"Uh, make it...an hour and a half. Takes a lot longer to achieve less and less when you're bumping up against fifty, you remember?" She roared at her own humor. "Not for you now, but someday," she vowed, "you'll find it more fact than funny—"

"Would you mind," Chelsea interrupted, "if we just go to my place? We can pick up something and eat in. I need your girl talk again."

"Talk, talk, talk. Is that all you ever want to do anymore?" Marianne chuckled, faking a pout, then added, "Yeah, sure. Gosh, I've missed you. Besides, I like more notice when I"—in her best Mae West imitation—"present my charms to the world, honey!" Suddenly all business, she continued, "I'll see you in one hour. Watch for me. I'll pull into the drive. They won't let me linger," she reminded.

"Thanks. You'll never know how much." Chelsea replaced the phone. She could hang on now. That lady was balm to her soul.

The rains had slowed to a quiet mist as Chelsea emerged from the vacuum seal of her office building into the 99 percent humidity mixed with exhaust pollution. Wrapped in her trench coat and incessant thoughts of Rand, she waited for her aunt, oblivious to the rush-hour nightmare. Marianne had to flash the car lights successively to get Chelsea's attention.

"Chelsea Norquist, I've tried for meditation like that when I took hatha and prana yoga! I never made it. How *do* you do it?"

Chelsea slid across the front seat and planted an affectionate kiss on the older woman's soft cheek. "Ohhh, I'm glad to see you. Sorry, I was distracted. Wow, you look great!" Marianne's silver-blond hair was partially coiffed; it was swept up and away from her face in short, worn-out curls. Her blue eyes not only sparkled; they zeroed in on the truth in a person's soul while mirth crinkled through layers of makeup. But Marianne viewed others from a rarefied vantage of wisdom; she lived life to the fullest possible measure. A hostess for all seasons, her widowhood was merry indeed.

This evening, Chelsea noted, Marianne was in one of her "dressed for life" costumes. A flambuoyant patterned caftan, in purple, red, and gold, was tied at the waist with a white extension cord, looped and plugged into itself. Her petite feet were in black canvas Mary Janes.

Marianne forced the car into the flow of traffic. An aggressive driver who sat on a pillow to see from behind the wheel, she had a compulsive need to stick to her rights.

The fragrance of fresh bread greeted Chelsea's olfactory organ. "What is that delightful smell?"

"You were born with perfect timing, uncanny timing. I had just pulled several loaves of my homemade bread from the oven when you called," she teased lovingly. "Oh, yes. I stuck in a hunk of cheese, some strawberry jam, and a jug of my homemade dill pickles. My special-occasion white wine is sitting back there in a blue cooler too. Oh, I'm so *good* to you," she teased, feigning righteousness.

Chelsea looked at the full larder in the backseat. "You really are something special to me. But about my timing—it's been off lately. Tonight must be the exception, Aunt M.; I felt better the minute you agreed to get together. You were just what I needed."

"Hmmm. That bad, huh? You really are in trouble, honey."

Chelsea jumped at the unexpected blast of the horn Marianne blared at the driver cutting in front of them. "The audacity!" Marianne spit indignantly. Chelsea hoped they would make it home.

"Now, what's his name again? He's the problem, correct?"

"Rand is his name, but the problem is me. I've let him take on too much importance in my life. You taught me to have my life centered and whole—in a career I enjoyed."

Marianne interrupted impatiently, "I know, I know. I'm the one who gave you that philosophy: 'to consider marriage an option, not an end-all. That it also requires work and you should view both as equally in need of your energies.' Now, aside from the party line, let me hear everything about your man. Everything. Don't leave out a single thing!" she rhapsodized.

While Marianne cleared a place at the glass coffee table and spread her homemade picnic, Chelsea changed from her moss-green blouson dress and panty hose into her warm, comfortable empire-style velour robe of royal blue trimmed with white lace. Barefoot, she padded to the kitchen for two crystal wineglasses, then joined Marianne.

"Let's have a little wine and a lot of your wisdom," Chelsea proposed as she seated herself on the floor Indian style around the coffee table laden with the bountiful feast.

Two hours later she had said all she had to say. The therapy worked every time. "I so enjoy talking with you. I feel better."

Marianne raised an eyebrow quizzically. "But I haven't said a thing yet! You did all the talking. I'm still thinking." She paused for a moment, then in portentous tones, teased, "Wisdom is a great burden...I unload in small lots."

Chelsea giggled, amazed at how good it felt to laugh, at how whole and happy she felt at the moment. "You silly, ol—oops, young lady." She smiled. Her placid green eyes showered love as they lowered directly at Marianne. "I love you."

Marianne's face grew quite passive and serious before she asked, "Would you still, if I advised you to go get him—and hold on tight? To fight with him, love with him, work and grow with him?" Her voice left the question in the air.

Chelsea eyed her suspiciously while she slowly tasted more of the bread and cheese. She rubbed her temples nervously before responding, "My heart would do that in a minute, but my mind knows that if I give this enough time—a lot of time—I'll see it for what it really is—or isn't. A better perspective will be mine—"

"Ha!" Marianne scoffed, and leaned forward to enunciate carefully, "You know, from where I sit, there are no such things as mistakes. You can throw all the decisions in a hat and pull one out blindfolded. It will work just about as well as another. It's just a matter of living with your choices or choosing another direction. It's flexi—"

The door bell interrupted.

Chapter Fourteen

The door bell buzzed several times. "Expecting anyone?" Marianne inquired, slowly alerting her guard.

"Not a soul."

"I'll get it, then. You can't be too cautious," Marianne warned. She crossed the room to the door and focused one eye on the peephole. She looked back at Chelsea, grinned, and her eyes crinkled with delight. With a lilt in her voice, she asked the door, "Who's there?"

"Some caution," Chelsea judged sardonically.

A muffled male voice asked, "Does Chelsea Norquist live here?"

"Young man, I'm not telling you anything until you identify yourself," Marianne explained, her voice warm and charming.

Chelsea heard an unmistakable voice boom forth: "Rand Korbet, ma'am." Her green eyes popped wide in disbelief.

Marianne looked at her for confirmation. Chelsea nodded woodenly. Her aunt unlocked the door and opened it wide, indicating this-way-please.

A wedge of lighted landscape illuminated the evening mist behind the well-dressed businessman on a midnight pilgrimage. Rand's upturned collar touched the edge of his flaxen hair; his hands were jammed in the pockets of his trench coat, which was belted against the cold, wet night. "I'm looking for Ms Chel-

sea Norquist. I was given this address,'' he volunteered
in his best, husky-velvet voice. Then he glanced past
the older woman into the room. His stern face relaxed
at the sight of his goal; a smile tugged at the corners of
his mouth.

"Hi!" His simple, boyish greeting seemed incongru-
ous with his unexpected appearance. Chelsea was still
stunned, unable to speak.

Marianne declared, "Come in, come in, for heav-
en's sake,'' and pulled the sleeve of his coat to help
him respond. She shut the door behind him and introduced herself simultaneously. "I'm Chelsea's aunt,
Marianne McClure," she said, and extended a hand he
didn't see, for his eyes remained locked into pools of
emerald green.

Not missing a thing, Marianne offered like a giddy
schoolgirl: "Your ears must be burning. We've been
discussing you for hours."

Her aunt's openness penetrated the shock. Chelsea
rolled her eyes away from Rand in embarrassment and
gasped, "Aunt Marianne!" as she slumped on the sofa
without looking at either of them.

Rand fixed his smile on Marianne briefly. "Nice to
meet you, Mrs. McClure." He paused, then added sincerely, "Appreciate your candor, too."

Like a magnet, he was attracted back to Chelsea,
and in three Texas strides stood gazing down at her on
the sofa. Enchanted, she watched as he shrugged out
of his coat; the fresh dampness misted the air around
her.

She was surprised to see him so traditionally dressed.
In the past his interesting, well-tailored dress casuals
had pleased her, but tonight his light gray flannel sport
coat showed impeccable good taste over dark navy
slacks. He could have been a Wall Street broker...or a
playboy, she mused.

Without blinking an eye, in husky, intimate tones,
he reminded her, "We must talk. Like I said on the

phone, we've got a lot of... unfinished business to discuss."

Marianne was thoroughly taken with Rand Korbet. She retrieved her jacket and winked at Chelsea as she announced, "I know when to make an exit. I'll get this stuff another time." She indicated the picnic basket. From the doorway she added, "Nice to have met you, Mr. Korbet. I, for one, hope to see more of you around here." She blew a kiss to Chelsea and signaled her approval of Rand to his back with an expression of sweet ecstacy on her face. Chelsea barely acknowledged her aunt's departure.

Rand, so drawn to Chelsea he stood basking in her presence, was totally unaware of Marianne's voice. He reacted only after he heard the door click shut behind her, saying a belated good-bye. Then, like a man remembering his mission, he walked to the door, secured both locks, and faced her. "I hope, Ms Norquist, these locks mean I have you alone." He sighed and raked fingers through his unruly hair.

As he returned to the sofa she asked, "But how did you find me?" Her gleaming emerald eyes opened wide, beseeching him to come closer.

Rand lowered himself to the sofa and pulled her tenderly into the curve of his arms while absently answering, "Connors gave me your address; then I took a plane, rented a car, and found a map..."

She was immediately crushed in his powerful arms and instinctively yielded. They both seemed to tremble as he hungrily sought her lips. His mouth drew nearer, and she unconsciously moistened her full, slightly open lips, parted to receive his claim. His warm, soft lips relaxed in a full sideways slant as if to savor the very first touch, unhurried but quivering with anticipation. The kiss was unlike any before. He lost control for a moment, and the increasing pressure of his mouth demanded oneness as his exploring tongue wreaked havoc on her senses. There was a rapid numbing of

Chelsea's defenses before he was in control again. Then he lightly brushed his seeking lips across hers, sweet, pleasing, tempting. When their mouths fused again, they shared a ravenous longing. It was as if her talk with Marianne had relaxed and somehow prepared her for this. Her body responded. A primitive rotation of her hips began a subtle movement to fit closer to him. Her arms grasped the flexed steel bands of his shoulders; her shaking fingers cupped his head. With matching intensity her tongue moved to seek and caress his.

Her aggressive compliance triggered a savage response. Wildly his lips plundered hers with a crushing, bruising pressure; then they were everywhere on her face, her neck, throat, behind her ear.... His right hand held the small of her back and forced her breasts hard against his chest. In torturous desire she clung to him; they moved as one. She found her position under him on the three-pillowed sofa.

All the desire she had ever felt for Rand was building, pulsating, coming forth more violently. The same mindless desire that had always preceded the inevitable pain and anger—and wounded pride. Deep inside, some part of Chelsea tried to kill the thought. But the eroding feeling began to grow in her awareness. She was appalled. Like it or not, her unconscious self-defense mechanism took over. Though she ached for him, she went limp in his arms.

He stopped and raised his head to search her face while the flame of desire sparked in his hypnotic eyes. His body jerked with the sensual tension. "What is it, Chels?" he gasped in a whisper.

She couldn't move to hide her face. Abruptly her jade eyes overflowed with tears of frustration that flooded quietly over her temples and into her hair in heedless disarray. "I...feel...damned if I do—and damned if I don't," she cried, bursting into sobs.

"Chels, Chels," he soothed her, his overheated

senses making his voice even more provocative. "It's okay. It's really okay. Don't cry." He tried to kiss her again, but she succeeded in pushing him away and struggled to a sitting position. He didn't understand.

"No," she breathed, filling her aching lungs and quelling her tears with the back of her hand. "You can't come across the Gulf"—she blurted, then paused, for she could hardly form the words—"to turn me on—and then turn me off again—in anger!" Her voice broke, and she wept more while choking out, "as you always have before."

Rand gently cupped her chin in his strong fingers and turned her face to look directly into his eyes. "I could say the same thing to you. Who came across the Gulf in the first place?" he teased, then tenderly supported her head in both his large hands and let his gorgeous eyes cast their spell. "But...I didn't come here to argue. We need to discuss, uh, to settle some things." His warm breath tantalized her as he bent closer. "First, let's hold each other again...to reaffirm what we felt in Pensacola...."

She fought for sanity in his mesmerizing nearness. The thought of Pensacola reminded her of more. "B.L." she uttered like an oath, and jerked her head from his hands. He looked perplexed. "Before Leslie!" she spat, as if the words burned her tongue.

With a deep sigh he looked away. He slumped forward, his elbows braced on his knees, his hands holding his head. "Please forget Leslie. She is nothing to me! She was never more than a prop for my ego—flashy, like my powerful red Porsche. I never went after any woman in my life until you, Chelsea. Leslie was always there, whether I wanted her or not. Handy, willing. I suppose I served some need of hers." Anguish wrinkled his brow and deepened the fine lines that webbed the corners of his eyes as he turned to gaze at her one more time. "I may be a southern chauvinist, as you put it, but when she intruded at the Danforths',

I knew it was up to me to remove her. If you had only seen it that way. She took nothing from my feelings for you, but your anger took you away.'' Once again he came so close she could feel his moist breath on her flushed cheeks. "Come back, Chelsea."

Her heart tripped wildly against her ribs while she waited to hear the age-old words *I love you*.

Instead he said, "Come back. Work with me and be the *Nor* of my newly formed *Norand* Enterprises, a subsidiary of Korbet Ship." The emotion and enthusiasm were evident in his voice and his body as his hands grasped her shoulders.

His touch was rare ecstasy, but his words stabbed her with confusion. She was feeling one thing from him and hearing another. In search of clarity she pulled away and stood up, rubbed her temples to clear the cobwebs, and walked to the kitchen, "I...guess I don't understand," she murmured. She returned with a wineglass for Rand. "What are you...suggesting?" she asked with a fragile hold on her composure. She poured both of them wine and cautiously sat back beside him.

He declined the drink, then said, "I know you talked to Connors this morning. Didn't he tell you?" He seemed dumbstruck. "I, uh... this may be quite a shock, but—" His voice grew soft and low. "Your grandfather... did *not* design *Triumph*!" He waited for her response, which she purposely withheld. He continued with a kind of reverence. "My father—Karl Korbet—was the genius designer." The sweetest, dearest eyes in the world bored into hers expectantly.

She was feeling more than hearing his revelations.

Rand pleaded for her understanding. "This means... the Korbet–Norquist team started with our parents! Your grandfather and my—father." Again he spoke the word *father* like a prayer.

Chelsea's soul received him wholly, even as her mind sorted facts. He nervously paced the room as he continued the story. "Because of a poker game, Connors said, my dad lost this prize design to Henry on a bet. Until this week my mom didn't know this was the way it happened. She feels he lost it on purpose. She said my dad just announced to her one day that he had given up his dreams and shoved all his designs into the garbage pail, saying something about one being safely delivered, a promise of a future with Henry Norquist. She said my dad had given up hope of ever building them at Korbet Ship, his will to clash with Herschel long since buried. Dad's will to live wasn't much after that, she admitted. He had no strength to clear out and start on his own, though she begged him."

Rand stopped for a moment, swallowed, then faced Chelsea and nodded. "The irony of this: if it weren't for a game of chance, lost on purpose, that thirty-six-foot design and my"—he paused—"understanding, uh, appreciation for—hell—my *love* for the person who was my father, would never have been a reality. If only I could have told him—" He broke off, shuddering with remorse. "I think I'll have a little of that wine now. He picked up the glass, sipped, and started pacing again.

In a moment he stopped in front of Chelsea. "Now, do you understand?" His eyes held hers; he knelt before her. "You little old curly-headed Chelsea." His hand touched her hair. "Such a female. You were the catalyst. *You* breathed life into two old men's dreams. *Triumph* lives because of you. The memories of Biloxi live again because of you." His voice hardened with bitterness. "And to think, I fought you!" His anguish tore at her. How could she comfort him? Her eyes offered him compassion. That was enough. Rand laid his head on her lap at the nonverbal invitation, and she discovered a new aspect of her womanhood as she stroked, patted, soothed him.

Chelsea struggled to understand what exactly he was

in Houston to offer her. Was it a business partnership in which they also shared a physical relationship... without declaring a commitment of...love...fidelity...soul?

He interrupted her maze of thoughts without lifting his head from her lap. His arms tightened around her lower waist. "Chels, when Dwight told me you'd sell the yard to me I—I realized how blind I've been. But you bailed me out. All week I've been through hell. I unfairly judged my dad...you...everything...wrong." He raised his head and looked directly into her loving eyes. "I've never in my whole life talked like this." He took a deep drink of the wine.

Chelsea was seeing a side of Rand she never dreamed existed. She never loved him more. She felt privileged. His emotional growth was tremendous. She spoke quietly. "I'm pleased, of course, with your plans. I had no idea this morning of all this, of the codicil. I just figured it would be better if some kind of ship-building traditions were carried forth rather than those awful commercial plans some new buyer had."

That triggered more zealous thoughts in Rand. "I hope to exonerate my father's name at Korbet Ship. Chelsea, it's going to take both of us. We—you and me—a team. We'll start mass production of the thirty-six-foot design at Norand. But I want to examine my dad's other designs, also. Mom showed them to me. She rescued them from the garbage and hid them away. She loved and respected him all along. His weakness, was simply...his weakness."

Love for his father was illuminating Rand's entire being. He moved back to sit beside Chelsea on the sofa, pulled her into his arms tenderly like a small child, and cradled her head on his chest.

"Chels, do you understand?" She felt certain the love and adoration that was evident in his gaze was all due to his rapture with his father's newly discovered value, and yet she felt like a treasure in his arms.

She offered tentatively, "I see a man... whose life has new facets, and I understand that." She left unanswered the questions of what else she didn't understand. Gently she pulled away to sit beside him, independent of his inviting arms, and said, "I must confess. When Uncle Dee told me briefly about the codicil, it didn't have the—impact—that hearing you, seeing you tell me. I guess it still hasn't hit me that my grandfather was not the great designer that I'd been lead to believe he was." She paused. Her throat ached, and she whispered, "It doesn't matter."

She could feel herself sinking into an emotional spiral. She was no less confused about where she stood with Rand personally. "Excuse me," she choked as she darted to the bathroom and slammed the door behind her just as the first wrenching sob broke through.

She hurriedly bent over and ran water in the bathtub to drown the sounds of her broken heart, which had erupted thunderously. She leaned against the bathroom wall and grabbed a big white towel to muffle her weeping. Why am I so miserable? Isn't this what you always wanted—to be centered in a fulfilling career, be an independent business person, and have a good personal relationship with no strings? Apparently she could have his physical love, for however long they both, or one... *No! That is not enough,* she raged inwardly, beginning to feel a cessation of the uncontrollable, spasmodic contractions in her lungs.

This is all driving me crazy! Crazy! Sherwood–Graham is nothing to me anymore. Rand is all I want. Yes, I do. I would love to be a part of his life, even limited, as he outlined. Build beautiful sailing vessels.... *But you also want to hear, "I love you," right?* Simple little phrase. It would feel so... complete, an inner voice added.

"Are you all right?" Rand called through the closed door.

She certainly didn't want him to know she was crying. That was the point in seeking the privacy of the bathroom.

"Are you taking a bath? I mean, we're in the middle of a rather important decision!" His tone was changing from perplexed to irritated.

She cleared her throat and tried to project a calm voice. "Just a minute. Uh, have another drink." Her traitorous voice cracked. She walked over and turned the running water off. She debated what to say or do next as she sat wearily on the edge of the bathtub.

"I don't want anything else to drink. I want to talk to you. And I don't like doing it through this door!" he shouted.

Chelsea couldn't respond. She remained seated, precariously balanced on the edge of the tub and her emotions. The hot steam from the full tub made the velour robe seem intolerably sticky on her skin.

"Chelsea" he bellowed, so angrily that she jerked in response and lost her balance. He threw open the door just as she fell backward, hitting her head on the soap dish and splashing bath water on the floor. "Wha—in your robe?" He glowered, shocked. Then a wicked grin began to play across his rugged face.

All she could do was sputter and flail about uselessly, still dragging her legs over the side of the tub.

"I'll never get used to your surprises." He shrugged as he started undressing. "Don't mind if I do. Seems as good a place as any to talk. But, *I* prefer these things with my clothes off."

The weight of her wet robe hampered her ability to get out with any agility at all. Finally she stood up in the tub, dripping, the wet velour a second skin around her breasts, waist, and hips. He stepped in. "Rand," she sputtered, exasperated at the whole situation. He calmly took the zipper at her neck and slowly started to unzip her robe.

He peeled the wet velour open to reveal two damp, pink buds. His indolent smile, arrogant stare, and wonderful, rough hands reminded her of their past encounters. She grabbed his arm and tried to stop him. "Enough," she growled, more like a spitting, ruffled kitten than a real threat. His hand dragged heavily against her slippery midriff, waist, abdomen, and furry mound under her bikini until the zipper stopped just above her knees. His swaggering hand retraced its path and fluttered across her skin on its way back up, awakening a dormant drummer deep inside. Rand's closeness smelled salty and steamy and mixed wonderfully with her sweet moistness. For a moment her life's most important decision was postponed.

She met him on his terms and held his gaze without embarrassment. He stood majestically naked before her and magically slipped the robe off her shoulders. It settled and caressed her ankles in the water.

His breathing increased perceptibly as his eyes stared hungrily at her high, firm breasts and the pointed tips that begged to be suckled. He obliged first one and then the other as he went to his knees in the warm bathwater. His tongue's provocative, stimulating sampling sampling hardened more than her aching nipples.

Ripples of electric pleasure followed his tongue as it teemed downward, swirling a place for himself, as he removed her lacy bikini. She didn't even realize they were gone until he pulled her down on him and he was half inside. The hot water enveloped them, the velour and lace mingling with their sensations. His large warm hands pressed her to him in slow motion. Her mouth found his lips, and they fed ravenously, increasing the pressure, crushing.

No words, no thoughts. Wonder and joy.

Chelsea was resilient, receptive. He was rising, thrusting. His eyes closed; his chest heaved. The ocean about them mounted with their gorging exultation. Their magnetic maelstrom crescendoed in a gasping thunderclap from Rand that she answered in a rolling echo.... Slowly, slowly, the seas were calmed again.

"Pensacola wasn't a dream. I knew it," he said in a husky whisper, bathwater teasing his chin as they lay side by side, legs still intertwined.

The water level seemed considerably lower, Chelsea noted as his hot hands roamed her spine, an unslakable thirst prodding them onward. She felt so languid she could hardly speak. "But you, here, in my bathtub. Surely this is a dream."

He groped behind him for the soap tray. "Just to prove it's not, I'll be practical. Dreams are not practical." He found the bar of scented soap and briskly rubbed the matted curls on his chest. "Don't be timid," he prodded, moving her hand to his soapy chest and starting a circular movement. He then held her eyes with his dynamic gaze and let the bar of soap paint a glossy trail around her breasts, into her valleys, and over her mounds. Her eyes never wavered, nor the circular motion of her hands as they made the diameter wider and wider.

He nibbled lightly at her wet ear as the soap in his hand made a foamy massage up and over her shoulder and around her waist, her hips...up and over and under.... She felt drugged. The sexually-induced stupor was hard to break.

"Your fingers look like prunes." He kissed them tenderly, absently.

She took notice of her shriveled fingers and inspected his. Yes, that did indicate some measure of time spent in the water. It was enough motivation for her to pull up and turn on the shower.

"What—wha'd you trying to drown me?" he sputtered, struggling up and out of the direct line of the spray.

And lose the love of my life? she thought, but said instead, "Time to rinse our prunes," as they stood together under the pelting warm rain.

She leaned against the tiled wall, out of the cascading water, one leg braced on the edge of the tub. For a long moment he appraised her, then made her a prisoner between his hands, one arm on either side of her shoulders, as he said a startling thing. "I hope all our little triumphs are built like you. Your body is perfect."

It took a moment for his remark to penetrate. She still wasn't sure if she'd heard him correctly. "What are you talking about?" she asked, the steamy fog making her vision somewhat blurred. She watched his softened face while she waited for the answer. He licked the water from his lips and with a crooked smile added: "Of course, if some are boys, they'd look pretty silly, but girls, now they should be built just like you, Chels." His lips lightly touched the tip of her nose; then his arms brought her nakedness to him; her satin-like legs were surrounded by his thighs of iron. His mouth sought hers as hungrily as ever.

The echo of his words shattered her lovely, loving aura. She was certain he had meant children. She was already moving out of his hold toward the faucets. "You're crazy, mister." Her disbelief was turning to that old, familiar, building anger. She shut off the mesmerizing warm rain, which she noticed was about to run the water over the edge of the tub. She released the plug and thought, So much for games; play is over. Aloud she snapped, "I haven't even said yes to building boats with you!" and stepped out of the tub.

"What are you doing...saying? I—we_haven't... finished?" He stood in the middle of the tub in totally nude innocence, waving his arms about in annoyance.

"Oh, yes, we have!" she sizzled, and flung him a towel while she bent over to get another from under the sink.

Still enjoying his euphoria, he stepped out of the tub and reached over to enclose her from behind. She straightened up, but her composure was totally threatened by the sword at her back. His magic hands massaged her breasts.

"We haven't even begun, Chelsea Norquist-Korbet.

Norand Enterprises is a very diversified company. While making babies and building wooden *Triumph*s, you can also start your own house agency for publicizing all Korbet Ship products.''

"Raaaannnnd," she shouted with more ferocity than she'd ever shown in her life. She jerked away from his hold, turned to face him, her hands on her hips, and hissed, "Your sense of humor is the blackest of the black." Dark green shards nailed him as never before. "It's true I'm a Ms and your independent equal." She inhaled, grabbed the towel from him, and held it to her for a modicum of dignity while she continued, "But nowhere in my ethics can I bring children into this world by the same mass-assembly process as a line of boats."

She stopped, her rage suspended in midair. Something he had just said reached home. "Chelsea Norquist-Korbet?" she questioned.

It was his turn to be disgusted. He crossed his arms and stood over her like a judge. "Are you going to be one of those liberated ladies who wants to keep your own name? I thought hyphenating our two names was what you would want. Maybe you're right. How can you give children hyphenated names, anyway? Where does it end? Who drops—"

His words became indistinct ramblings under the music playing in her heart. *Am I the dunce?* She brushed the frizzy tendrils from her eyes and cheeks, "Rand?"

He hushed.

"Have you asked me...to marry you?" she asked breathily.

He moved his head from side to side, incredulous at her question. "Chelsea, not just *marry*—merge in absolutely every way. I thought I'd made that clear." His voice, incredibly soft and husky, begged her to believe him. "I love you, Chels."

For a long moment they lingered, his word resonating, their eyes open windows to their souls. "I love you dearly. I thought you knew—I'll never assume—I'll tell you over and over, forever." He crushed their naked bodies together, forgetting his strength in his overwhelming surge of devotion. "I cherish you," he whispered in her ear, "for being you. You with your strength of will, your power to excite me, your body...." His hands dropped to cup her hips and allow him to look again into her emeralds, which became more liquid with each word. "You, Chels, gave me all that and more. Your boatyard and my chance to feel love." His voice grew more hoarse. "For my father, too."

"Shhh," she breathed, and placed her fingertips on his lips. Her voices were a heavenly chorus in her ears as salty tears of unbounded joy spilled down her steamy cheeks. She cried, "Oh, Rand," and raised up on her tiptoes to place her arms around his neck. "I love you, I love you, I love you, love..." she sang before he swept her naked body into his arms. Her voice trailed after them as he carried her to the bed. His senses were drunken as he reminded her huskily they had plans to make as soon as they got some more "business" out of the way.

The cool sheets reminded her of where and who she was as he lay down beside her. Contented, ecstatic, she happily placed him at the center of her life and being. The first of many productive mergers was just beginning.

Get this book FREE!

Mail to:

Harlequin Reader Service

In the U.S.
2504 West Southern Avenue
Tempe, AZ 85282

In Canada
649 Ontario Street
Stratford, Ontario N5A 6W2

YES! I want to be one of the first to discover **Harlequin American Romance.** Send me FREE and without obligation *Twice in a Lifetime.* If you do not hear from me after I have examined my FREE book, please send me the 4 new **Harlequin American Romances** each month as soon as they come off the presses. I understand that I will be billed only $2.25 for each book (total $9.00). There are no shipping or handling charges. There is no minimum number of books that I have to purchase. In fact, I may cancel this arrangement at any time. *Twice in a Lifetime* is mine to keep as a FREE gift, even if I do not buy any additional books.

Name _____ (please print)

Address _____ Apt. no. _____

City _____ State/Prov. _____ Zip/Postal Code _____

Signature (If under 18, parent or guardian must sign.)

AR-SUB-200

Take these
4 best-selling novels
FREE

Yes! Four sophisticated, contemporary love stories by four world-famous authors of romance FREE, as your introduction to the Harlequin Presents subscription plan. Thrill to **Anne Mather**'s passionate story BORN OUT OF LOVE, set in the Caribbean.... Travel to darkest Africa in **Violet Winspear**'s TIME OF THE TEMPTRESS....Let **Charlotte Lamb** take you to the fascinating world of London's Fleet Street in MAN'S WORLD .... Discover beautiful Greece in **Sally Wentworth**'s moving romance SAY HELLO TO YESTERDAY.

Harlequin Presents...

The very finest in romance fiction

Join the millions of avid Harlequin readers all over the world who delight in the magic of a really exciting novel. EIGHT great NEW titles published EACH MONTH! Each month you will get to know exciting, interesting, true-to-life people .... You'll be swept to distant lands you've dreamed of visiting .... Intrigue, adventure, romance, and the destiny of many lives will thrill you through each Harlequin Presents novel.

Get all the latest books before they're sold out!
As a Harlequin subscriber you actually receive your personal copies of the latest Presents novels immediately after they come off the press, so you're sure of getting all 8 each month.

Cancel your subscription whenever you wish!
You don't have to buy any minimum number of books. Whenever you decide to stop your subscription just let us know and we'll cancel all further shipments.